mardi
gras
murders

mardi gras murders

phillip scott

alyson books
los angeles

© 2000 BY PHILLIP SCOTT. ALL RIGHTS RESERVED.

MANUFACTURED IN THE UNITED STATES OF AMERICA.

THIS TRADE PAPERBACK IS PUBLISHED BY ALYSON PUBLICATIONS,
P.O. BOX 4371, LOS ANGELES, CALIFORNIA 90078-4371.
DISTRIBUTION IN THE UNITED KINGDOM BY TURNAROUND PUBLISHER SERVICES LTD.,
UNIT 3, OLYMPIA TRADING ESTATE, COBURG ROAD, WOOD GREEN,
LONDON N22 6TZ ENGLAND.

FIRST PUBLISHED BY PENGUIN BOOKS AUSTRALIA LTD. (AS *GET OVER IT!*): 2000
FIRST ALYSON BOOKS EDITION: FEBRUARY 2005

05 06 07 08 09 a 10 9 8 7 6 5 4 3 2 1

ISBN 1-55583-758-1
(PREVIOUSLY PUBLISHED WITH ISBN 0-14-028279-3 BY PENGUIN BOOKS AUSTRALIA LTD.)

COVER PHOTOGRAPHY BY STEVE COLE/GETTY IMAGES.

In memory of "Johnno" Mulock, May 24, 1999

chapter one

My best friend is a celebrity. This amazes me since, (a) he's not spectacularly good at anything and (b) he's gay.

I've known Paul for four energetic, exasperating years. We first met when he answered my advertisement in the trade papers. The ad was for Italian lessons, entirely legitimate and above board—I'm Italian born, after all—but through some mishap my innocent paragraph made its initial appearance on the phone sex page, with the result that every one of my callers could already speak perfect if somewhat colloquial Italian. I had the placement changed in the next issue. From then on, SPEAK ITALIAN AND AMAZE YOUR FRIENDS. CALL MARC appeared under Languages, between Landscaping and Latex Mail Order.

Paul absolutely amazed me. He took to the Italian tongue like a duck to sump oil.

I still sometimes wonder what we see in each other. He's twenty years younger, we've had no lovers in common, he's no great fan of opera nor I of dance parties. We're both partial to champagne, the big difference being that Paul has an aversion to paying for it. And there was never anything sexual between us, despite the epidemic of raised eyebrows in my circle when Paul first swanned into it.

Of course, I was besotted—for about five minutes. He is an attractive boy and a compulsive flirt. Like a reformed sexaholic, I can now admit that I did think twice about those dark eyes with the fluttering lashes that are rarely stilled. I did on a couple of occasions, late at night and the worse for wear, conjure up an image of that slim but true dancer's body to get me through. I'm only human.

Paul has since admitted, in a flurry of frivolous candor, that he also weighed me up as one-night-stand material. He'll say anything to ingratiate himself, but in this case I believe him. He's never confined his casual partners to one particular race or age group; if variety is the spice of life, then Paul's been through the entire rack. And yet, for some reason—apathy, or plain old instinct—we bypassed those messy preliminaries and simply settled into a snug, inexplicable friendship.

When we first met, Paul was a chorus boy with big plans. *Chorus boy,* as a phrase, conjures up the gay '30s of Noël Coward more than the gay '90s of George Michael, but it's the correct job description. He sang a bit, danced a bit, and camped it up a lot in mega-musicals.

At one point, fate hauled him out of the chorus to costar in a production of *The Rocky Horror Show* which toured to far-flung disadvantaged communities. The sole reviewer described Paul's performance as "lightweight and strident" but Paul remained resolute, still convinced that acclaim was only a pelvic thrust away. His constant refrain was "I want it all and I want it by 30"— although as 30 loomed ever closer the refrain lost some of its freshness and took on a crabbier tone.

And then, just short of the deadline, it happened: Paul was elevated to minor eminence in the medium of television.

It caught me completely unaware. Of course I own a TV set, but I think of it solely as a helpful device that tells me what sort of weather to expect. For the rest of the time I avoid its endless parade of bad actors pretending to win the lottery and weird, exultant women pouring green liquid onto maxipads. Television is not called a "medium" for nothing. It is, nevertheless, the only road to genuine fame.

Recently, Lachie Turner, a young friend of ours and the star of a teenage soap opera, outed himself at a big TV awards night. Far from killing his career, the revelation did our friend nothing but good because gay was suddenly in—specifically, the kind of gayness associated with youth, good looks, and self-confidence.

Paul, who has those things in abundance, was quick to cash in. He'd had a part to play in Lachie's story and was determined to tell the world. In a nutshell, Lachie's partner had been wrongfully accused of murder and it was only through the fine sleuthing of Paul and I that the real culprit was discovered.

Armed with all the juicy details, Paul targeted the press like a moth fluttering around a follow spot. Gradually, the subject matter of his interviews broadened to include love, life, and fashion, and before you could say "blabbermouth," Paul was invited to host an "around town" segment on cable television. His task was to yap about where he'd been during the week: the movies he'd seen, the clubs he'd frequented, and every dance party he could remember. He quickly picked up a cult following, most of whom he'd probably picked up in person.

Even so, I felt no great need to shell out good money for cable. I'd been getting Paul's infotainment free and unsolicited for years.

Of course, his new vocation had a downside. If he was unreliable before, now he became impossible. For instance, we've always had a more or less regular arrangement for Sunday mornings. I'd stock up on croissants and champagne and Paul would come over to consume them. We used to call it brunch. Four Sundays after Paul's cable debut I was ready to call it off.

Croissants are temperamental creatures. They're French, after all. You can only keep them warm in an oven for so long. If they sense the slightest inkling of neglect, they spontaneously combust.

On this particular Sunday in early winter I was scraping the poor charred things into the trash and considering the alternative of stale date loaf when a loud screech of metal made me jump.

I hobbled to the window and peeked between the curtains. Just outside sat a bright red truck with the slogan MOVE IT printed in stark white letters on the side. The offending vehicle was crammed snugly into a space in front of my car. I rushed out to check the car for damage: Yes, there it was, a telltale scratch in vivid moving-van red. I saw red myself! Resolutely, I marched up the steps of the house next door.

My previous neighbors, a Greek Cypriot family, had sold and moved away months ago. Since then the terrace house had been renovated inside and out. The noise had been constant, but when you live under the flight path, what difference do a few jackhammers make? The results were certainly impressive: The stone block facade had been restored to its pristine glory and painted a gentle cream; the original railings and fittings had been replaced with brand-new copies; and through the open door I could see where walls had been scuttled, floors buffed smartly, unobtrusive lighting installed.

I took a deep breath and knocked loudly. There was no answer, so I stepped through the doorway and stood, bathed in the glow of a subtly placed skylight.

"Excuse me?" I called out in my most authoritative tone.

"Just a moment."

Down the stairs swept one of the most attractive men I'd seen in quite some time: tallish, probably in his mid 30s, with a neatly trimmed beard, slightly graying, and a broad, open smile. His T-shirt clung perfectly atop a neatly pressed pair of chinos.

"I'm Marc," I began. "I live next door."

"Do you? Excellent!" With masculine authority he shook my hand, giving off a distinct but not overwhelming odor of cologne. "I'm Gavin. Which side are you on?"

"Pardon?"

He chuckled. "I don't mean *that*! We take that as a given, don't we? I mean, which terrace is yours?"

"The one on the left." I pointed.

"Ah! With the liquidambar. You're the man who plays opera. The agent mentioned you."

"You like opera?" I asked cautiously. (He would be the first neighbor of mine who ever did.)

He shrugged. "I subscribe, of course. I just wish I knew a little more about it. Well, now. I'm afraid I can't offer you a drink or even coffee; nothing's unpacked."

"Oh, that's all right. Look, I wanted to mention—"

"If I ever *can* unpack! There's an old car—I think it's abandoned—sitting there blocking the truck and I can't get my things out. I should have hired professional movers, I suppose, but I'm a bit of a do-it-yourself fiend."

"That car is mine," I said, almost apologetically, "and I'm afraid you've scratched it."

Gavin scarcely batted an eyelid. "You own that car? Ah. Marvellous!" He placed a warm hand on my bicep. "Could I be so brazen as to request a neighborly favor?"

"You'd like me to move it."

"If you would. And let's have a look at this scratch. I don't recall doing it, but of course if there's the slightest damage just send me the bill. I insist."

My anger was swiftly evaporating as Gavin proceeded to charm the pants off me. Manners always make a good impression, especially in the right package. What's more, he was unpacking alone, which meant a "double A" rating: Attractive and Available.

"Perhaps you'd care for a coffee *chez moi*?" I asked brightly.

"Love to. Give me a couple of hours to shift furniture, and I'll turn up at your doorstep with bells on."

Waving gaily, I sped off in search of another parking space. I found one five blocks away near the shops, so I grabbed some dolmas and Lebanese bread. Once home again I made a hasty attempt to tidy the house. I'm quite neat, but sometimes one is inclined to let things lie. Socks under the sofa, for example.

I've been living at Villa Petrucci, my rustic retreat in Sydney's

Inner West, for two decades—and it looks it. When I bought the place as a deceased estate it required a lot of sprucing up. I took my time. It wasn't until five years down the track that all the old carpets had been ripped out, the roof patched up, and protective antirust applied to the wrought iron railings. With the help of my then–loving partner Andrew, since relocated, I interior-decorated in pure '70s *Better Homos and Gardens* style. We deployed rough Tibetan scatter rugs, hanging bathroom ferns, Thai-dyed cushions, and their ilk. The cushions have long gone (along with the ilk), but I've never had enough capital to do anything more drastic. At least the roof doesn't leak in the same places it did originally.

The best feature, inside or out, is the ancient liquidambar. I love how it shades the place in summer and flings its leaves over the neighbor's fence in autumn.

Around 4 I heard a seductive *bing-bong* at the front door. Checking my hair in the hallway mirror, I flung the door open in a hearty gesture of welcome.

"Caro!"

It was only Paul. He bounded in.

"What are you doing here?"

"Brunching, what else?" He threw himself onto the couch. "Aren't you expecting me? Where are the croissants?"

"They died and went to hell." I checked my watch. "And you can join them. It's 4 in the afternoon! You've lost all track of time since you got that silly job."

"It's going fabulously, thanks for asking. Did you catch me last week?"

"You know I can't afford cable."

He smiled mischievously. "Stingy old bat. Which is why I brought you a special treat. Ta-dah!"

He held up a plastic bag with a video cassette inside.

"What's that?"

"My show reel. A compilation of every one of my 'what's on' segments, lovingly collected for posterity. I've been flogging it round the commercial networks, and I thought I'd take this opportunity to show you exactly what you've been missing. So break open the champers and force this into your slot."

He threw the tape to me.

"Uh, right now?"

"When else? Let's start with Show 3. I said the wittiest thing about biopeel facials. On second thought, let's take it from the top."

"We can watch for a minute, I suppose…"

He suddenly leapt up and sauntered to the window. "Are you aware that a sexy older man is moving in right next door? Older than me, I mean."

"Yes."

"I caught a glimpse just now. He was carrying a lamp single-handed. I love what he's done to the house. Makes your place look like a dump. But it was sweet of you to tidy up for me."

"Think nothing of it. How's your own flat looking?"

"Hideous." His eye alighted on the Greek delicacies. "Yum, dolmas."

"Put those down."

He peered into the street once more. "I'm sorry to be the one to tell you, but your car's been stolen."

"No, it hasn't. I moved it. Get away from the window."

He slunk over, slid his arms round me and gave my cheek a nuzzle. "I'd really like us to watch my video. Don't you want to?"

"We had all day to watch it."

"I know I've been neglecting you, but it's so time consuming being a celebrity on the TV."

"Even a minor one?"

"'Specially a minor one! I have to do all the work myself. But I love it to death! And I'm good at it; it comes naturally, like acne. People in high places are saying my segment is the best thing to happen to infotainment since smokers' toothpaste." He smiled a gleaming smile. "You know, I've got a spooky feeling. This could be the moment I've been waiting for after all those fame-challenged years." He squeezed me harder and began singing softly in my ear. "Could it be? / Yes it could / Something's coming…I've got wo-o-ood…"

"Paul, will you let go!"

"Not till I get a big kiss and a fuck."

"Oh, sorry. I beg your pardon."

Startled, we both looked up. Gavin was standing in the room.

"Ah, Gavin, there you are." I wrenched myself free.

"I can come back later if you like," he said. "The door was open…"

"No, no. Sit down!" I gushed, pulling myself together. "This is Paul," I added as an afterthought.

"Hi, Paul."

"Howdy, neighbor!"

"I'll put on coffee. Do help yourself to…uh…" I saw the empty plate sitting innocently on the table, a hundred percent dolma-free. "Bread?"

"No, thanks."

From the kitchen I could hear Gavin and Paul chatting away as I wiped down my maternal grandmother's silver coffee service. So much for a neighborly tête-à-tête, I thought, but hopefully Paul would be off soon. He must be late for other appointments by now.

I brought the cups in on my best tray.

"What's all this fancy stuff?" Paul asked tactlessly.

"Italian antique."

"Like you."

"We were just talking politics," said Gavin earnestly. I looked askance. "It's very interesting just now with the state election coming up."

"Oh, yes, extremely interesting," I lied.

"A lesbian friend of mine is standing in this seat," Gavin continued, "though between us, I don't like her chances."

"They changed the electoral boundaries," explained Paul.

"I know that," I snapped. "I'm not completely ignorant."

Gavin was getting quite excited. "The government created a new electorate out west—Grayhurst?"

He turned to me for confirmation. I looked blank.

"Yes, Grayhurst," said Paul.

"They think it'll be another safe seat for them, but the plan may possibly backfire. An independent is running and he's very popular."

"Ugh," said Paul, "you don't mean that redneck who sells cars on late-night TV?"

"He's the one. Stan Cahill."

I was staggered to hear Paul sounding so unnaturally well-informed. I resolved to redirect the conversation. "What kind of work do you do, Gavin?"

He smiled in broad cat-with-cream mode. "Corporate promotions...events management...in a small way, so far, but at least I'm my own boss. How about you, Marc?"

"I'm sort of retired."

He glanced dubiously around the room; a swift professional evaluation. "Made your pile early, eh?"

"You could say that."

"You two been here long?"

"Oh, Paul doesn't live here," I exclaimed with indecent haste.

"I did for a while," Paul grinned.

"No, you didn't."

"I did too."

"You stayed here. That's not the same as living."

Gavin looked faintly embarrassed. "Trust me to stir up trouble," he remarked.

"It's nothing like that," I explained. "You know, you're my third neighbor in that house. The first was a wonderful old woman, Russian, I think..."

He interrupted one of my best stories. "I enjoy doing a place up. Starting from scratch. I've achieved something very special with my little terrace here."

"It's gorgeous," I agreed.

"But I get restless. I like to sell and move on." He hesitated. "Not that there's anything wrong with this area. It's increasing in value out of all proportion."

"Onward and upward," Paul enthused.

A fleeting, predatory look brushed across Gavin's face as he reappraised my soon to be ex–best friend. "Excuse the old cliché, Paul, but you look familiar."

"Paul's an out-of-work actor," I said bluntly.

"Not anymore," Paul crowed and rushed over to the video. "Allow me to show you exactly what I do."

"Anyone for champagne?" I asked glumly. I felt a sudden desire for alcohol. If I wanted to play Getting to Know the Neighbor, it clearly wouldn't happen today. Paul's overwhelming enthusiasm for the subject of himself had temporarily thrown a wrench into the works.

chapter two

It was about this time I realized I had a more pressing problem to deal with: It came under the heading of the Petrucci Fortune. Namely, there wasn't one.

Since my early retirement from teaching hefty rich girls, I had been living on a dwindling bequest from a widowed aunt in Rome. My private Italian lessons provided the financial icing on the cake, covering little luxuries such as food. Of late, however, these lessons had completely dried up. I'd kept up my advertisement in *Queer Scene,* but obviously the readers had found alternative ways to amaze their friends. I was forced to face the unpleasant truth: I had to find gainful employment.

This was clearer than ever on the Monday morning after Paul had regaled Gavin and me with *Australia's Most Egocentric Home Videos.* Setting out to retrieve my car, I happened to glance back towards home sweet home. It was shabbiness personified and practically cringing with shame next to Gavin's gleaming showplace. My facade needed a little work, and a little work costs a lot of money.

By one of those eerie coincidences, I had parked outside an employment agency. With nothing to lose but poverty, I wandered inside. It was a new establishment, sleek and pastel-colored with a vase of fresh flowers at the reception—one of those arty vases designed to inspire confidence.

I filled out the complex paperwork, and then after a waiting period during which civilizations rose and fell I found myself seated opposite a tiny angular woman. According to the name-plate on her desk, she was called Ariadne.

"You're 50," she said brusquely, as she glanced up from my brief but pithy résumé.

"That's right."

She exhaled slowly through her nostrils. "Are you on the dole, or the pension?"

"I've been living off investments. Now I'm after a job."

"I'm afraid we specialize in corporate placings." She chucked the pithy résumé into the permanent out tray at her feet.

"But don't you have the government contract?" I asked.

She looked, if possible, even more pained. "You're not on the dole, so the government won't reimburse us for placing you."

"Oh."

"Still, let me see what I can do. Your last job was teaching, was it?" She began searching through a drawer.

"Excuse me—Ariadne?"

The woman looked up. "Ariadne's no longer with us. She was downsized."

"Sorry. I thought...anyway, the thing is, I'd rather not go back into teaching."

She slammed the drawer shut. "What *do* you want to do?"

"I don't know, really."

"You're not qualified for anything else."

I smiled winningly. "I make an excellent cup of coffee."

"Well, there are eleven cafés in this street. I suggest you do the rounds. Good afternoon."

The nearest café was two doors down, its doors open wide to the street. I slunk in and meekly ordered a cappuccino. As I sipped I watched pedestrians amble past in the wintry sunshine. They all held jobs, I assumed, yet very few of them looked clever or capable.

The latest copy of *Queer Scene* slouched in a magazine rack, already spattered with the remnants of multiple breakfasts. I perused the back section but found no offers of employment for opera-loving 50-year-olds. There were just the usual rent boys and young groovers in clubs, all half dressed with their mouths hanging open. These bleak pictures made me feel more than usually out of touch. In my clubbing days, I reflected, we wore clothes. If you wanted to strip, a darkened area was provided out the back. And we kept our mouths shut. Standards were clearly falling.

Then a familiar, distinctive face caught my eye.

Bernard Angelovski, known to his intimates as Angel, was one of the movers in the gay milieu. He'd been around a long time, even predating the pivotal protest march that had blossomed into Mardi Gras. I'd hung out with a more political crowd then, and Angel had been a big part of it. Lately our paths crossed less often.

Angel's picture appeared beside an advertisement for an adult education center: Gay Lifestyle Enhancement and Education, or GLEE, of which he was the creative director. The center was funded by the usual sponsors—travel consultants and wax 'n' tan studios—but this sponsorship didn't mean classes were free; a seven-week night course appeared quite pricey. Moreover, the center was situated at the Paddington end of Oxford Street, all of which suggested that whoever taught courses at GLEE might just possibly be paid. *Well,* I thought, *why not me?* It had to be better than teaching schoolgirls, who were only ever interested in clothes and each others' boyfriends. It would be a breeze for someone with my experience. I began to get quite enthusiastic, but once again my hopes were dashed: The courses were starting this week. Angel would have hired everyone he needed long ago.

A pallid girl with spiky pink hair swooped on my cappuccino. "I haven't finished it," I snapped, but she took no notice and whisked it away. I was about to complain when *Queer Scene*'s lead headline diverted my attention. "Gay Hate Murder," it screamed. Murder is a special interest of mine—what's more, I was in just the mood to read about somebody worse off than me.

The victim was a man named Quentin Butler. From the blurry picture he appeared to have been a handsome-ish older man, bald with a neat black mustache and goatee.

His body had been found in an inner city park, situated not far from where I live. This vast, hilly reserve had once housed a heavy industrial park. A dark, disused shot tower was the only original building remaining; all the rest had been long since demolished. Unhappily, every subsequent landscaping and beautification project had failed due to the high level of toxins left in the ground. Parkland authorities had given up trying to do anything with the place. As a result, it contained no kiosk or children's playground or even public toilets. The only citizens who got any use out of it were single gentlemen walking their dogs at dusk. In other words, it was a beat—and, in my limited experience, an area to avoid.

In one boggy corner, trees had been successfully planted in a memorial grove. This was colloquially known as the AIDS glade, and it was here Butler's body had been discovered by an overzealous malamute.

The police had nothing to say to the *Queer Scene* reporter, except to ask anybody with information to come forward. However, the owner of the dog who had made the gruesome discovery was more than happy to bask in his moment of notoriety. He described, with no little relish, how Butler's half clad body had suffered multiple stab wounds. It was the viciousness of the attack which lead *Queer Scene* to dub this murder a gay hate killing.

The whole gruesome story was hugely absorbing, but one particular sentence jumped out at me like a maternal funnel-web spider: "Butler was well known for his work at Sydney's GLEE Center for Gay Studies."

The Petrucci brain ticked over. If this Quentin Butler had taught courses for Angel, there could be a vacancy after all. It felt tacky, but my desperate circumstances called for desperate measures. I decided to visit GLEE without delay.

I found the building easily. At street level it was an art gallery, which I had occasionally passed by without realizing (or indeed caring) what lay upstairs. At the moment the gallery seemed to be between exhibitions, having nothing to show for itself but a vast, white-walled space, a staircase, and a heap of refuse against the far wall. The door was open and I made my way upstairs.

The second floor was cluttered with stacked chairs, room dividers, and whiteboards. The walls were covered in posters and notices.

A series of grunts emanated from behind a door at the far end of the room. I tiptoed across to peer inside and discovered a tiny makeshift office. At a desk, which bent precariously under the combined weight of phone books, take-out food, and a computer, sat Angel. He was on the phone.

"Mm," he snorted. "I hate to say it, but I'm not surprised. He was giving a lot of people the shits."

Without showing any sign of recognition, he waved me to the only other chair. I removed the coffee percolator from it and sat down to wait.

"I need to know now," he said, sounding impatient. "Either you can take this on, or you can't…"

I marvelled anew at the sight of this strange human being who, so far as I could tell, was completely hairless from top to bottom. His head gleamed and his beady eyes were set back in his face like sultana raisins wedged in dough ready for the oven. His outfit consisted of baggy jeans and a bleached hemp shirt under a teeny leather jerkin. Even when seated, the most striking thing about Angel was his size. He was shaped like some experimental giant pear.

"Sorry to burst in," I said, as he put down the phone.

He made no response, but peered briefly in my direction, then fumbled about on his desk to produce a pair of glasses. These had the effect of turning his pupils into sinister alien pods trapped inside goldfish bowls. They all stared at me as his face broke into a wide grin.

"Marc!" he gurgled, lunging over the desk. His large gut swept all before it, including a plastic tub of fried rice, which split open upon hitting the floor. He grabbed my face with two fleshy, oily mitts. "Well, well! You got yourself a new boyfriend yet?"

"You alwaysh bring thish up. No, I haven-n."

"Hopeless. How long is it since you and Andrew split? Must be five years!"

"Teh."

He let go of my face. "Ten, did you say? Slip out of that little black frock at once. What *are* you waiting for?"

"A stunning 28-year-old who adores me, knows nothing, and owns Microsoft."

Angel threw back his head and emitted his oft-imitated, deep-throated laugh. "Welcome to GLEE. Want to sign up?"

I bit the bullet. "Actually I was wondering if you needed any more teachers at all. To teach...things."

Angel looked momentarily taken aback. He drummed his fingers distractedly on the table. "We call them facilitators," he grunted. "Of course, you're a schoolteacher, aren't you."

"Retired, but..."

He pursed his lips. "Yes. Well, the fact is, we've had an unforeseen glitch in the schedule. To put it bluntly, one of our facilitators has been killed."

I believe I blushed. "I just read about it."

"Marc Petrucci. You filthy opportunist!"

I smiled weakly.

"But you could be a godsend. What do you know about the Warrior?"

"Who?"

"The Warrior as Icon: A Gay Perspective. That's Quentin's course."

I blanched. "Not much."

"No," he muttered to himself, then looked up hopefully. "Did you have something similar in mind? Something, you know, a bit butch?"

"I know lots about Italian opera."

Angel buried his face in his hands. I didn't read this as a good sign.

He looked up. "You see, Marc, most gay men aren't all that concerned with opera anymore. Icons have changed. It's not like it was when Maria Callas died. Everyone was opera mad back then. Couldn't get enough. Well, you'd know; you're a Callas freak."

I bristled. "Tebaldi, actually."

He stroked his jaw in the vicinity of where a chin would have existed on any other face. Suddenly, he slapped the table.

"Oh, the hell with it. Buggers can't be choosers, hey? You can do your opera. Throw in a few recipes to spice it up." Heaving himself to his feet, he lurched around the desk and planted a big wet kiss on my forehead. "Report for duty Tuesday night. Welcome aboard."

"OK." I instantly panicked. "Today's Monday."

"Tomorrow should be Tuesday then, by all accounts."

"But no one will know about the change," I remarked limply, stalling for time.

"Let me worry about that. See you at 6:30."

"Um, do you have a CD player there?"

Angel paused. "I can get one, but you'll have to keep the noise down."

"There's no such thing as soft opera."

"True, but another course will be in progress in the same room. It's nothing for you to worry about. They don't speak."

It wasn't until I was heading home that I realized we'd never discussed payment.

I prepared all the next day. However, by the time I'd photo-copied the libretto of *La Rondine* Act 1, accompanied by my own thoughtful translation, there was little time left to think about facilitation and what it entailed. I'd have to wing it.

The evening brought a downpour. As I bustled through pelting rain towards the door of the GLEE building, most of the precious photocopies slipped out of my hands and wafted into the gutter. I swore as I watched them dissolve into useless pulp; hardly an encouraging start to my new life in the workforce.

Angel was upstairs, setting up chairs. A row of partitions was now in place, dividing the space into two segments, one twice the size of the other. Groups of men stood around holding polystyrene cups and arguing vigorously. They wore woolen suits and single earrings.

"Ah, Marc!" called Angel, and rushed over to hug me. "Ooh, hon, you're all wet! Go and dry off. There's a towel in my office."

I made my way through the cluster of attendees into the office. Instantly, I stopped dead. A towel was there all right, but a boy was wearing it.

"Hi," he said, smiling. "I'm Stewart."

He had shortish red hair and a rather asymmetrical face, his nose being rather long with a slight kink in it. But his body! Perfection, as a descriptive term, didn't begin to tell the tale. It was one of those bodies you see in ads for beauty products and think, *It can't be real, they must have assembled this picture in the lab*.

I swayed, slack-jawed and moronic. "Towel?" I drooled.

"Oh, sure," said Stewart. He stood, unwound his towel, and handed it to me.

He was naked. If I'd been impressed before, I was now visibly moved. I felt an overwhelming impulse to throw myself at Stewart's feet and start worshipping from the toenails up. Incidentally, that long nose with the kink began to make perfect sense.

Like a priest handling the Shroud of Turin I cradled the towel as Stewart lowered his priceless bottom onto the desk.

"Hope the heater's on out there," the boy remarked. "Look, my nipples are sticking up."

"Orgh! So they are," I gagged, vigorously rubbing my hair.

"I'm posing for the life class," he continued.

"Uh, uh, my name's Marc," I replied, inconsequentially.

"Hi, Marc. Which course are you doing?"

"Um...I don't know. Which one are *you* doing?"

"I'm posing for the life class."

"Oh. Lovely. What's that?"

"Sketching. You know. I'm, like, the model." He lowered his voice confidingly. "The life class is the most popular. Some of the guys in the warrior group told me they only picked that one 'cause it's on the same night."

Just then, Angel poked his head around the door and grinned. "Stew, Gerda's here. Could you go and drape yourself all over the place? And Gerda says will you please not wriggle this week."

"Yeah, yeah."

I shambled to one side to let Mr. Perfection squeeze past. His electrically charged thigh brushed my fingertips.

"Marc?" whispered Angel. "What's that odd sound you're making? Are you hyperventilating? There's no need to be nervous. I'm going to introduce you and explain why we're switching over." He scratched his forehead. "You're not doing Wagner, I s'pose? Millions of warriors in his stuff."

"No. Puccini."

"Well, anyway, I've set up the CD, and we've cordoned you off so the sketching people don't get too distracted. And please, not too loud, or Gerda won't be happy. All righty?"

"What girder?" My brain was still delightfully addled.

"Gerda rents the gallery space downstairs and runs our art classes. I'll introduce you."

I glanced towards the door. "Introduce me to Stewart. He's…I don't know. Words fail me."

"You bet they do."

"Remember what you were saying yesterday—about new boyfriends and so on…"

"Read my lips: There's a queue a mile long. Now off you go."

Seconds later I found myself facing a semicircle of men, all eager and 30ish. Timidly I fiddled with CDs while Angel addressed the group, sotto voce.

"This is Marc," he announced bluntly. "Marc will be the facilitator for this course, as Quentin Butler can't be with us. I'm sure you all know why. I don't want to go into it now, except to say it has been a great shock to us at GLEE. Marc has kindly stepped in at ridiculously short notice. His subject is Italian opera."

A lanky man in a leather tie spoke up. "Does this have *anything* to do with the warrior as a gay icon?" His bearing was unashamedly warlike.

"I'll leave it up to Marc to bring in related themes," Angel answered smoothly. "But I will say this: opera has played an enormous role in the formation of gay sensibility. Our radically evolving lifestyle may have rendered the opera queen a thing of the past"—I glanced up, to find them staring at me as though I were an exhibit in the Poof Museum—"but he is relevant because history is always relevant. We must explore our past if we are to define our present. How do we know where we are, if we don't know where we came from? Gay history is a vibrant, oral history." There was a groundswell of interest at the word *oral*. "So I'll hand you over to Marc. If anyone wants to talk refunds, which I doubt you will, please do it afterwards."

With that, Angel ambled off to join the life class. The group eyed me expectantly.

"Well," I said, rubbing my hands with feigned confidence. At that precise moment I discovered that I could see Stewart through a gap in the partitions. There he lay in languid repose, propped up on one arm, legs slightly apart, staring straight back at me. He winked cheekily. My mouth went dry.

"Well?" said the man in the leather tie, sounding slightly cross.

"What? Oh, yes. Um, what?"

"What are we supposed to do?"

I cleared my throat. "We're going to listen to *La Rondine* by Giacomo Puccini."

A fragile, bespectacled man meekly raised his hand. "Will opera design and costuming be covered in this course?" he asked.

"Not tonight."

He looked shattered.

"Was Puccini a gay composer?" asked another man. Two or three others held pens poised to take notes.

"Not as such," I admitted. "But he did live in a de facto relationship for twenty years and his partner was insanely jealous. At one point she suspected Puccini of getting it on with the housemaid and hounded the poor girl to suicide. I'm sure, as homosexual men, we have all…uh…been in a similar situation."

"I certainly haven't," said the leather man.

"Well, no, neither have I, come to think of it. So, *La Rondine*. It's a vehicle for the soprano, as most of Puccini's operas are."

I made a final rash attempt to put a gay spin on the piece.

"The story is about Magda, a middle-aged woman who has led a full life in every sense of the word. Just like you or me, she's had plenty of lovers but never found real love, if you get my drift. Then into her life comes this handsome, naive boy…like you."

I pointed directly at a pretty boy sitting quietly at the side. Everyone turned to stare. He flinched, a look of genuine alarm flashing across his face.

"Let's plunge in," I said, handing out the few remaining photocopies. "I'll stop from time to time and tell you what's going on."

So I let Puccini do the work and, of course, the moment the orchestra struck up their opening chords I began to enjoy myself to the hilt. I encored Magda's first big number, simply because it was so beautiful, and I did the same with the sweet, nostalgic waltz tune, "Fanciulla, e sbocciato l'amore," in which she recalls her long-lost days of innocence.

With a minimum of interference and no discernible queer perspective whatsoever, we reached the end of Act 1. As it closed gently, with the orchestra recalling each of Magda's tunes in turn, and some gorgeous soft singing from the lady herself, I surveyed my audience. Surely, I thought, music this ravishing must be having some effect. My "Once Were Warriors" group exhibited the full spectrum of expressions from polite interest to utter boredom. I craned my neck to take a peek between the partitions where the delectable Stewart seemed to be fast asleep. Overall, I confess, I was disappointed.

Then my gaze came upon the boy whom I had singled out so abruptly before. He was leaning forward, his elbows on his knees, staring into the middle distance. His eyes were filled with tears.

chapter three

Trash is the vortex, the epicenter of what's left of gay old Oxford Street. Situated on a corner atop a well-stocked basement sex mart, haphazardly spilling stainless-steel chairs and tables almost into the path of oncoming traffic, Trash is the brasserie where every self-respecting gay boy meets, greets, and dishes dirt. Many spend their entire day there, lounging and languishing, macchiato untouched but SMS in constant operation. It is the first café to get *Queer Scene* delivered each week, and the last to close every night. Trash has a kitchen—somewhere—but no habitué ever orders anything to eat. The waiters become dazed and confused if you do.

I didn't know this and was coolly perusing a menu while I waited for Paul. During the week he'd rung to suggest a Sunday brunch out—probably feeling guilty for spoiling our last few— and had dropped several mysterious hints to the effect that he might have some exciting news for me. Of course, I had news myself, namely my blossoming career in facilitation. Two can play at one-upmanship. I also wanted to speak to him quite seriously about Quentin Butler's murder.

The gay rags were by no means the only media to cover the story. During the week Butler's grisly death had made a sensational appearance in the mainstream press, and I'd found out more than I really cared to know. Butler and his "partner" ran a movie memorabilia shop in Sydney's tourist area: the Rocks. Nothing was mentioned about the victim's link to GLEE, but there were reams of unsavory details concerning the murder itself. The knife attack had been swift and frenzied, with many of the blows striking the poor man in his groin and face.

Like all gay readers I suppose I felt especially unnerved because until this happened I'd regarded gay hate crime as a redneck sporting event that happened far away in the backward parts of the USA. Now that our own soap-opera demigods and high court judges were coming out, I'd simply assumed there was greater tolerance among right-thinking people. A false assumption, as I was quickly discovering.

Most worrisome of all, Butler had been a middle-aged man, like myself, savagely cut down at the tail end of his prime. The similarities between us were not something I cared to dwell upon, but how could I not? I had literally stepped into a dead man's shoes. The more I thought about this fact, the more it seemed like tempting fate—historically not my greatest ally. Once or twice over the preceding few nights I had woken up in a cold sweat.

I would have liked to have broached the subject with Gavin (or any subject, come to that), but he wasn't around. Evidently my new neighbor was yet to take up residence in his flashy new house.

At last a combination of fear, guilt, and, yes, embarrassment had forced me to a decision: Paul and I would investigate this crime. We had a good track record, having solved two murders already, and I felt I owed it to Quentin Butler. I just needed Paul himself to agree.

When he eventually materialized at my side, radiant and only slightly late, his face froze in an expression of horror.

"Caro, stop! What in the sacred name of Beulah do you think you're you doing?"

"Getting ready to order."

"Don't be a fool. This place is for meeting, not eating. For heaven's sake!"

He waved to the waiter who casually breezed over. This doe-eyed boy wore a muscle shirt that didn't come close to containing his bulk. That he could survive in such a garment without succumbing to first degree frostbite was a miracle.

"We do *not* need the menu," Paul snapped.

The waiter shrugged. He understood perfectly. "Your friend here asked for it."

"He didn't know any better," answered Paul. "Please just bring us two lattes." He grinned, all mysterious and sphinx-like. "And now…my big news."

Mine would have to wait, naturally enough. "Let me guess. You're pregnant."

"Wrong. It's work related." Paul squeezed my hand. "I'm hitting the big time. Ta-ta, obscurity! Fare thee well, Never-Heard-of-Her!"

"You're leaving the cable show?"

He nodded solemnly. "They've been heaven to work with. Supportive and absolutely wonderful. But fuck 'em! I had a capital-M meeting on Friday with Sonia Porter-Hibble. She wants me for *NOW!*" He sprang up and kissed me all over the head, practically up-ending the table.

"Let me get this straight. Sonia Porter—"

"Hibble is the Editor of *NOW!*—the glossy magazine for girls. Well, for grown women, really, but they call themselves girls, same as we do."

"You're going to be a journalist?" I blinked. "You?"

"Not exactly. *NOW!* has a cross-media deal with Channel 6. They put out a weekly infotainment lifestyle program. *NOW TV!* Sonia adores my around-town pieces, and she wants me in their show."

"What does your sordid existence have to do with women's interests?"

"Don't know," he replied blankly, "I didn't ask. I guess queer is where it all happens first. That's certainly true of fashion, except in your case."

"Thanks."

"Sonia's keen for me to keep on doing the same type of thing, but on a more lavish scale. I'll take you to the opera! There's no reason I can't embrace cultural activities along with Martyrdom and Tumescence."

"Sorry?"

"They're dance parties." He clapped delightedly. "Oh, look! GayLez FM is doing an outside broadcast."

I peered through the window. Since my arrival the curbside tables had been cleared away to make room for a disc jockey's microphone, desk, and turntable. A heavily made up girl with tired eyes seated herself at the desk and lazily donned a set of headphones. Nearby, a second girl poured buckets of steaming water into a plastic kiddies' pool, transforming the plain household object into a lathery spa. Having completed this task, she placed both index fingers in her mouth and gave a piercing whistle. From the bistro kitchen emerged three pink, pumped up musclemen wearing skimpy gym shorts. One of the musclemen was our waiter.

"We'll never get our coffee now," Paul remarked.

The men bounced up to the spa, flung their shorts at the water-carrier, and stood nude on one of the busiest intersections in the city. One by one, with much good-natured teasing and slapping, they lowered themselves into the tub.

"Are we on?" murmured the DJ, her nasal tones disagreeably amplified. "Hi, you're with GayLez FM, 191 on the dial, I'm Trish and we're outside Trash, makin' a splash! Let's have some music."

"Paul, can we go somewhere else?" I begged. "I'm famished."

"I wanna watch the steroid promotion."

"But it's getting loud, and I've got some news of my own."

"What is it?"

"Well…"

He jumped up with a huge grin on his face. "Wait. Look!"

The water sports were attracting a certain amount of attention, not all of it welcome. A drunk was lurching towards the pool, cursing and swearing colorfully. It seemed these gym bunnies were cavorting in his favorite spot. The DJ looked around for help, unwilling to abandon her duties.

One of the musclemen started flicking foam at the drunk. "Piss off," he whined. "We're doing a promo here."

The drunk took this as an invitation to join them. His weathered face lighting up with joy, he attempted to climb into the pool. A couple of the boys tried to stop him, but slipped on the plastic, splashing foam into the gutter and lowering the water level perceptibly.

"Those sweet innocent kids," Paul chortled as he hauled me to my feet. "They're only trying to show off their body work."

"They don't look too innocent to me," I said.

We elbowed our way through the crowd that had now formed outside the café and hurried down Oxford Street.

"Let's find a Thai place," Paul enthused. "It's time for lunch."

"Do you want to hear my news now?" I inquired testily.

"Sure."

"I thought you'd never ask."

So I told him about GLEE and my first opera session, describing it as a glowing artistic success, and casually mentioned that the man I'd replaced had been hacked to death. Pretty sensational goss, I thought! Paul knew about the killing, of course, and immediately hit upon the salient point.

"So you rushed right over to grab his job," he squealed.

I grimaced. "I feel terrible about it too. Every time I think about it I'm sick."

Paul's mouth fell open. "Why?"

"I feel guilty."

"Caro, you did the humane thing. Is this gig worth a packet?"

I smiled wanly. "I'm sort of waiting for them to bring that subject up."

He skidded to a halt. "And you've already started? You're nuts."

"Possibly."

"Still, I don't suppose you need the dough."

"I do," I protested. "Desperately! That's the whole point."

He took my hand with a look of condescending pity. "I didn't know," he said.

"I'm sure you did."

"Oh, well, I must have forgotten, which is the same thing." He winked. "I'll treat you to a celebrity lunch."

"Who's the celebrity?"

"Be sensible. My new celebrity is me! You know, I was thinking about those boys in the pool. That's the kind of stuff I want to bring to *NOW TV!* I want to push the envelope. To shock and delight."

As Paul continued in this vein, it became clear that an unpaid murder investigation was the last way he'd care to spend his precious time. He had his hands full letting success go to his head. If there was any snooping to be done, I would have to do it solo— and GLEE was the obvious place to start.

chapter four

I spent all of the following Tuesday preparing for my opera class. It was one thing to improvise stunningly on the spot, but to remain impressive, research was required. I wasn't comfortable with the local Internet café—the scent of marijuana put me off—so I took myself down to my local library.

In an attempt to be user-friendly, I selected a popular piece which would be familiar to the class: Bizet's *Carmen*. It's full of hummable tunes and Carmen herself is your basic sexual predator. A slut, to be frank. Surely this would strike a chord. I went to the added expense of borrowing all three of the library's recordings so we could compare famous Carmens: Supervia, Crespin, and Horne. The most important thing a gay man needs to learn about opera is that some divas are better than others. In fact, divas fall into two categories: the divine and the dreck. There is no in-between.

Heartily I threw myself into these detailed comparisons. It was only when packing up my copious notes that I remembered a sobering fact: Carmen is stabbed to death in the last act. In the light of Quentin Butler's demise, my choice of *Carmen* suddenly struck me as rather tasteless.

It was too late to rethink.

School night was chilly but at least this time it was not rain-ing. The GLEE door stood open and I rushed up the stairs a pair at a time. The facilitation room was set up as before, and groups of the artistically challenged were hanging about. The delectable Stewart wasn't among them, but I did not fret. He was probably toweling himself somewhere very private at this precise moment. I practically scampered into Angel's office.

I found Angel sitting moodily at his desk. His discarded coffee bobbed with cigarette butts.

"Ah, Marc," he said flatly. "You're early."

"Just keen, I guess. I'm doing *Carmen* tonight." I hesitated. "You don't think that will be too…pointed?"

He looked at me blankly. I made stabbing motions with my hands.

"I'm sorry," he said, "I'm a bit preoccupied. I only just got here myself. I intended to ring you, but I didn't get around to it."

My face fell. "My session's still on, isn't it?"

He shrugged. "There were a few cancellations after last week. Perfectly nice about it, of course…"

"Not everyone, surely!"

"We'll have to cool our heels and see how many show up. You don't mind if I smoke, do you?"

Without waiting for an answer he threw a cigarette between his lips and picked up a cheap lighter. He flicked it and shook it but it simply refused to ignite. With an explosive "Fuck!" he hurled both lighter and cigarette against the wall. I jumped. His hands were shaking with barely suppressed rage.

"Don't let anyone tell you the cops have changed over the last twenty years," he snarled. "I'm sorry, but they're as homophobic as ever. Do you know, Marc—can you imagine!—they were practi-cally accusing me of Quentin's murder this afternoon?"

"That's ridiculous," I murmured.

"Of course I would kill one of my best teachers! Of course I would put the damn place in jeopardy. Jesus!"

"Facilitators."

"What? Oh, yes." He took a deep breath. "The police get me

to identify the body—you know, to do their work for them—and then they expect me to provide an alibi. I was here. I'm always bloody here! I don't know who else was around. People come and go all the time."

Angel started to sip his cold coffee but luckily noticed the cigarette butts in time. He frowned. "Quentin's a bigger pain in the tits now than when he was alive, if you want the truth."

It was time to do some Petrucci-style detective work.

"Sounds like you didn't get on with him," I remarked noncommittally.

"That's what someone's been telling the cops, I suspect. The thing is, nobody got on with him lately. Still, he knew his stuff, I'll give him that. The Warrior thing would have been terrific. He had a real sense of gay iconography. He was a prime mover in LAV."

"Pardon?"

"Haven't you heard of it? Leathermen Against Vanilla? It's a loose association dedicated to broadening the parameters of sexual expression. Quentin was devoted to it. The movement meant everything to him."

I made a mental note to look into LAV. "But lately...?" I prompted.

Angel raised his eyebrows. "Oh, we had the occasional difference of opinion. I don't like to see young gay men abused and belittled. There's enough of that out there." He waved a fleshy paw in the direction of the homophobic world-at-large.

"What happened?"

"Oh, there were incidents." He snorted dismissively.

I tried a different tack. "Do you think it was a gay hate crime?"

He shrugged. "I don't know. It was certainly a hate crime. He was doing the beat, of course."

"Beats have always been dangerous."

"That's why some people like them," he remarked. "I wouldn't have thought Quentin was the type."

"Maybe he was out walking his dog."

Angel shook his head. "Cat man, through and through."

"I see. He didn't walk his cat, then?"

He smiled faintly. "Not that I know of." I was relieved to see him calming down. "It's just that Quentin wasn't someone you'd pick on. He kept himself in shape. A man's man."

I nodded. "It's a tragedy." I craned my neck to take a peek through the office door. "Speaking of keeping in shape, is young Stewart around?"

Angel lurched to his feet. "No, and that's another bloody thing I have to deal with. He's a lovely person—"

"So I saw."

"But such an airhead. He rang an hour ago, says he's spooked by the murder and too frightened to come in. The poor baby feels vulnerable posing up there in front of everyone. What utter bull-shit! That boy's vulnerable like Fort Knox. Anyway," Angel patted his stomach, "the police have kept me too busy to find somebody else, so I guess I'll just have to be the model myself."

"You?" I could just imagine the faces of the sketch artists when they discovered the substitution—especially those whose work was only half completed.

"Why not?" Angel answered gruffly. "It's not all flab. Feel that."

He flexed his bicep for me. I was stunned to find a large, tight muscle not too far beneath the surface.

"See? I'm not to be trifled with." He grinned. "Come on, I want to say a few words before we start."

By now the main group had finished setting up. Gazing around, I recognized nobody from my own course. The six chairs on the operatic side of the partition were empty.

"Looks like tonight's performance of *Carmen* is cancelled," Angel whispered to me, then strode out in front of the class. I expected him to say something smooth and apologetic about Stewart's absence, but Angel's thrust was quite different.

"GLEE has no official political affiliations," he began, "but as you know, there's a state election this weekend and I would urge you to check out the candidates very carefully on the mat-ter of their sexual politics. An election is one of our rare opportunities to challenge the status quo. For those of you from the Inner West, there's an out and proud lesbian contesting your seat. She's a professional lobbyist, former journalist with *Queer Scene*, and in my opinion well deserving of your vote. Ms. Celeste Ireland."

The name rang an unwelcome bell. I had once been the subject of Ms. Ireland's investigative journalism, though I had never clapped eyes on her. In the affair in question, murder at a gay and lesbian resort, her report had mixed up a lot of half truths and painted me as some kind of underworld mastermind. I somehow doubted she'd be getting my vote.

"Our model can't be here for this session," Angel added casually. At this, the air temperature in the room dropped by several degrees. "But please continue to set up. I've got a real treat in store for you! Back in a sec."

Angel's promise of a treat created a buzz of interest. He immediately went into a huddle with a short woman who had been standing patiently nearby. She wore jeans, heavy black-rimmed spectacles and her gray hair was severely cropped. The two of them spoke for a moment, then Angel waddled over to me. He glanced at the empty chairs and shook his head.

"Oh, well," he murmured, patting me on the back. "Would you like to do it?"

"What?"

"Model for the class?"

I gulped. "Me? Stark naked?"

"Of course. Come on, don't be a wuss."

"But what about you?"

He shrugged. "Gerda thinks I'm too easy to draw."

"No. No, I couldn't!"

He poked his finger into my chest. "You see, this is your trouble, Marc. No wonder you don't have a sex life. You have to value yourself more highly. You need to get out there. It'll be good for you." He smiled sympathetically, then wandered back to the life class, pulling off his shirt as he did so. The gasps were audible.

"Excuse me?" It was the art mistress. She was holding a CD. "I am Gerda."

I nodded. "Pleased to meet you. I'm Marc. I'm the opera—"

"I know," she interrupted. "You will not be using the machine tonight?"

"No. I guess I won't."

"I will put some music in," she said brusquely, brushing past and sliding her CD into the player. A pulsating drum pattern emerged. My temples began to throb in perfect time.

Listening to this mindless racket as I packed away my *Carmen* paraphernalia, I couldn't help but feel disappointed. Maybe Angel was right. Maybe opera queens were dying out. I looked across at him, posing in the exact position Stewart had adopted the week before. He was twice the man Stewart was—in terms of bulk, at least.

Could he be a murder suspect? Surely not. Yet I couldn't truthfully say I knew Angel well enough to rule him out.

I thought about our chat. He'd admitted arguing with Quentin Butler—and Angel unquestionably had a temper. Physically he was more formidable than he might appear. And something else had struck me: the police had asked him to identify the body. From the reported state of Butler's injuries, that should have been an appalling, traumatic thing to do—yet Angel's only comment was that it inconvenienced him.

I'd have liked to bounce these impressions off Paul, but that's showbiz. Instead, I faced the exciting prospect of going home and listening to three performances of *Carmen*.

I trudged downstairs. The ground floor was in darkness. Not bothering with the light switch, I edged towards the door. I was halfway there when I knocked my elbow on a filing cabinet and dropped my entire bundle of CDs and papers. As I scrabbled around on all fours trying to pick them up, the front door swung open and someone came running in. Whoever this person was, I had no time to warn him or get out of the way: he flew straight into me, trod on my fingers, and hurtled ass over pecs to finish up flat on his back.

Aching from hand to foot, I stood up. The other person hadn't moved; he was moaning softly. I found the wall and felt for the switch. A blaring neon flickered on, revealing a young man in black jeans and a khaki windbreaker. A cut on his nose was seeping blood. His eyes flickered open. I recognized him right away: it was the boy from my previous session, the one who had been moved to tears by *La Rondine*.

"Are you all right?" I asked him.

"I tripped over something," he whispered.

"Me," I said, and kneeled to staunch the cut with my handkerchief. "Can you move? Nothing broken, I hope?"

"I hit my nose," he replied, as I helped him carefully to his feet.

"Sit here on the stairs for a while," I counselled. "Keep the hanky. I'm Marc, by the way."

"Tim." He smiled painfully.

I hadn't really noticed him the previous week, except to register a vague plus on the cute scale. Now, I took the opportunity to peruse at close quarters Tim's shock of thick, dark hair, deep set dimples, and extraordinary cool blue eyes. It was the eyes that got me in: They were large and trusting, not unlike those in mass-produced artworks depicting children or puppies. His eyes were set close together, which gave his facial expression an added intensity, further enhanced by a pair of stainless steel studs on either side of his nose.

"Don't you think you should take your, um, nose studs out?"

"Not supposed to. They're new."

He got up, coughed and started to sway. Automatically I reached out with both arms and grabbed him. He rested his head on my chest as I hung on, sensing the solid body beneath the wind cheater. We stood frozen in this unexpected embrace. After a long intimate moment, I spoke.

"My session's cancelled tonight. Nobody else turned up."

"Bummer."

"How are you feeling? I'm going to let go of you."

"OK."

He grasped the railing as I stepped back. "I think your nose has stopped bleeding," I remarked.

"Yeah. Thanks." He smiled once again. The dimples were truly dazzling. I decided to take Angel's advice and be forthright for a change.

"Tim—since the opera's not happening—would you like to go for a drink?"

"OK."

I blinked. I hadn't expected it to be quite so easy.

Conversation flagged as we briskly headed towards a nearby pub. The boy was reticent, hardly your typical GLEE-going yuppie. He was probably still supported by his parents, I decided, or by a sugar daddy. I hoped not.

The bar was not one of those thriving establishments on Oxford Street catering to a queer clientele but merely a no-nonsense watering hole left over from the days when Paddington was a working man's domain. It was empty.

Tim ordered a beer and ambled straight to the men's room to clean himself up. I secured myself the ever-reliable vodka and tonic.

"Any trade?" I grinned, as he shuffled back to the bar. He glowered and clutched his drink. Obviously light camp banter was not the way to go.

"I'm glad you turned up," I admitted, with the utmost candor. "It would have been profoundly tragic otherwise."

"Yeah, well. You gotta give things a chance."

"I wish the others in the class felt that way. But perhaps it was the murder that put them off rather than the opera."

Tim didn't reply but stared directly into his glass.

"A shocking thing. This murder, I mean. I feel awful about it, particularly as that's how I got my job at GLEE." I laughed brightly. "You know people often say 'I'd kill for that job'? I sort of know how they feel."

My companion shifted in his seat.

"Anyway," I added quickly, "let's not talk about that, it's too depressing. How about you? What do you do? For a living, that is."

"Haven't settled on anything. I worked on a movie set at Fox Studios for a while. That was cool. I'd go for something else like that."

"Mm. Times are hard, aren't they? I was practically thrown out of an employment agency the other day."

"Don't you have a real job?"

"I used to be a teacher. I retired, but lately money's a bit tight. Still, I can afford another drink. Beer for you, is it?"

"I haven't finished this one yet."

I fidgeted with my empty glass. "I was going to play *Carmen* tonight. Do you know it?"

"I've heard of it."

"Oh, it's a brilliant work. And here I've done hours of preparation for nothing...I know! Why don't I play you some of it at my place?"

"I dunno…"

"It's not far," I persisted. "Scull that down and we'll go."

"Well…"

"I'll make us a nice hot coffee," I wheedled. Angel would have been proud of me.

He nodded and uttered the magic letters: "OK."

I practically capered around him as we hurried back to my car, swamping him with the story of the opera and making a few shaky attempts to hum the Toreador song. Tim never uttered a syllable. He really was the strong, silent type. But, I reminded myself, it's the quiet ones who go berserk in the bedroom.

We parked and I literally led him up the garden path. I was unlocking the door when a sound close by scared me out of my wits: a loud, vicious snarl. I jumped, involuntarily, into Tim's arms.

He gently pushed me away. "Don't. Not here."

The snarl transformed itself into a ear-shattering bark.

"What the hell's that?" I whispered.

"A dog?" suggested Tim.

I peered over the fence. It was dark, but I could vaguely make out a slavering Baskervillian form. It glared at me from next door's step.

"You're right! Gavin's got a dog," I muttered. "I'll bet the bloody thing wakes up yapping every morning at 5 o'clock, come rain or shine."

The dog growled in confirmation.

Tim stared at me quizzically. "Don't you like dogs?"

"They don't like me, for some reason." The creature barked again. "Stop that!" I snapped.

"Hector," a voice called out. "What is it, boy?"

Gavin's door burst open and he appeared, looking cute but fierce in his neatly pressed football shorts. The dog trotted innocently inside.

"Who's there?" Gavin demanded.

"Me! Marc from next door," I called, waving a cheery hand. "I'm just getting home."

"Oh. I hope Hector didn't disturb you. Good night."

"Night."

"G'night, Paul," Gavin added.

"Uh, this is Tim," I explained hastily. "One of my students."

"Oh, right. Can't see you there. You should get an automatic light installed, Marc, it's much safer. We can't be too careful with this gay killer around. Well, enjoy yourselves."

Gavin retired and all was quiet once more. I unlocked my door.

"Here it is," I announced, "my humble abode. Do come in."

Tim didn't budge.

"Is everything all right?" I asked solicitously.

"I've changed my mind," he murmured.

I cursed inwardly as I gave his shoulder an avuncular squeeze. "Look, you're getting all tense. Let's put on some music and relax. Mm?"

He took a step back. "Who's this Paul? Does he live here?"

"No! Just me. You needn't worry, nobody will disturb us."

"No," he said firmly. "I can't. I think I'd better go."

I could hardly believe it. What had gotten into the boy? "How about one more drink and we call it a night?" I pleaded. "You've come all this way…"

"No, I said!" Without another word he scampered away into the dark. Then and there, I decided I never wanted to hear *Carmen* again.

Once inside, I poured myself a scotch and settled back to soak up the siren song of Tebaldi soaring above the stave in *La Bohème*. I tried not to feel frustrated, but it did seem like I was strolling into one brick wall after another these days.

As the opera eased my mind, the situation gradually became clear. It was obvious Tim had been frightened off by all this talk of gay-hate murder. Stupidly I'd even brought the subject up myself. In fact, after my crass joke about killing for a job, he probably thought I *was* the murderer! I was now more determined than ever to lend my investigative prowess to this case. After all, I reflected, I had plenty of time on my hands to do it.

Or so I thought. That aspect of my life was about to change radically.

chapter five

"Hello? You're a busy little bee for someone with no life! Pick up the phone! Not there? *Ay caramba.* OK, well, relax. I've been on your case. Don't say I neglect you, *caro mio.* I've dedicated my entire day to making your existence worthwhile. You'll flip when I tell you how." The voice on my answering machine giggled. "Now, let me see—I'm not contactable tonight, I'm going out. Oh, and guess what? My date is a hairdresser who works at the TV studio, Raymond. My hair takes forever to get right, so I'd better stay on his good side. Well, every side's a good side from what I can see so far. What was I talking about?"

Beep. The voice cut off abruptly midflow. If I'd been able to save every message ever recorded on my machine, I would have the makings of a long-running soap opera called *The Life and Loves of Paul Silverton*. His next call followed seconds later.

"Me again. What I really rang to say was, I hope you're not busy Friday because we are booked in for a business lunch. You, me, and Sonia Porter-Hibble! She'll adore you, and she's so-o-o important even though I know you've never heard of her. Glance through this month's *NOW!* if you get the chance. Or at least cast your eye over the cover. We're lunching at Xadok at Bondi Beach. Pure trendoid. We'll have the best table and get shit-faced at someone else's expense. I'll meet you there at 12:30, downstairs. Wear something retro. What am I saying? You always do. Ciao!"

Some winter days you curse the fact that you ever have to get out of bed. You lie there listening as loose segments of your roof rumble, buffeted by gale force winds, while rain pellets strike at the window like small persistent birds with no concept of glass. Such days are hideous, but at least you know where you stand. The other kind of winter mornings—the ones where the sun's out and the world appears serene—are even more treacherous. They contain traps for the unwary, like sudden gusts of wind direct from the Antarctic which cause your lips to shrivel and bleed and age you beyond recognition.

The day of Paul's surprise business lunch was one of these sneaky ones. In the moderate confines of Villa Petrucci, a natty black polo-neck and a lightweight shaggy sports coat provided all the comfort my body craved, but out in the pallid sunshine I was soon chilled to the heart.

The surf was up at Bondi and a few rubber-coated diehards braved it on their boards. I was early for my appointment so I watched these graceful creatures, bracing myself against the building for protection from the elements. As an ardent inner-city urbanite I rarely make the trek to the ocean; when I do, I prefer to go during that first warm spell before Christmas, when the locals pack away their fake winter tans to start working on the real thing and nobody has a stitch on.

I waited. No sign of Paul or anyone else appeared. Every so often I glanced at my old reliable watch to note with surprise that I was still early. Finally I realized the watch had stopped—petrified by the cold, no doubt. Cursing, I rushed upstairs into the restaurant.

Xadok inhabited a large L-shaped room with floor to ceiling windows looking out over beachside parking lots. Very light and uncluttered, it sported white walls with minimalist art—for example, a framed question mark fashioned from a piece of string—and a polished floor of blanched wood, miraculously free of dust.

A slick waiter greeted me, wearing the full knee-length navy blue apron with matching corkscrew accessories.

"Do you have a reservation?" he droned over the hubbub.

"I'm meeting friends." I glanced at a minimal clock on the wall, hewn from a lump of sandstone. I was twenty minutes late. "They should be here…" I could see nobody among the throng who looked like my party, least of all a table of what I took to be circus performers in the prime ocean-view position.

"What name was it?" the waiter asked. His tone suggested he would shortly be required to escort me downstairs with force.

"Silverton?" I ventured. "Paul Silverton? Or Porter Something?"

"Porter-Hibble?"

"Yes."

His eyelashes quivered in exquisite disbelief as he pointed to the circus table. "There," he said, giving my outfit a derogatory once-over.

At that moment, a circus person sprang up and came heading towards me. It was Paul.

"Caro! At last! Don't say a word." He did a double take at my coat. "When I said retro I didn't mean something out of an archaeological dig."

"This is timeless," I answered. "What about you? You look grotesque."

His hair had been cut short, evidently using two blunt rocks, then peroxided until it had settled into a series of stiff yellow spikes.

"I'm not totally committed to it myself," he admitted in a stage whisper. "It's just a look. Anyway, come on and meet the girls!"

"What's this lunch all about?"

He winked. "You'll find out. Did you catch this month's cover?"

I had, but it meant nothing to me. Two blurry photos of supermodels, not caught at their best, were divided by a jagged red line. The words BITTER FEUD were splayed across the pictures in pseudo graffiti style. Who these bitter combatants were or what the feud was over remained a mystery.

"Yes—" I began.

"Good! Be sure to toss it into the conversation."

He dragged me to the table. Seated there were two women. The younger was verging on plump and had a pleasant, open face. She wore a simple outfit in fiery red and glasses with frames the same color. She extended her hand as Paul did the honors.

"Helen Jamieson, Marc Petrucci."

She nodded.

"Helen is Sonia's private secretary," explained Paul.

The other woman, presumably Ms. Porter-Hibble, was mid phone conversation. She was of indeterminate age, her thick, pale makeup quashing any chance of making an informed guess. Her hair had been tortured in exactly the same style as Paul's, except that it extended upwards by a further six inches. Her face was long and square, as was her body, wrapped tightly in a burnt orange business suit. From a distance she would have looked remarkably like an HB pencil.

"No, but that's terrific," she blared into the smallest cell phone I'd ever seen. "Of course they can…cut it! Cut it! She repeats herself to death, God knows…repeats herself to death. OK, I want the new layout on my desk when I get back in ten minutes." She folded the cell phone into a ball and palmed it, then shot her hand in my direction. "Matt! You made it, I thought I was going to miss you."

"Sonia Porter-Hibble, Marc Petrucci."

"No need to introduce us. I'm sure we've met, haven't we? I think it's terrific you're gay. My first husband was, you know. Poor dear. Years ahead of his time! My God, that coat takes me back."

"Marc is *Mister* Retro!" Paul gushed. "He just doesn't know it."

"How wise not to know. Do sit down."

Befuddled, I sat. My chair was smack in the path of a back-numbing breeze. I couldn't work out where it was coming from. I ached for a bowl of steaming hot soup.

"I've ordered us a green salad," Sonia enthused. "Energy food. Rush, rush, rush!"

"I'm sorry I'm late," I said. "My watch—"

"Heart, you had a meeting. When *don't* they run over? I know, it's sheer hell." She wriggled over to Paul and rewarded him with a big kiss. "Isn't he very special? You two are lovers, I can tell."

"No!"

"We work together," said Paul. "A business partnership."

"Oh, yes, all right then! Keep up your little charade! Paul tells me— Heart! Another drink? Paul tells me you practically *invented* television." She patted my hand. "I'm a print journo from way back. A mag hag! But the TV show is my little fling on the side. Bloody good idea, don't you agree? Bryce oversees all that. You'll meet him this afternoon. You *have* managed to clear the afternoon?"

"Yes," answered Paul.

"I appear on the show personally," Sonia went on, "purely in the interest of sales. I'm no star, but I have my fifteen seconds of fame. Or was it fifteen years? Whatever the man said. But the point is, nothing like the acclaim our Paul is about to experience! How *astute* of you to find him, Matt. This kid's going places."

"I'm very serious about my career," said Paul, very seriously. "This is my life, you know? It's not a rehearsal."

Sonia's jaw dropped. "That's brilliant! So NOW!"

The secretary coughed quietly.

Sonia continued. "Circulation's never been higher," she crowed. "Helen's got the latest figures somewhere."

I remembered the magazine cover.

"What about that bitter feud?" I exclaimed chattily.

"Which feud is that, Matt?"

"Marc."

"Yes."

"I meant the—uh—feud between those two supermodels. On the cover."

Her heavily mascaraed eyes focussed in on me like lasers. "Nicci's on the cover, surely. 'Nicole's Cancer Shock!' Isn't that right, Helen? We lock these things in months ahead. I scheduled Nicci's photo shoot the *second* those test results came through."

The other woman spoke for the first time. She had a London accent. "*Bimbeau* has the supermodel feud."

I'd glanced at the wrong magazine! Well, they all look the same, after all.

"Oh, *Bimbeau*," Sonia seethed. "Yes, Matt, I see your point. You're absolutely spot on. *What* bitter feud indeed? A beat-up if ever there was. We didn't look twice at it." She grinned viciously. "I can see you're *devastatingly* perceptive."

Sonia's secretary regarded me with justifiable scepticism.

"'Fraid I can't wait around for salad, the deadline looms." Sonia leapt out of her seat. "Terrific to have you on board." She gave me a wet peck on the lips. "Helen'll take care of details. Paul, walk me to a cab, I like to be seen out with a hot young guy."

As the spiky-haired duo left the room arm in arm, heads turned, exactly as Sonia had predicted.

I settled back to meet the secretary's wry gaze.

"Sonia does love a challenge," she said drily. "She won't rest till she's got that boy exactly where she wants him."

"You mean in bed?"

"It has happened before. What are you drinking?"

"Nothing."

"I'm *asking* you what you want. Relax! I'm going with champagne myself."

"Perfect," I replied with some relief.

The laconic waiter arrived at our table, lugging a glass bowl of greenery. He didn't even get the chance to put it down.

"Cancel the salad," commanded Helen, quietly but firmly. "Bring us a bottle of Dom and the dessert menu." She winked at me. "You look like you've got a sweet tooth, *Matt*."

"It's Marc."

"I know. I bet you'd like me to fill you in about what's really going down."

"I would, actually."

"You ever worked in media?"

"Never."

She sighed. "Well, even so, we're offering you a job if you want it."
I was amazed. "Really? What kind of job?"

"Paul starts with us next week. We also have plans to try him out with a column in the mag. The two feed off each other, as Sonia was saying. Paul has asked for a personal assistant. Specifically, you."

"Oh! That's wonderful, but I—"

"You have no idea what to do. That's cool. Sonia's indulging him. He's her fluffy new toy. If he wants you on the payroll, you're on…for the time being. Don't misunderstand me; she's a very shrewd lady, and your friend is fiercely hot and he's going to be hotter. But some time in the near future Sonia will get over him and latch on to someone else, and he'll be dropped. And so will you. I'm only telling you this because I think you need to be clear about it. You don't strike me as an operator. Nothing personal."

A subdued pop caused me to glance around. The waiter was opening champagne behind us.

"By the way," Helen added with a subtle grin, "their zabaione's super here—and they serve it *warm!*"

"Two zabaione, *per favore*," I said to the waiter as he poured. "Served warm."

"Cheers," Helen grinned. "I don't suppose you need a moment to think about the offer."

She was right, I reflected grimly. "Well," I answered, "since I've cleared the afternoon and everything."

"Good! I'll take you in, and we'll set it in motion. Studio day is Wednesday. Got any questions?"

As it happened, I did. I was not about to make the same mistake twice. "What's the money?" I asked.

"Speak to Bryce about that. He's aware of the situation."

"You mean I can name my own price?"

"Don't go to town." She laughed wickedly. "You won't be on salary; you'll just invoice NOW! Holdings. That way we don't need to concern ourselves with holiday pay, etcetera. It makes your contract easier to terminate when the time comes. Are you a company?"

"No."

"Doesn't matter. We can still do it." She leaned forward. "Now tell me, how well do you know Paul?"

"We're not a couple," I repeated. "Honestly."

"I can see that. I mean as a friend. The reason I'm asking is, you could be genuinely useful. Sonia likes the way Paul free-associates; he'll say anything that comes into his head. Now, that's not a problem in magazines; they're planned out weeks in advance down to the last comma. Everything's considered and reconsidered and the editorial process lets nothing iffy get through. Telly, on the other hand, has no editorial process at all—a lot of the show goes live to air. Sonia doesn't see the potential problem.... How shall I put it? The very quality she likes in Paul could also be his downfall."

"You mean he could say something stupid on the air?" To my way of thinking, this was merely a matter of time.

"We need a person Paul trusts; someone who can keep an eye on him without cramping his style. And when I say we, I don't mean Sonia. This comes from the top." Her voice fell to a whisper. "Our beloved publisher himself, Mr. Flynn."

She lowered her gaze while we observed an instinctive minute's silence. Even I knew of Justin Flynn, the entrepreneur whose touch turned other people's garbage into his own personal gold. He was one of Sydney's favorite sons. Rising from rags to riches in the dizzy '80s, Flynn positively reveled in the subsequent recession. For a pittance he'd taken a clutch of ailing magazines off the hands of one of the large media giants and then proceeded to turn them around until they'd wiped out most of the competition.

"You're not trying to tell me someone like that is taking a personal interest in Paul?"

She smiled elusively. "Justin Flynn takes a personal interest in everyone and everything. Obviously he trusts Sonia's gut feeling, that's why he headhunted her, but he still believes in insurance. Mostly, he hates controversy."

"I don't think I could control Paul." I blanched at the thought. "He's an impetuous boy."

"Try. Ooh, here comes the pudding! Dig in and enjoy yourself. And finish the champers."

We both eyed the waiter's compact derriere as he sashayed back to the kitchen, then tucked into our dessert. One thing about Helen puzzled me slightly. For someone who was purportedly Sonia Porter-Hibble's private secretary, she was extremely au fait with the thoughts of Chairman Flynn.

"Who do you work for?" I asked her. "I mean, really?"

"I work for *NOW!* magazine," she answered, stuffing the delicate sweet into her mouth with gusto. "But I skip the diet pages."

The zabaione was indeed a marvel. Like a wartime melodrama filled with stolen glances and enforced goodbyes, it left behind a warm glow and a craving for more. By mutual agreement, we ordered seconds. Outside, across the water, sharp icy rain started to fall.

chapter six

If Australia's hottest publisher had an agenda for me in my new position at *NOW!*, so did Paul. He revealed it over a quick caffe latte at Trash.

"We'll have the most fabulous time," he enthused, running his fingers through blond-tipped hair that I was pleased to see had been despiked. "We can go to opening nights, dine out.… We'll be seen everywhere and never pay for a thing."

"I'm sure there's a catch," I murmured, mindful of my role as undercover watchdog.

"Actually…" Paul hesitated slightly. "There *is* something else you can do."

"What?" Already I was beginning to feel overutilized. I'd have to give myself a raise.

"I'm suppose to write an advice column for the mag—Get Over It!"

"Pardon me?"

"That's the name. I answer people's letters. Solve their problems in a smart, noncaring way."

I had an instant vision of some poorly advised reader creating a huge stink and all the parties ending up in court: Paul, me, and a furious Justin Flynn.

"If we work on it together," Paul continued, "we can make the letters up. You can write the questions, and I'll do the answers. It'll be a hoot. We could turn to ourselves for inspiration. Let's start with you, caro. What irritating little problem do you have at the moment?"

"I'm talking to it."

"No, really. Any murmurs of the heart?"

I thought briefly of Tim. He had seemed so promising. However, there was no way I'd be publishing that little episode in some trashy magazine.

"The only thing bringing tears to my eyes of late is a bruise on my shin," I quipped. "I keep knocking it against my bed in the dark."

"Fascinating, but of cult interest only. We need to come up with something juicier."

"Nothing personal," I cautioned, "but do you think you're the best person to be doling out advice to the lovelorn? Do you have the runs on the board?"

"Natch! I've had more lovers than you can shake a stick at."

"Exactly what I mean. How many of those relationships could be described as, uh, a success?"

A frown crossed Paul's forehead. "They weren't relationships, they were sex." He tossed his head. "Caro! Are you calling me a slut?"

"Never! But in terms of your qualifications for this advisory role...well, maybe you had better be careful."

Paul slapped his hand down on the table. A man close by peeked up from his newspaper.

"Careful! That's so typical. Nobody hired me to be careful. What's wrong with 'sensational'? What's wrong with 'fantabulous'? That's where *I'm* going, but if you're not interested, fine. Don't worry about it! I apologize for dragging you into my glamorous new life."

I was shocked by this outburst. Where had it come from?

"I've got to see a man about a vote." Paul shoved back his chair and stalked off.

"Oh, God, the election's today. I'd forgotten." I followed him out into the street. "Wait a second, will you? Paul!"

Abruptly, he flung himself down onto a bus stop bench. I joined him. Neither of us spoke for a moment.

He cleared his throat. "I'm tired and emotional," he whined defensively.

"There's a lot resting on your shoulders."

He nodded. "We can handle it. Say yes to success, caro. That's going to be our motto from now on."

"Do you want a lift?"

"Natch!"

I dropped him off, then rushed home, still slightly rattled by our little scene. Clearly it would be no easy task to keep Paul's manic ego in check. As for our friendship, it could easily end up in tatters unless one of us was careful. No prizes for guessing which one that would have to be.

The dull morning had turned into one of those dark, overcast afternoons. Random slabs of rain were falling—they were too big to be called drops—and I only just managed to rip my washing off the line before a storm hit. In typical Sydney fashion it pelted down with a fury that was ultimately unsustainable. By 4:30, a pale sun peeped through the debilitated clouds. I threw on a warm jacket and headed for the Orbost Road Kindergarten, four or five blocks away, to cast my vote.

This kindergarten was housed in a double-story terrace with substantial grounds. The building had once been very grand and was still in good condition, so it was a shame to see the windows and lattices blocked out in blaring reds and yellows. Neither did I care for the synthetic lawn, a nauseous green, in the center of which sat a slippery dip and another kiddies' plaything that looked as if it could be used to distill liquor.

Today the playground was cluttered with tables and stalls, all dispensing propaganda of various shades to the good citizens who wandered in to make their compulsory choice. Aside from the major parties' candidates, there was also a refugee from the rabid right-wing One Nation party. His table, in prime position closest to the gate, additionally offered homemade preserves and chutneys for sale. Lined up in quaint crocheted jars, these foodstuffs looked delicious, though I had a suspicion that mingling small goods with rhetoric was somehow in breach of electoral guidelines. I was debating whether the purchase of loganberry jam constituted a political act when I was startled by a familiar snarl. Tethered by the slippery dip lay Gavin's dog, eyeing me with blatant distrust.

"Marc!"

I peered. There was Gavin himself, looking spruce and businesslike, seated behind a card table piled high with How to Vote cards. He waved me over.

"Hello," I said. "I've hardly seen anything of you since you moved in."

He grunted distractedly.

"Is something wrong?"

"Reports from Grayhurst suggest Cahill is going to do well. Remember the guy your friend was talking about? The Car and Truck King?"

"Oh, yes."

"Of course, we won't know the whole story till the polls close."

"What's the trouble with him again?" I asked timidly.

"Renegade independents are too unpredictable. What's his platform? Roadworks! Highways! Irrelevant. Where does he stand on vital issues like gender parity? That's what counts. From one or two things he's said, we think he may not be very socially enlightened."

"Mm."

"We can't go backwards, Marc. Let's face it, gays are powerful. We deserve strong representation." He broke into his broad smile and handed me a How to Vote card. "Well, I hardly need to give you the spiel, do I."

I glanced at the brochure. It featured a picture of a woman with shiny black hair and intense eyes. She was the strong, unsmiling type.

"Is this Celeste?" I asked.

"Yep! She's our man."

Scouting around at the polling booth for a sharp pencil, I realized I had given no thought whatsoever to this election. My usual approach is to go with the flow and vote for whoever is already in—a "better the devil you know" policy. But maybe Angel and Gavin had a point. As a gay voter, clearly I should give Ms. Ireland my support. Still, I held back. Why couldn't I do it? The answer was staring me in the face—straight off the brochure. I simply didn't like the woman.

When I returned to say bye-bye to Gavin, Celeste was with him in person, much to my horror. She was leaning over the table, haranguing him with sharp, earnest gestures. I started to sneak away, hoping they wouldn't notice me. I didn't really want to meet her.

"Yo, Marc!" Gavin called. "You've been forever in there. What took so long?"

"Oh," I smiled, doing a swift about-turn. "I made a mistake the first time. Uh, if I'm interrupting anything…"

Gavin was expansive. "Not at all. Have you met our candidate in the flesh?"

Celeste stared at me. I felt as though I had a tattoo on my forehead saying "I didn't vote for you." She shook my hand fiercely, then returned to her diatribe.

"I could have stood for the Upper House," she moaned, crankily tossing her head. "But I took the hard road. I assumed the gay community would rally. Pfft! Should've known." She turned on me. "You disco queens, pumping iron like there's no tomorrow—but when you get a chance to show some political muscle you go limp."

"I've never pumped iron in my life," I said.

"Do tell," she replied flatly. "So what's *your* brand of escapism?"

"Opera," I replied.

She rolled her eyes. "Nothing galvanizes you people. Look at this homophobic murder the mainstream press are enjoying so much. Do you think that'll be the end of it? Not on your life.

Don't you want to fight back?" I winced. I thought she was about to slap me. "But you're too busy going to the opera! You wouldn't give a shit unless you knew the dead guy personally. Like Gavin."

Gavin stood. "I think Celeste and I need to talk. Touch of damage control. Mind the shop, would you, Marc?"

"Me?"

"Just for five minutes. Ta."

I stumbled around behind the table. "But what do I do?"

"Just give out the card," he called over his shoulder. "And don't get into an argument. At the end of the day, it's not really worth it." He ushered his cranky candidate out of sight.

I sat, utterly bemused by this sudden promotion to queer spokesperson. Fortunately no one seemed to crave Celeste as their parliamentary representative, so I could relax and mull over the information I'd just heard. Gavin knew Quentin Butler. I was almost sorry to hear it, although I couldn't really regard him as a suspect. Gavin was far too...well...handsome. It was probably a coincidence. Lots of people had known Butler. I could even ask Gavin about him; I might learn something useful. Also, it would be a good excuse to pick up where I'd left off in the friendly neighbor department.

My train of thought was interrupted by a severe old woman, all in black, hastening in my direction with remarkable swiftness. Her face seemed to be fashioned out of recycled cardboard.

"Can I help you?" I stammered.

She pointed at Celeste's photograph. "Greek girl?" she inquired. "She Greek?"

"Could be, I suppose. She's the lesbian candidate. As in, you know, Lesbos."

At this moment a low-flying jet flew overhead. The old woman cocked her head to one side.

"Eh?"

"*Lesbian!*" I shouted. I now had the undivided attention of the other volunteers and most of the public.

The old lady considered her options, rocking her head from

side to side. "Lesbian, lesbian…" All of a sudden she made up her mind. "OK!" she said, and grasping one of my How to Vote cards she scuttled off to the poll.

"Any luck?" asked Gavin hopefully when he came back—alone, thank heaven.

"Just one. An ex–One Nation supporter, I think."

"Oh." He placed a hand on my shoulder. "Marc. I wonder if I could ask you a favor."

"Please do!" I said, ever anxious to put our relationship on a more intimate footing.

"As soon as the polls close at 6 we're all getting together for a meeting. It may go on a bit."

I was flattered. "You want me to come?"

"No, no. I just wondered if you'd take Hector home for me."

"Hector—your dog?"

"I promised him a walk. You don't mind, do you?" He gave me his most seductive smile. "Drop in later on for a drink and we'll watch the election results."

"Yes. Oh, yes, all right."

"Great."

He strode to the slippery dip and untied Hector's leash. The dog made an immediate dash for my left leg. He was clearly tossing up whether to soak it in urine or rip it to shreds. Taking advantage of this momentary indecision, Gavin yanked him away.

"Marc's walking you home," Gavin explained.

At this news, Hector exploded. Heaving himself up, he firmly planted both front paws on my hitherto spotless jeans and licked my face in a frenzy of warm spray and gravy-breath.

"Just let him know who's boss," Gavin advised lightly, "and he won't give you any trouble. I can't believe how friendly he is with you."

Neither could I. "Come on, boy," I muttered with little or no conviction, taking the dog's leash.

For the first two blocks, Hector could scarcely have been better behaved. He trotted ahead at a gentlemanly pace, instinctively realizing where ultimate authority lay. The two of us developed a tangible camaraderie and, for a moment, I even considered getting a dog myself. Some breed that wasn't too demanding and lived on scraps.

This plan, along with the camaraderie, was abruptly terminated when we reached the highway. While I waited for the lights to change, Hector wrenched himself free, lead and all, and plunged headlong into the traffic.

"Oh, my God! Hector!" I bellowed.

Cars honked as the idiotic creature padded along the median strip and plunked himself down, tail wagging. His leash trailed halfway across the road; an enormous mobile home cruised over it. Trucks whizzed by on both sides, but Hector wasn't remotely disconcerted. He was enjoying every second.

A passing motorist slowed down. "Get your bloody dog off the road," she screamed.

"It's not mine," I called back. If people thought I was about to risk my life over the neighbor's pet, they could think again.

With a ping the WALK sign flashed green and I rushed onto the street. Hector sprang playfully into action and dashed across to the other side. Now he was running like the wind.

Panting and wheezing I bounded after him, but he had the advantage over me, carrying less weight and using twice as many legs. He raced up alleys and back streets, and unlike every dog in the movies, he headed unswervingly away from home. I prayed the vile mutt would skid under a van or into a pit of lime on an open building site.

Eventually he disappeared around a corner. When I got there, he was nowhere to be seen. I looked up and down the busy road in breathless frustration.

"Hector?" I croaked.

Then I caught sight of him. Less than a block away, among the few stunted trees on the fringe of our large local park, Hector gamboled in blissful defiance of every command he'd ever been forced to obey. As I watched in dismay, he vanished over the rim of a hill and was gone. At the same moment the street lights flickered and lit up. If I were to recapture him, I'd have to move.

I didn't pause for breath until I'd reached the summit of the hill. From this vantage point the park spread out before me on every side. It was huge—and filled, of course, with no sign of dog whatsoever. Hopelessly, I scanned the endless grassy knolls and lonely patches of scrub in the dwindling light of dusk. A chill touched the air.

I set off along one of the paths towards a clump of trees. It was only as I approached that I remembered where I was. A sign confirmed it. I was about to enter the AIDS glade, the very area where Quentin Butler's corpse had been discovered. I steeled myself.

"Hector?" I called, though the call came out as more of a whisper.

The glade, undoubtedly peaceful and calm on a summer's afternoon, was now desolate, its eeriness compounded by wind whistling through the trees in classic style. My heart leapt as I spied my own dim shadow out of the corner of my eye. I was ready to turn back when a distant, muffled bark lured me on. I followed the path into the darkness, simulating a confident stride which fooled none of those present. When I emerged on the other side I found myself at the foot of a second hill. There, against the skyline, illuminated by the blaring neon of a distant sports ground, were three figures in silhouette. One was clearly a dog, another equally clearly a man. The third I couldn't quite identify. A Shetland pony? Strangely, none of them moved. I began to wonder if the trio formed some locally funded sculpture installation. (Those things turn up in all sorts of pointless places.) Then the dog barked.

"Hector!" I cried.

It was indeed Hector. He jumped excitedly but was restrained by his leash, held firmly by the strange man. I ran towards them. Half way there, I came to a sudden halt as I realized the third presence on the hill was not, as I'd imagined, a horse but another dog. A frighteningly large one.

"Is he yours?" the man sang out.

"More or less," I answered. "Um, come on, boy! Come to Marc." I had no intention of moving any closer.

"I shouldn't let him off the leash," the man called back in sonorous tones. "You'd better come up and get him."

The very big dog grinned, in anticipation of an unexpected feeding frenzy.

"Uh, no. I won't, thanks." I called.

"Why not?"

"Umm. Can't, right now. Just send him down."

"I don't think that's a good idea. *Sit!*"

Both dogs dropped at this sudden decisive command. As for me, I trotted meekly up the hill to confront a solid, granite-like man with a round, reddish face. He was unsmiling as he handed me Hector's leash. At least I think he was; I was keeping one eye on the big dog.

The man must have sensed my discomfort. "Don't be frightened of Connelli," he said. "She won't hurt you." He paused. "Unless I tell her to."

I nodded. "Sizeable, isn't she."

"Still a puppy."

"Gosh. Well, we'd better go. Come on, Hector."

Hector responded to my command by refusing to budge. I wagged my finger at him, so he wagged his tail, then sniffed around the other animal who responded with disdainful interest: the canine equivalent of small talk.

The man moved closer. "Didn't expect to bump into anyone today," he murmured.

"I'm Marc."

"Denis." He extended his free hand, clad in a black woolen glove. "This dog of yours. I'm wondering, he's a crossbreed, but...?"

"Hector? Oh, I don't know. Beagle kind of thing."

Denis raised his eyebrows and nodded slowly.

"What sort of dog is...that?"

"Connelli's an Alaskan malamute."

"A malamute!"

He grimaced with pride. "Connelli found the dead body. You probably read about it."

"Well, yes."

"Want to see where it was? It's about time I got back anyway."

Clearly he was bursting to show me. I shuddered as I recalled the relish with which he had described his grisly discovery in the papers.

"OK," I answered. We had to return that way, after all.

Without another word we ambled down the hill, flanked by our dogs. Halfway through the glade, which was now almost pitch black, Denis halted.

"The body was in there. Face down in a ditch."

Denis pointed at some shrubbery, but it was too dark to see beyond the pathway.

A shiver ran through me. "How can you bear to come back here again?"

"Connelli likes this park. The cops had it all cordoned off for a while, but nobody tells *me* where I can go walkies. Anyway, I don't think the guy died here."

"What makes you say that?"

Denis paused dramatically. "He'd been stabbed, right? But there was no blood around. And then there was the bandages."

"The what?"

"Rags and stuff. Even Band-Aids. Like somebody had tried to patch the guy up in a hurry after it was too late."

"How weird."

"Maybe." Denis put a hand on my shoulder. "This sort of thing doesn't scare me. I've been in some tight places. Just got back from Indonesia, actually. Winding up business interests. They're not too crazy about Australians up there right now." He laughed grimly. "But I never thought the first thing I'd stumble across when I got back would be a corpse with no eyes."

A shiver went through me. I felt Denis's heavy breath on my neck.

"Want to get something to eat?" he asked in a hoarse whisper.

"There's a good Malaysian joint near here. P'raps we can get to know each other. I like doggy people."

"Well, I—a-a-agh!" I almost jumped out of my skin as a siren erupted next to my ear. Connelli was howling.

"Shh, good girl," cooed Denis, stroking her furry flank. "She's hungry," he explained. Connelli bared her fangs, suggesting that she too fancied Malaysian—a whole one.

"Afraid I'm busy," I gibbered.

"Too bad."

"Can we please get out of here?"

I started to rush, but Denis held me fast. "No need to go back up the hill. We're right next to the road."

An excited Connelli and Hector led the way down a barely noticeable side track, and we soon stepped into a covered clearing adjacent to the quiet road which bordered this side of the park. Overgrown bushes sheltered the entrance to the clearing, but if you knew where to stop it would be a quick and simple matter to drag something in there.

Denis broke into my thoughts. "The main road's back that way." He pointed.

"Oh, right," I replied. "Well, bye."

"Might see you here again, hey?"

Malamutes might fly, I thought, but waved cheerily as we strode off in opposite directions.

Hector, having gone berserk earlier, trotted home beside me as though he'd won every obedience prize in Christendom. No doubt his acute animal sense told him my nerves were shot to pieces. Denis was the kind of person you wouldn't want to meet on a dark night—and I had. Even so, I didn't consider him a suspect. He was far too delighted by the whole thing. The police would have checked him out carefully. Besides, he appeared to have an alibi.

Nevertheless, I felt a surge of relief when I finally reached my front door. Gavin was still out, so I tied Hector's leash to the liquidambar, which he didn't seem to mind, and fed him a couple of cold sausages.

While waiting to join Gavin in our electoral postmortem I ran a bath. (There's nothing I like better than soaking under scented foam while a glorious aria unfolds in the background—it's the height of self-indulgence.) Even so, I couldn't shake off a persistent creepy feeling. I kept recalling eerie details: the bandages on the body, for example.

As a distraction I flicked on the bathside radio to hear what was happening with the election. The result was close, I discovered; too close to call at this stage. Neither of the major parties could claim victory, and the commentators speculated about a hung parliament with independents holding the balance of power. There was no mention of Celeste, but much talk of this Stanford Cahill character who had already won his seat.

As I wafted in and out of a cozy stupor, the program crossed to a live interview with Cahill at his home, perched on the outskirts of his brand-spanking-new electorate. Cahill was ranting about his personal vested interest: roads.

"Roads are a very good indicator of where the country's going," he insisted loudly. He sounded blustery and aggressive—ghastly, really—but he did have a point; the street outside my place, for instance, needed urgent repaving.

I must have nodded off, because when my eyes blinked open, I realized the water had grown cold and distinctly unfrothy. Cahill was still speaking, but he was now travelling down quite a different road.

"What kind of image of our beautiful harbor city does that parade send overseas? The mind boggles."

"But surely," replied the reasonable voice of the ABC, "Sydney's Mardi Gras brings in millions of tourist dollars every year."

"Oh, no doubt. I bet tourists would come if we brought back public hangings too. It's high time something was done. A lot of decent ordinary people are with me on this. These homosexuals are getting away with absolute bloody murder. Who do they think they are?"

The tenor of this speech rang alarm bells, even for underpoliticized me. Bells I hadn't heard in twenty years.

chapter seven

My diary for most of the next week was already booked up with meetings, briefings, and whiteboard scribbling sessions as Paul eased his way into his glamorous new life. I was to be officially employed from Wednesday, one full week before *NOW TV!* foisted its new celebrity presenter on the public. As I ran through the schedule, it dawned on me how inconvenient a day job might become. When was one supposed to nap? Meanwhile, although my sleuthing time was running out, I still resolved to give the murder my best shot.

There were possible leads I could follow, but I needed a little more information about Quentin Butler. For example, what were the incidents Angel had referred to? Who was the young man Butler had been annoying? I decided to pump Angel further on the subject. Luckily, I had a good excuse to drop in and see him: my opera course. I wanted to assure him that even with my full schedule I wasn't about to let him down—although Tuesday nights would be a tad inconvenient from now on. Perhaps he could shift my class to the weekend.

When I got around to listing murder suspects, I found I didn't really have any. Angel, I had to concede, simply wasn't the type. He could be lethal if he threw his weight around—I remembered a protest march long ago where he'd turned on some taunting bystander and bashed the man senseless—but stabbing was hardly his style. It was too premeditated. And Angel's argument with Butler sounded more political than personal. I could scarcely imagine him gutting somebody over their sexual politics. Celeste, yes. Angel, no.

So my next move would have to be the old fallback position: When in doubt, the boyfriend did it. As soon as possible I planned to have a chat with Butler's partner in the film memorabilia shop, Celluloid Sisters.

Late on election night, when Gavin had finally arrived home to take headstrong Hector off my hands, I'd made a fleeting attempt to sound him out on the subject of Quentin Butler. Gavin had been depressed by the election results and seemed disinclined to open up.

"Oh, I knew the man briefly, ages ago. Must be ten years," he said, dismissing the subject. "I'm sick of hearing about this murder. I don't want to think about it. Look, Marc, I think we'll give the drinks a miss. Celeste got nowhere and I don't greatly feel like watching that homophobic asshole's majority soar higher and higher. It's been a long day."

And that had been it. I felt a quiet wave of relief to know Ms. Ireland wasn't about to become my local member. She was tough enough already; under the protection of parliamentary privilege she'd be a monster.

Midmorning, at about 11, I made my way to GLEE headquarters. When I arrived the place was abuzz with activity. At least twenty people stood milling around a long trestle table set up in the ground-floor gallery. Others sat on folding chairs or on the floor. An art class seemed to be in progress. Under Gerda's direction, three men were painting signs and I noticed several placards stacked neatly against the wall.

Among the crowd, facing away from me, strutted a well built young man in jeans and a leather jacket. He was laughing. As the boy threw his head back and turned his profile towards me, I realized it was Stewart. It's a tired observation, but I honestly hadn't recognized him with his clothes on. He was talking to Angel, who spotted me and beckoned me over. I pardoned my way through the crowd.

"Marc!" Angel enthused. "Perfect timing."

I just called by to have a word about…something."

I gazed momentarily at Stewart. He still had the uncanny ability to make a girl forget her train of thought.

"Have you two met?" Angel asked, with a mischievous twinkle.

"No," Stewart said, offering me his hand. "I'm Stewart."

"We have met, actually," I smiled. "You were wearing a towel."

"Oh, yeah?" he answered, patently not remembering the first thing about it.

"What's going on here?" I asked Angel.

"Organizing ourselves, hon! We can count on you, can't we?"

"Well, yes. But what—"

"Marvellous. I always say, you can't keep a good man from going down." He clutched my forearm, his eyes glistening. "It's just like the old days when we marched arm in arm against all odds." Angel flashed Stewart a wicked grin. "Round about the time you were conceived."

Stewart nodded dumbly, scarcely able to comprehend the idea of such extreme old age.

Finally I twigged. "Oh, it's a protest march."

"A sit-in! That's what I persist in calling it, in spite of the strange looks I get from these generation Z babies. It's about Stanford Cahill, of course."

"I heard him on the radio last night."

Angel shook his chins angrily. "Nothing'll stop that idiot now. He won't be satisfied till he's dragged us screaming into the Middle Ages. But GLEE is ready! Oh, yes. I've been expecting something like this."

He reached over to the table and produced a clipboard and marker. "We'll be camping on the lawn outside Parliament House, starting Wednesday, every day for a week. And this is just the beginning. There'll be more protests as the parliamentary term gets underway. We don't plan to disrupt anything, we just want to be a tangible, undeniable presence, like in real life. There's a rotation system, because let's face it, no one makes a living sitting around on their bum. Except politicians! What else do you need to know? It's catered, of course."

With a wave of his pudgy wrist he indicated the placards. "I can give you a choice of signage. You can have HAPPY AND GAY: WE WON'T GO AWAY—or advertorial—I WORK OUT AT THE STONEWALL GYM. Hmm. Not for you, I think. Or you can write your own. I like CAHILL'S A CUNT, but apparently there's a gender-specific problem with that. So?" He smiled expectantly.

I hesitated. "I don't know if I can go. I have a full-time job. It starts on Wednesday too."

"Good for you." He seemed put out.

"Until my timetable is settled, I'd better not commit to anything else—what with the opera course as well…"

Angel grunted. "Oh, don't worry about *that*. I've suspended all courses for at least a month. I'm turning my GLEE people into activists." He peered around the room with glee—appropriately enough—then swivelled back to me with a triumphant glow. "But you'll be pleased to know I'm planning a special Summer Queer Arts program, specifically featuring opera."

"Well! That's wonderful. I had great hopes for the *Carmen* session, you know." Several other topics instantly occurred to me; foremost was "Renata Tebaldi: An Appreciation of Her Life and Genius."

"I hope you'll come," Angel continued excitedly. "I've secured an actual opera person to run the course."

"Oh?" I picked myself up off the floor.

"Yes, a member of the Sydney Opera chorus, so there'll be practical singing work and, one hopes, a bit of insider goss. Plus he's a dish. There's quite a bit of interest already. So there you are, Marc. You paved the way."

"I…" I was speechless.

Lustily, he took Stewart's arm. "Can't stay chatting. We're off on a recruitment drive. Sorry you won't be coming to the protest. While you're here, you might see if you can give Gerda a hand with the signs. Cheers!"

They disappeared through the crowd while I remained rooted to the spot. My brain could scarcely comprehend what it had heard. Angel had hired some second-rate, spear-carrying nobody from the opera company—some *comprimario* in padded tights— to do my job. And to give kindergarten class karaoke as an extra! Charming. A man who could do that would commit murder with no hesitation. Angel was back at the top of my list of suspects, at least for the rest of the day.

I saw Gerda walking towards me, her jeans and old torn shirt splashed carelessly with black paint.

"How are you?" she asked in her dour Germanic accent. "If you want to paint, you'll have to wait a while."

"I'll probably go," I answered. "I only came to see about the— course." I almost choked on the word.

She nodded. "*Ja.* I told Angel he is stupid to cancel everything. But he is too excited to listen. Like a kid, heh! I will continue to hold classes downstairs." She shrugged.

"With Stewart?"

"No. That boy is no model. He hasn't got it *here*." She tapped her temple. "But I have a big class project in mind. This murder, such a terrible thing. So! I will get my class to paint it. They talk about nothing else. It will be therapeutic for them to release their deepest fears onto the canvas."

I nodded sagely. "Excellent idea. I'm very impressed."

A flicker of agreement crossed her face. "I must wash my hands."

"Tell me about Quentin," I asked slyly, following her to a sink in the corner. "I didn't even know him."

"Neither did I. He never bothered with me." She pulled a wry face. "I am a woman."

"I believe he had a fight with Angel?"

"*Ja.* They are shouting. Not just Angel. There were others."

She thrust out her jaw defiantly. "I told the police this."

"Who were the others?" I hazarded a guess. "Stewart?"

"Of course! Quentin is always wanting to do the pick-up. He would not leave Stewart alone. But the boy is used to this, I think."

"Did Quentin and Stewart argue recently?"

Gerda gave me a skeptical look. "Recently he is dead."

"But if Quentin already had a boyfriend..."

She frowned. "So what? This is the normal thing around here." She wiped her hands vigorously on a filthy towel.

"Well if Quentin was *my* partner I wouldn't like him to, uh, do the pick-up all over the place."

"I did not know Quentin. I do not know this boyfriend." She gripped my wrist. "But I know the heart! Love is never simple."

"That's true."

"I must go back to work," she said, releasing me. "See you around."

chapter eight

The Rocks is the oldest settled part of Sydney, harking back to convict days—way before my time. It's a heritage area, carefully preserved, nestling under the southern span of the bridge. The preservation, interestingly enough, has taken two forms: the residential section has remained untouched for decades, so it's shabby and decrepit, whereas the tourists' shopping section has been nurtured, repainted and repaved until it's come to resemble a cartoon version of the old city. Dividing these two disparate halves are the harbor bridge and a public toilet.

It was my final day of unemployment. I parked at the top of the Argyle Cut and ambled down through the bustling tourist domain, window shopping as I went and gawking at the price tags. Over a thousand dollars for a leather *Crocodile Hunter* hat with teeth in the brim! At that price the teeth must have belonged to Mother Theresa.

On the wharf road I stumbled across a lone busker, a dishevelled hobo scraping away at a musical saw. The sound was agonizing: the swan song of a distressed mosquito. "It's a dying art, mate," he croaked as I furtively trotted by. I fumbled in my pocket and flipped him a fifty-cent coin—hopefully not enough to save the art from dying.

I sauntered among alcoves and warehouses which had been sensitively converted into craft galleries. At last, at the end of a narrow back street, I found myself staring at a row of repulsive mugs, each one shaped and painted to resemble the face of James Dean. They were on discount and, I suspect, had been so ever since Mr. Dean's demise. The sign above the shop window read CELLULOID SISTERS — MOVIE MEMORABILIA.

The tiny interior was dingy. Book shelves lined the walls beneath fast-fading posters of *Spartacus*, *Pillow Talk*, and a more recent addition, *Matrix 2*. (The latter was signed "With love, dude!") At the far end of the room, beside an open door, stood a long glass counter covered in boxes filled with black and white stills of long-dead divas. There was also, to my surprise, a stand featuring leather and steel sex aids.

Nobody was in attendance, so I browsed among the books. I hadn't realized there were quite so many biographies published of Agnes Moorehead. Moving on, I encountered a small, bronze-colored object: a model of a snail-like creature whose random patches of fur suggested it had undergone chemotherapy. I picked it up. Although utterly formless it appeared to have orifices, one of which displayed zig-zag teeth. The thing was cute in a sick sort of way. Playfully I stuck my finger in its "mouth" and, to my horror, triggered some inner mechanism. The teeth clamped shut on my finger.

"Agh!" I cried, trying unsuccessfully to shake the ugly thing off.

A slight, weasely man with patchy skin and a wispy mustache appeared at my side. "Are you intending to purchase that item, sir?"

"Certainly not!" I snapped. "It bit me! What am I supposed to do now?"

He smiled wanly. "The release mechanism is here…" He pressed a red button. Nothing happened. "Not again," he moaned. "The whole batch must be faulty." Without warning he grabbed my wrist and wrenched the predatory merchandise off my finger. The pain was searing.

"Oo-o-oh!"

"There," he remarked calmly. "No harm done. I'll send them back."

I shook my hand in the air. It was numb. "What on earth is this thing anyway?"

He looked surprised. "It's Pokkle from *Alien President 2: The Penultimate Solution*."

"Good God." Red welts were forming on my sore digit. I sucked it lovingly. "I thought dangerous toys like this had been banned."

He pursed his lips. "Pokkle's not a *toy*, sir, he's a *collectible*." He marched over to the counter. "I'm afraid I'm closing for lunch in five minutes."

I cursed under my breath. A sleuth can't work properly under random time restrictions.

"What are these doing here?" I asked brightly, indicating the sex aids.

"They're celebrity cock rings. But we tell the tourists they're key rings." He pointed with a skinny finger. "That's the Rock Hudson, and the Randolph Scott. We've got a Ramon Novarro but we don't keep it on display." He sniffed. "No one has *that* many keys."

I glanced at the *Matrix 2* poster. "Got a Keanu Reeves?"

"We'd have to order it in for you. We go through them. Is there anything else?" He was sounding a touch tetchy.

I adopted my most charm-laden manner. "How long will you be closed? You see, I've been searching for this place for ages and I'm dying to treat myself to a good long browse! All those Agnes Mooreheads…"

"She was great, wasn't she." He shot me a tepid half-smile. "You're an actor?"

I played coquettish. "Why do you ask?"

"Only actors are interested in other actors." He leered knowingly. "I used to act but I gave it up when the shop opened. Or it gave me up, I should say."

I was suitably awestruck. "Have I seen you in anything?"

"I doubt it," he replied. Then, suddenly, he brightened. "I'm about to step out for a sandwich. You could come back in an hour, unless…?"

"I'm starving!"

We were soon sitting on a bench overlooking the harbor, grasping our soggy tomato sandwiches. The musical saw player had departed, which was a relief.

We introduced ourselves between mouthfuls. He was Doff McKew, which I could only assume to be a nom de stage adopted on the advice of some malevolent prankster.

I waxed lyrical over the James Dean mugs for a while, then ever so casually dropped GLEE into the conversation. "I'm so glad somebody mentioned your shop to me! A film buff was raving about it at GLEE. That's Gay Lifestyle Education and…Encouragement."

My companion went pale. "Enhancement," he choked in correction.

"Yes, right. I was teaching a course there."

"So you knew Quentin?" he asked tentatively.

"Quentin Butler? Before my time."

"You must be recent," Doff remarked, then he paused. "Quentin was my partner."

"In the shop?"

"And in life." His mustache twitched and his eyes began to moisten. He resembled nothing so much as a mouse looking over a bit of straw.

"I'm so sorry," I said. "We've all been in a state of shock."

He smiled sadly. "I'm afraid I was rude when you first came in. I must apologize. I hate all that attitude they have in shops now. But I've been getting so many people coming around just because of the murder. Just to have a look."

"How could they," I exclaimed guiltily.

"I'm going to take a long holiday, as soon as the police will let me."

"Have they charged anyone?"

"Not yet. They think *I* did it," he confided. His tone betrayed a very slight hint of Bette Davis. Or was it Barbara Stanwyck?

"But why should the police suspect you?" I inquired.

"I don't have an alibi. That's probably it. And they haven't come up with anyone else. When in doubt, the boyfriend did it.

That seems to be their attitude." His eyes darkened. "It doesn't help that our relationship was falling apart. Thanks to LAV." He spat the word out.

"That's a leather group, isn't it?"

"That and more." He made a fist. Unluckily his tomato sandwich was in it. "I've got nothing against leather! I sit on leather chairs, I wear leather when it's cold. That doesn't mean I crave it internally."

"Someone told me LAV was into—what was it?—'extending the parameters of male sexuality'?"

Doff sneered. "I went to a couple of meetings but I couldn't see the point. I'm so over all that 'queer' stuff. You're gay aren't you, Marc?"

"Definitely."

"Well, you look like a plain, ordinary person—and what's wrong with that? I'm sure you don't prance around announcing your sexuality on every street corner."

"Only Oxford Street corners," I quipped in my plain, ordinary way.

"Quentin had such a ghetto mentality." Doff touched my sleeve, smearing it with tomato. "We had some awful fights." He leaned close to whisper. "The last one was right there in the shop: a screaming match, and in front of customers too. Dear, oh, dear."

"Don't talk about it if it upsets you. What happened?"

"We argued about LAV, as usual. In the end, I just stormed out. Quentin never came home that night…but I didn't expect him to. He said he was leaving me. I thought he'd done it! I just sat there alone in the flat, thinking nasty, terrible things about him—and he was dead. So, you see? No alibi." He paused. "I don't know why I'm telling you this. It doesn't seem prudent."

I pressed him. "Get it off your chest."

He sniffled, wiping tomato seeds into his mustache with the back of his hand. "I wasn't even asked to identify Quentin's body. I'm his partner, but was I the one they informed? I don't *think* so! His sister rang from Adelaide to tell me what had happened. His sister, who he hated!"

"How dreadful," I said consolingly. "Weren't they on speaking terms?"

"Oh, they were on speaking terms all right. She nagged him nonstop. She's got capital invested in the shop, you see. She distrusts me because I do the books. Whenever she rang, Quentin would be in a black mood for days."

"Ah."

"You know, I haven't mentioned all this to anyone—I don't have many friends anyway, not to talk to…" His voice trailed away.

I gently took his clean hand. By now I was feeling genuinely sorry for him.

"Doff," I said quietly, "what do you think happened?"

He took a deep breath. "I think Quentin was in the wrong place at the wrong time. I've never known him to go to a beat, but, well…things weren't too good at home…and he met a bad person. It can happen. I sneak off to the movies when I'm depressed. Much safer."

I nodded. Actually it was a very reasonable theory.

"And Quentin wasn't himself lately. He was getting some very strange notions. You've no idea the things those LAV people like to do." He stared into the distance. "Whatever happened to the man I fell in love with? The man who shared my passions? The man who once met Sylvia Sidney?"

He stood awkwardly, suddenly embarrassed. "I've been raving on and on, I do apologize. Thank you for being sympathetic. I'd better get back. Call me next week. I'll get you the Keanu." He literally ran away.

I stayed on the bench and gazed absent-mindedly at the Opera House. It sat forlornly on the other side of the quay like a big abandoned baby, shoved and hustled out of the way by advancing apartment blocks.

Doff was an embittered little man, undoubtedly, and he had no alibi for the time Butler was killed. But I had been in that park, at the spot where his partner's mutilated body had been found, and I couldn't see Doff there in a month of Sundays. I was strongly inclined to go with that other old rule of thumb: The boyfriend *didn't* do it.

In fact, our conversation had completely taken the wind out of my sails. Sitting there that afternoon, I had to admit defeat. None of the evidence I'd found so far amounted to anything: just a couple of arguments that hardly seemed worth following up.

Doff's scenario seemed the most probable. Quentin Butler was clearly a sleazebag, in a failing relationship. He tried to get it off with Stewart at GLEE and Stewart had knocked him back. In the end he'd picked up a stranger, who killed him—somewhere— and dumped his body in a park.

The wind picked up as I trudged back to the car, putting all thoughts of the murder behind me. Really, I mused, it was up to the police to arrest the person who did it, and the sooner the better.

chapter nine

For Paul's first appearance on *NOW TV!* he covered a film fes-
tival launch and a drag talent quest. In both cases an unobtrusive
technical person had hovered alongside, capturing every nuance
of Paul's involvement on video. This footage was then edited into
bite-sized chunks, to be inserted into the live studio segment for
added visual interest.

The piece was to close with the first of what would hopefully
be a series: Inside Celebrity Bedrooms. Paul had been inside
quite a number of bedrooms in his time but none of them
belonged to celebrities, so he had brazenly put the inaugural
request to Sonia Porter-Hibble.

"Heart," she'd roared with more than a hint of salaciousness.
"This is a first. I'm a *notoriously* private person but you can twist
me round your little finger. I hereby grant you access to my
boudoir any time you like."

She'd teed up a photo shoot for the magazine to coincide with
Paul's debut, posing with him in unnatural positions around the
aforementioned room. And what a room: It was the crowning
glory of Sonia's 3.4-million-dollar coastal abode. A huge picture
window and balcony presented views of the ocean and the sheltered beach below. The room faced due east, so the heart-shaped

bed was hit by the first rays of the sun every morning. Within a week of settling, Sonia had invested in thick curtains.

"Fucking sun pours in at some ungodly hour. It could blind a girl," she explained.

Paul could hardly contain his raw, seething envy after such a brush with luxury. "I'm going to buy my own penthouse," he vowed, "now that I'm up there with the big players. Why shouldn't I get everything I deserve?"

"You should," I agreed, "when you deserve it."

We were sharing a taxi ride back to the studio. By the time we got there, Paul's mantra of "Why not me?" had become practically unbearable.

The Channel 6 buildings were interred deep in suburbia, on the lower north side of Sydney. The main studio and company offices resided in a huge edifice shaped like an aircraft hangar, but the network also owned an entire street of cottages nearby. God knows what had happened to the original homeowners; they might have been abducted by aliens, judging from the peculiarly frozen state of the gardens and lawns. Whatever the story, the TV people had moved in and now squatted there quite happily.

Each cottage was allotted a different program, and it was to the *NOW TV!* house Paul and I made our way. Because the show had only one set and minimal crew, it was literally made "in-house." This left the main studio free for the taping of gritty award-winning dramas, such as the current feather in the network's cap, *Precinct Hospital*.

A scruffy, thin young man with long hair and a single headphone greeted us in what was once some elderly couple's front parlor.

"Hi!" chirped Paul.

"Could you go straight into hair and makeup?" the boy mumbled, then glanced languidly at me. "And you are?"

"Marc Petrucci."

"Oh, yeah, the personal assistant." An unpleasant smirk settled across his roughly shaven face.

"Wait out here please, caro," commanded Paul grandly.

I sat awkwardly, feeling patronized on all sides.

"Is that my boyfriend?" came a high, mellifluous voice from one of the rooms. As the assistant scurried off, blathering gibberish into his mouthpiece, a graceful creature swanned into view. "It is, it *is!*"

"Hi Raymond," replied Paul. He seemed slightly uncomfortable.

"You haven't called me for hours," Raymond snapped and lunged towards Paul, smothering him in a major bear hug. Paul struggled, but the boy was powerfully built. His bronzed arms were a sculpture. His legs were tanned, taut, and savagely defoliated. He wore a jazzy shirt over a tight red singlet: summer wear, though the weather was still cool. His wide smile and dark eyes had an Asiatic tint, and speaking of tints, his hair was dyed bright pink.

The hug lasted for aeons. As Raymond's dark eyes dreamily fluttered open he spied me, grinned broadly, and winked. "You must be Paul's friend. I didn't know he liked older men. I'll run some silver through my hair right now." He chuckled lightly as he let go of a panting Paul, took my hand and kissed it courteously. *"Je suis Raymond.* Charmed to meet you." He arched his eyebrows. "Mm. I could fix your hair." He gave it a pat. "This way you wear it now, it's a teensy bit Danny Aiello."

"Raymond's a film buff," said Paul.

"That's right," he squealed, cradling Paul's head between his palms. "The Christina Ricci look for you on your first day? I think so. Or early Heather Graham. What are you wearing?"

He started to drag Paul away, then swivelled back to me.

"This is gonna take for*ever,*" he crooned. "Why don't you run up to the canteen? Or there's a *Jeanette* McDonald's two blocks away if you're real peckish."

Everyone was trying to get rid of me. Raymond waved a supple wrist towards the back of the house. "If you want the canteen, darling, nip through and hop over the fence. It's much quicker."

I looked at Paul. "Don't you need my moral support?" I asked.

"*I'll* give him that," said Raymond. "And *so* much more."

"Just do my hair," Paul snapped.

"Ooh, yes, my lady! The diva commands."

They disappeared into a room the size of a closet—inappropriately enough.

I glanced briefly at the piles of old *NOW!* magazines and the plastic mug full of instant coffee. Perhaps I'd amble over to the staff canteen after all. What mischief could Paul get up to with his hairdresser? Apart from the obvious. My job was to watch over his behavior on air, not in confined spaces. He had run through his chat for me in the cab and it seemed perfectly harmless— what there was of it. Unfortunately, he expected to rely heavily on spontaneous inspiration.

I wandered down the hallway. In the center of the house a wall or two had been removed to create a larger area which functioned as the *NOW TV!* studio. A table and couch were placed there, in front of a fake window with a blurry photo of the Sydney skyline behind it. Technical people and thick cables were everywhere. I gingerly picked my way through and slipped out the back door.

Like the front, the rear of the house suggested a memorial shrine to suburbia. There was even a laundry under the stairs with big old tubs for rinsing. However, half the picket fence had vanished and a pair of thick planks had been shoved through the gap. These led to the grassy rim of the helipad behind the main studio building.

I carefully negotiated my way up the steep planks to the other side of the helipad, where an insignificant back door opened onto the bottom of a cement stairwell. I crept up the stairs and arrived in a maze of corridors.

After a few false starts I found what I was looking for. The canteen was pretty ordinary as cafeterias go; what was surprising were the number of hungry people there. Whereas the rest of the building had seemed deserted, here I was surrounded by men and women of all ages, queuing up with their trays or squeezing onto Laminex tables. Many wore plain white smocks over their clothing. Nobody appeared to be paying for their meals. Assuming this was company policy, I joined the queue. I was next in line to order when an officious girl with the ubiquitous single-ear headset and mouthpiece barged through the double doors.

"People! We need you now!" she shouted.

Coughing and grumbling, the crowd put down their cutlery and began to shuffle out.

"Where are they going?" I asked an obese woman who was making short work of a greasy crumbed chicken breast.

"To the set! We're extras on *Precinct Hospital*. There's been a big train wreck."

"What?"

She laughed. "In the show. Isn't that why you're here?"

"No, I'm just killing time."

"Well, come and join in, lovey! We're only shooting the one scene and you'll get a hundred bucks for doing nothing."

I must say the idea appealed. After all, how long could one scene take?

"What do I do?"

"Follow me."

So I joined the shuffling throng. We made our way down another stretch of corridor which opened out into a cavernous studio. The ceiling was crammed with lights and electrical apparatus. On the floor stood hefty video cameras, ready to be wheeled into place. The central feature of the studio was the set: a hospital ward, complete with beds, drips, glass doors, trolleys, doctors, and nurses.

The girl who had fetched us from the cafeteria began shouting again. "Everyone back to the same spot where you were before the break!"

At this, people climbed into the beds or draped themselves over trolleys. One elderly woman crumpled in a heap next to the wall.

I tapped the TV girl on the shoulder.

"Yes, what is it?"

"Where should I go?" I asked.

"Where did we put you before?"

"I wasn't here before."

She looked momentarily confused. "Have you been to makeup?"

"No."

She suddenly smiled. "Oh, right! You're the dead guy. Come with me."

She led me through the false hospital doors. The shiny corridor behind them came to a sudden halt against the studio wall. Stuck in the corner was a trolley bed.

"Climb up there," she ordered, "and lie completely still. I'll get Props to put a sheet over you. From then on, you're dead meat. Whatever you do, don't move."

"OK."

"Jack, we need one of the bloody sheets," she called to a fat man in overalls. This struck me as unnecessarily harsh, but the man simply lumbered off and returned clutching a sheet with blood spattered across it.

"Rest in peace," he grinned, draping the grisly article over me from head to foot.

The TV girl leaned in close. "Put your hand outside the sheet—yes, that's right. Keep your face covered up. The doctor will feel your pulse and say, 'There's nothing we can do.' Got it?"

"Yes."

"Good. Relax for a minute."

This would be the easiest money I'd ever made. I closed my eyes and listened to the hubbub. Somewhere in the distance, I heard the girl calling. "Let's move it, people!" Other voices shouted to each other over the groundswell of babble.

As the minutes crept by, I began to worry about the time. Nothing seemed to be happening. Slowly I moved my covered hand up towards my eyes to sneak a look at my watch.

"The dead guy's moving," said someone nearby.

"It's *The Night of the Living Dead*," a second person remarked.

At that moment, the sheet was pulled away from my face. I blinked. Staring at me, upside down, was a young man in white.

"Stewart!" I exclaimed.

"Oh, hi," he answered vaguely. "You're from GLEE, right?"

"Marc," I reminded him. "How's the protest going?"

"I dunno. I'm going over there later. Angel's pissed off, but it's not every day you get to be in a soapie—I mean, medical drama."

"Are you playing the doctor?" I asked, hoping he would be the one who had to hold my hand.

He giggled. "Nah. It's a woman doctor. I'm just an orderly. I wheel you in."

"I see. So you push people around," I remarked wittily.

He gave a shrug.

"Look at the blood all over this sheet," I said, watching for his reaction. "I feel like another victim of the gay hate killer." I couldn't resist probing a little.

"Yeah," he answered vaguely.

"I suppose you knew Quentin Butler." He frowned. "The murdered man," I added.

"Oh! Nah." He yawned. "Not really."

"I heard Butler tried to pick you up. Didn't the two of you have words over it?" I could see what Angel and Gerda meant; the boy was exasperatingly vacant.

"That's what the police kept asking me." His brow furrowed in concentration. "I s'pose we could've done...probably did." He smiled. "The police are usually right."

"You must find yourself in that situation all the time."

He nodded. "Shit, yeah."

"Standing by," called a distant voice. There was immediate silence.

"Are we doing the scene now?" I whispered.

"Scene 18," called the voice. "Quiet, please! Take 1!"

I lay my head back and held on tightly as Stewart pushed the trolley along the false corridor and through the hospital doors.

"Cut!" cried the TV girl.

We came to a halt. Cautiously I sat up. The girl was listening intently to her headpiece. She gazed at me.

"You moved," she said.

"I was putting the sheet over my face," I confessed.

"Don't move! All right?"

"Sorry."

"Set up for another take!"

Stewart wheeled me backwards out the doors. He covered my face again and we waited. And waited! I was getting anxious. *NOW TV!* must have been well underway by this time.

"There's some real cute guys in the crew," Stewart remarked.

"Too bad I'm dead," I quipped.

The voice came again. "Quiet on set. Scene 18, Take 2!"

The trolley began to move and this time I remained absolutely rigid. We slammed through the hospital doors and veered to the right. The trolley tilted; I hung on like grim death. Then we hit something. A woman screamed.

"Sorry," Stewart mumbled.

"Cut!"

I let out a sigh; we'd stopped again. All around, voices began screaming at each other.

"Can't you steer this thing?"

"He ran over my foot. That body weighs a ton."

"She wasn't there before."

"This is exactly where I was!"

"Where's Continuity?"

"It's going to bruise. I bruise easily."

"Then you're in the wrong business, pet."

"Quiet, please, everybody! The director's coming down to the floor."

There was an appalled silence. I peeked over the top of the sheet as a pale man with a beaky nose and tinted glasses came storming onto the set. I knew his face immediately. Ten years ago, he had been highly celebrated as a controversial director of plays and operas. I could still recall his daring *Tosca*, set on Easter Island. Tosca had hurled herself from the top of one of those ancient monumental statues while a volcano erupted in the distance. It had been terribly artistic.

Now he was directing television.

"What the devil's wrong with you people?" he growled. "It's the simplest thing in the world." He pointed at Stewart. "You! What's your name?"

Stewart flashed a seductive smile and eased his frame into a GLEE-like pose. "Stewart," he answered proudly.

"Mm." The director stared as though he'd only just noticed him. "Try to do better next time."

Stewart nodded vigorously.

"Where's the woman he ran into?"

"Here."

"Move your foot out of the way, for Christ's sake. That's what a *real* injured person would do." He turned to my trolley. "As for you, all *you* have to do is play dead. A dog could do it."

I decided to defuse this awkward moment with a little flattery. "I loved your Rapanui *Tosca*," I uttered meekly.

"My what? My *Tosca*?" The effect was extraordinary. The man simply crumpled, as though all the air had been sucked out of him. "Uh, once more, please," he croaked and trudged back to wherever he'd come from.

The actress playing the doctor gave a whistle. "Well done," she exclaimed.

We set up for yet another take, and this time Stewart steered the trolley to a halt without mishap. I, in my turn, simulated rigor mortis perfectly.

The scene unfolded. The dialogue struck me as puerile.

"We can't take any more of them," a man shouted in my ear.

"Don't you understand?" I heard the voice of the lead actress. "There's been a train wreck. We *must* take them."

My back began to itch desperately. I tried an unobtrusive squirm. Suddenly I felt someone grab my wrist and lift it. I held my breath.

"There's something we can do for him," murmured the actress, lowering my arm gently.

I waited to be wheeled away.

"Cut," said the TV girl.

"Now what's the matter?" the actress demanded.

"You said something."

"Of course I did! I said the line."

"The line is, 'There's *nothing* we can do for him.'"

"Shit."

"We'll have to go again."

I glanced at my watch, then hopped to my feet. "I'm sorry," I said, "I can't do it anymore." I handed my bloodstained sheet to the startled floor manager. "You'll have to get a new body."

"And where will you be?" called the actress as I hurried out. "In your trailer?"

I arrived at the *NOW!* studio, sweating and out of breath. Sonia Porter-Hibble, dressed today as a blue pencil, was babbling away at the camera. A girl in the crew looked up sharply in my direction and made a shushing sign with her forefinger. I froze. Finally Sonia wound up her spiel and a silent commercial flashed onto the TV monitor. The crew began to pack up.

Sonia rushed over to me. "Matt, where have you been? Did you see it? Paul was divine! And so wicked. Some of those things he comes out with, I thought I'd die. Weren't you impressed?"

"Immensely."

"You watched it up in the control room, did you? I've never been able to *find* the place. Where is that sweet boy? He was here...*heart*?"

Paul, freshly scrubbed, sauntered in with his hairdresser Raymond hovering lightly in the background.

"Caro, we thought you'd disappeared."

"Matt was in the control room," explained Sonia.

"We have to leave *right now*." Paul shot me a piercing look of utterly impenetrable significance.

"Oh! Must you?" Sonia moaned. "I thought we might snatch a drink to celebrate."

"No, we have to go to that...that...thing," Paul said emphatically.

"What thing?" asked Sonia, grabbing my arm. "Matt, where are you taking him?"

I glanced at Paul. He nodded in frantic encouragement.

"Uh—to a gay protest meeting outside Parliament House."

Sonia was aghast. "For God's sake, why?"

"It's a matter of principle," I answered, as Paul dragged me towards the cottage door. A taxi was waiting—he'd already ordered it—and we sped off towards the city.

"What on earth was all that about?" I demanded.

Paul frowned. "I didn't feel like hanging around. Just take me home!"

"Since when can't you handle praise?"

He patted my knee. "Caro, it's no great drama, but I have to get away from Raymond. We went out twice and now he considers himself my husband. He's a bit full on, even for me."

"Yes, I could see that."

Paul sighed. "Oh, you know what these hangers-on are like. I can't bear a star fucker."

I could scarcely believe my ears. One show, and Paul was already turning into the celebrity version of Medusa.

"Anyway," he continued, "the important question is, how did I look? How was the hair?"

"I have no idea," I answered lightly. "I'm afraid I missed the whole thing."

"Oh." He stared out the window and never said another word.

chapter ten

It was a clear, clean Friday afternoon. I was sitting at my desk—or rather Paul's desk, which he never used—gazing at the corporate cityscape of which I was now a part.

In the three months since I'd started working for *NOW!* Holdings Ltd., I'd become a completely different person. Unlike the easygoing Marc of old I was driven—for two reasons. Firstly, the more time I spent in the office, the more money I received. Secondly, I'd seriously underestimated how hard the work would be.

Strangely enough, the job I was doing for Justin Flynn—which Helen dubbed "Paul wrangling"—was less trouble than I'd anticipated. The *NOW TV!* segment was Paul's all-consuming interest and he was good at it. Once or twice, his boyish spontaneity led me to the brink of panic, but as yet no lawyers had been in touch.

Getting our advice column in on deadline, however, was a nightmare. Paul kept erratic hours and he refused to accept that sitting at a computer keyboard was part of his celebrity workload. Initially, I'd concocted the letters and Paul had answered them, but this soon proved unworkable. Even though the column was titled "Get Over It!," Paul's use of the phrase in answer to every query became a tiny bit predictable. Eventually, he blew up—which he was increasingly wont to do—and I ended up taking over the whole thing.

Soon, genuine letters from the public began to roll in, but these made life even more difficult. Several involved tricky situations requiring a knowledge of the law. Most were utterly incoherent.

Increasingly, I relied on Helen as a sounding board. Sonia did yoga every Monday from 12 till 2, so Helen and I took ourselves off to lunch. We sampled every trendy bistro in the vicinity. During these expense-account binges we would check my oft-rewritten copy, discuss correspondence, run through the functions Paul was to attend during the week, and plan strategies to steer Paul (and Sonia) safely through the Wednesday show. Over the course of our Mondays we became close friends. (Anyone who buys me lunch with any regularity is promoted to the rank of lifelong friend—it's automatic.)

Today, however, was Friday, and the pressure was off. Paul's spot for the following week had been set up, and Sonia had been especially delighted with the last one.

"He's getting it down to a fine art, Matt," she'd confided. "That comes from working with pros, and I do mean you."

"Thanks," I replied humbly, though to me it all seemed like a confidence trick. Paul had rambled on about the opening of a new cabaret venue in town, raving about the talent and the ambience—whereas in reality he'd only stayed for ten minutes, just long enough to consume four glasses of pink champagne, before heading off to premises where the ambience and the talent were more to his taste.

He'd followed that up with a piece about furniture aimed at young homemakers. (Every story had to "target" somebody.) This involved a historic tourist town two hours out of Sydney with a low-security corrective facility in its midst. On weekends the jail was opened to the public, and people could buy imitation antique furniture made by the inmates in their spare time. During our visit I secured myself a rough but cheap pinewood coffee table.

Paul had closed the piece with an unfortunate crack about the prisoners stealing the furniture back once they'd been released;

he'd advised potential buyers to paint the goods a different color. This comment had caused a few prickles to rise on the back of my neck, but otherwise everything had gone smoothly. I had nothing left to do today except the one aspect of my job which I was coming to loathe: answer Paul's phone.

Three lines on the console were flashing. Lazily I picked up the receiver.

"*NOW TV!*" I droned. "Paul Silverton's extension."

"Is that Paul?"

It was the whispering man again.

"Mr. Silverton is in a meeting. Can I help you?"

"I'd love to speak to Paul…"

"He's busy all day. Can I take a message?"

"No," he breathed and hung up.

A stream of calls flowed in every day. Some were from the promotional directors of various organizations, others were from idiotic fans or persons who remained annoyingly anonymous. A lot of the callers were women. I couldn't quite understand the attraction; Paul was witty and attractive on screen but quite clearly off limits to the female sex. It was so obvious Helen Keller could have spotted it.

The whispering man was something else. He'd been calling more frequently of late, but although I found it peculiar, he didn't strike me as dangerous. He actually sounded quite chirpy!

Today, however, I was in no mood for him or anyone else. I zapped all calls back to the switch, snuggled down in Paul's chromium designer chair and lost myself instead in random thoughts of murder.

I'd continued to follow the Butler case in *Queer Scene*. The frenzy had died down in the mainstream media, but the gay press remained vigilant. There was ongoing concern that, after all this time, no arrest had been made. *Queer Scene* was pushing the line that because it was a gay hate crime, the police weren't terribly interested in solving it. The police commissioner hotly denied this.

My own interest in the case had been rekindled when I'd

attended a candlelight vigil in remembrance of Butler—organized, of course, by Angel. Lots of interested parties had been there, including Stewart and Gavin, both looking fabulous in the flattering glow of flickering candlelight. Gavin in particular. I kept meaning to see more of him, but I could never find the time. Maybe later on tonight…. Glancing at my notebook, I discovered that my doodling had taken a graphically phallic turn.

The sound of a throat clearing startled me. Helen was leaning over my desk, scrutinizing my draftsmanship.

"Is that work?" she inquired with mock innocence.

"No," I dithered, snapping my notebook shut. "It's the end of the week. I'm sorting out my timetable."

"Don't forget to keep *that* appointment." She grinned. "Let's sneak away from the office for five minutes, unless you're too busy. Bring the Get Over It file."

Five minutes later, we were ensconced at my favorite corner café, Eccocina. It was one of the first in Sydney to take advantage of the revised liquor laws, which meant you could buy a drink without having to eat—in Helen's view, a dangerous precedent to set so close to the financial district. However, the reason I liked Eccocina had nothing to do with chardonnay and everything to do with the waiter, a young Milanese going by the name tag of Fabio. Dark hair bound tightly in a pony tail, dark skin, perfect teeth, and stubble arrested miraculously at two days' growth were his trademarks.

"Marco," he carolled, gracefully handing out menus as Helen and I seated ourselves at an isolated table. "So the *signore* has turned back to women? It was in the stars. I am devastated."

"You're still my only love, Fabio," I answered.

"I do understand Italian," Helen remarked icily.

Fabio colored. "I will return to take your order, *signora*," he said, this time in English.

"Just bring two glasses of semillon."

"At once." He swished off.

"We always do this sort of operatic flirting," I apologized.

Helen was unimpressed. "Any sensible woman would run a mile from his type," she said. "There *is* such a thing as too sexy."

She perused the menu and came down on the side of a sloppily rich banana and caramel pie. Only when it arrived did Helen start to unwind.

"I've had a hell of a week," she burbled through caramelized lips. "Sonia?"

"Everything."

I sipped stealthily. Wine in midafternoon was conducive to only one thing, in my experience: a nap.

"Was there something you wanted to talk about?" I asked. "I thought we were OK for this issue."

"It's still a bit light, though I do like the tattoo question."

"That's actually one of Paul's."

I opened the file I'd brought along and found the piece. Unusually, Paul had provided both question and answer. It read:

Dear Paul,
    My boyfriend wants me to get a tattoo. He says it would be specially for him, so he'd like it in a place where only he will see it. What do you think? Also, will it hurt? Pain scares me.
    Sasha

Dear Sasha,
    I'm not convinced about tattoos. For one thing, they're blue, which limits your wardrobe to one color scheme. If you're a blue singlet kind of girl, that won't be a problem.
    Your real problem is your boyfriend. He sounds like the insecure type, more interested in fashion than the well-being of his partner. Are you sure he's not gay? And you're dead right about pain. Don't go there.
    Tell your boyfriend if he wants a tattoo where only he will see it to get one himself—on his dick.

"I think we'll get away with 'dick'," Helen said, "if we balance this one with something genuinely helpful. Take a look at this. It was faxed in this morning."

She handed me a neatly printed-out sheet.

Dear Paul,

I have a serious problem and I think that while you're funny and everything you're also very wise about relationships. I would really like to "get over it," so here goes.

I am 20. I love this successful guy. He's very hot when we're together, but he can just as easily turn it off and pretend like he doesn't even know me.

The thing is, I work for him. At work he doesn't want anyone to know we're seeing each other, and this is making my life impossible.

We have great sex but I want more than that. I want commitment. I want everything! Is he just using me? Will he change? Or will I have to leave him and my job? I don't want to do this as it's a good job. Please tell me what to do.

"We'll have to give her a name," Helen muttered. "The fax wasn't signed. I've transcribed it, of course. The original was practically illegible. What do you think?" She pursed her lips. "Mr. Flynn believes it would be nice if Paul revealed a caring, sharing side occasionally."

"He's not the only one," I answered wryly. "Do you have any suggestions as to how we might answer it?"

"No," she said off-handedly, "but I think the girl's a complete moron." Helen drained her glass and indicated to Fabio to bring the bill. "She doesn't realize all the power's with her. The man she's shagging doesn't want it to get out, and he's bullying her into keeping mum. If I were in her shoes, I'd be dropping the odd hint round the office. All she has to do is threaten him with exposure and the situation's turned on its head. He'll be forced to put his money where his mouth is."

"*Il conto, Signora.*" Fabio presented the bill with a swish.

"*Grazie.*"

"*Prego.*"

Helen lunged for the complimentary chocolate and devoured it. "So you think I should advise the girl to threaten her employer?"

Helen examined her fingernails. "That's what I would do." She smiled and checked her wristwatch. "Break's over. Back to the grind."

In the office I cast my eye across the letter once again. It was different somehow from the inane complaints we usually received. I folded it and stuffed it into the "too hard" pocket of my shirt. I could think about it on the weekend.

The wine had induced a pleasant midafternoon lethargy, and I put my head down for a moment. Two hours later I awoke in a blur. It was 5:30 and everybody was packing up. I cursed. Now I'd be stuck in peak-hour traffic, and I had to meet Paul at a product launch at 6. I splashed cold water on my face in the men's room, then hurried outside in the direction of the parking lot.

"Oh, Ma-a-arc…"

My heart sank as I looked around to see the lightly made-up and grossly underdressed hairdresser, Raymond. Today he was wearing tight slacks with a wallpaper design and a loose black gym top.

"Raymond. What are you doing here?" I hoped the explanation would be succinct.

"Is Paul coming out?" he asked.

"He did that on his sixth birthday," I replied.

Raymond was unamused. He gripped my arm. "Is he inside? Is he coming down this way?"

"No," I answered. "He's not here today. Please, I'm in a rush." I tried to pry his fingers away, but they remained fast. Unexpectedly I found Raymond snivelling on my shoulder.

"Hey," I muttered uncertainly. "What's the matter?"

"I'm a *tragic mess*," he whimpered, smiling through his tears and settling into a sniffle.

"Because of Paul?" I asked. He choked and nodded. This was no surprise. Paul had been getting increasingly curt with Raymond at the studio and had even lobbied Sonia to have him replaced—something Raymond would certainly have heard about on the grapevine.

"Here, take my hanky," I said. I was sure he couldn't be carrying one in those tight pants he was wearing. He blew his nose then hugged me limply. In turn I slid my arm around his lithe and beautifully proportioned body.

"Shh, now," I whispered. "Pull yourself together, and we'll have a drink somewhere."

My earlier impatience vanished. Quite frankly I was angry with Paul for treating this perfectly sweet boy in so cavalier a manner. If I missed the function and Paul was forced to muddle through on his own, it would serve him right!

I led Raymond to the nearest pub, a quaint old tavern. The front bar was wood paneled and the walls were decorated with framed photographs of long-dead racehorses. In one corner a large and loud TV set bombarded the atmosphere with trivia. Drinkers were crammed in everywhere, unwinding after their week's work. The air was soggy with masculine camaraderie.

Raymond secured a table directly in front of the television while I battled my way to the bar to get us a couple of vodkas. On my return, I was relieved to find him looking more composed and less overtly emotional.

"Thanks," he said, shouting above the hubbub. "Lord knows I need it. Love's a curse."

"You've fallen for him pretty heavily."

"Can you tell? Where the heart takes her a girl must follow. I've seen it happen time and again: Bette Davis, Susan Hayward—my God, even Kim Novak."

I tried to be gentle. "Paul's never been strong on commitment."

"You know how many dates we had? Two. *Two*!" He counted on his fingers. "One...two...three...hell, we only had sex five times!"

"Mm. Appalling."

"And then, ignored. Used and abused like some old hooker in the lockup." He sipped his drink pointedly. "But you wait. Nobody's gonna treat *me* like that. Not again!"

The last thing I wanted to get into was Raymond's past history.

"Paul's not his regular self lately," I said soothingly. "All the pressure of the new job…"

"Crap, darling. She thrives on it."

"I'm sorry. I'm only trying to help."

He leaned forward and placed his hand firmly on my knee. "You're a kind, kind soul, Marc, and I won't forget. So tell me, have I blown it completely? They say you should never use the L word with a Virgo."

"You did that?" I was horrified.

"Guilty."

"Let me think."

The irony of the situation dawned on me. Here was I, the ghost writer of Paul's advice column, orchestrating his love life! I felt a tingle of deviousness.

"Make him jealous," I announced.

"Play hard to get? The oldest trick in the Glo-mesh, but will it work?"

"With Paul, yes. He always wants what he can't have. Be seen out with somebody else, preferably someone stunning. Make a big deal of it. Tell Paul you're deeply in love—that it surpasses any thrill you've ever experienced before. Especially sexually!"

"You scheming old cunt!"

"Thank you."

"Another vodka?"

"I have a function…. Oh, all right. One."

Raymond bouréed over to the bar, leaving me with no alternative but to watch TV. The 6 o'clock news had started.

The news reader, a seriously neat woman, trawled through the usual litany of international assassinations, failed peace talks and environmental catastrophes. Then came the top domestic story.

"Stanford Cahill, the independent MLA who holds the balance of power in the lower house, announced today that he will be drafting a private members' bill to make homosexual acts illegal. The controversial proposal has already caused an outcry among gay rights groups."

Onto the screen flashed the intimidating image of an apoplectic Celeste Ireland.

"The legislation protecting gays and lesbians is imperfect and incomplete," she snarled, "but we've come a long way since gays were treated as criminals. This retrogressive bill is a joke! Cahill will never get it up. In fact, I bet that's his problem."

The scene changed to the steps of Parliament House, and a close-up of Cahill bustling through a crowd of reporters. It was my first view of him. He looked tall and rather on the well-fed side. His rugged face and disconcertingly blue eyes revealed nothing. I searched in vain for any sign of his overhyped "everyman" quality: the phenomenon which apparently made people buy cars from him and frivolously vote him into parliament.

"Stan!" cried a reporter. "Is the government with you on this?"

Cahill didn't even slow down. "I support their legislation, they support mine," he called out. "That's why they're *in* government."

He was followed by John Garland, the state premier. In contrast with Cahill's self-confidence, this seasoned politician showed every sign of a having undergone a charisma bypass. He was short, weedy, and aging, and while I generally think hairpieces look grotesque, in his case anything would have been an improvement.

"No comment," he muttered, shuffling through the crowd. Then, swerving at the last moment, he glared into the camera and became uncharacteristically forthright. "There is no way the recriminalization of homosexuals will see the light of day," he blurted out in a small, whiny voice.

I lay back against the wall and scanned the noisy pub. No one had been following the bulletin, thank goodness. A shudder went through me: Were we returning to the bad old days? I remembered those early protest marches. They were wonderful times, exhilarating and liberating, but surely we wouldn't have to do it all over again? My arches throbbed at the prospect.

Six-thirty loomed. What was keeping Raymond? I could just make out his colorful form leaning sinuously across the bar. I squeezed my way over and discovered he was chatting to Fabio, my favorite waiter.

"*Buona sera*," I called.

"Ah! my friend," Fabio gushed. "Allow me to introduce my new friend, *Raimondo*." The name sounded much classier in Italian.

"I know Marc already," Raymond sang. "We're sisters."

Fabio's brow wrinkled. "Your brother?" he queried.

"*Sister*, honey."

"It's a politically incorrect expression," I explained.

"Here's your drink," said Raymond, handing me a double vodka.

I gulped it down. "I'd love to join you both," I said, "but I must rush. I'm already late."

Fabio nodded solemnly. "I understand," he uttered in his smooth, liquid baritone. "*Addio*."

As Fabio turned away to light a cigarette, I whispered in Raymond's ear. "Good choice, he's just Paul's type."

"That's what I thought," he replied conspiratorially. "Mine too."

chapter eleven

The function that evening was a whisky tasting, designed to launch a new company of liquor importers onto a saturated market.

It was taking place in a cocktail bar atop an old skyscraper from the 1970s. Once famous as the Talk of the Town, the bar had looked serenely out over the glittering lights of the city. Now only remnants of this panoramic view remained, dissected by thrusting towers and apartment blocks. No longer the talk of the town, the bar had been abandoned by all but a handful of loners—but this proved to be its saving grace, ensuring that its '70s furniture and fittings remained in good condition. Recently, the place had been rediscovered as a retro sensation—indeed, Retro Sensation was its new name—and it had begun to fill up again, much to the chagrin of the city apartment-dwellers whose domestic dramas now provided the bulk of the view.

Tonight it was packed even tighter than the bar I had just left. I searched for Paul among the spirited throng as I inched my way through the room. I was late, but it seemed that Paul was later still. No surprise, really. I soon found myself in a corner, jammed up against a large flat-leafed cactus protruding from a rough pseudo-Mexican pot. A waitress, juggling a tray of drinks, eased her way past.

"Help yourself," she smiled, maneuvering the tray under my nose. It contained several shot glasses and a few large tumblers, each one brimming over with free alcohol.

"Are they all the same?" I asked.

"The shots are the tasting whiskies, the tumblers are the quaffing whiskies. But between you and me, most people are quaffing the tasters."

"Can I get some ice?"

She craned her neck, peering over the crowd. "Might be a while."

"Don't worry." I grabbed a taster and downed it in one, throwing my head back. "Ow! Oo-o-oh!" I cried, biting my lip.

She seemed concerned. "Didn't you like it?"

"No, it was fine," I panted. "I just leant against this cactus."

"Better have another. Take a quaffer too in case I don't get back here in a hurry."

"Thank you."

I quaffed away joyfully, then decided to remove myself from the proximity of the barbarous plant; I was developing an itch between the shoulder blades. Progress was difficult but I finally reached the exit, having made a full circle of the place. Still no Paul. I gently untucked my shirt, trying to free the remaining cactus spines from my back; this made me look unkempt, but I was leaving so I didn't care.

As I lunged for the door and the outside world, the crowd thinned and I found myself collapsing to the floor in filmic slow motion. I'd grown accustomed to the crush of bodies supporting me, and now they'd suddenly departed. I giggled quietly, and rolling over, managed to sit up on a step. Somebody had deposited a half-finished tumbler on the floor, within reach. It seemed a pity to let it go to waste.

"Marc?"

With some effort, I looked up. Paul was standing beside me in the doorway, hugging his digital video camera.

"Where've you been?" I inquired.

Paul put down his equipment. "Look at you. You're pissed," he announced bluntly.

"It may seem that way," I replied carefully, "but let me explain. There's quaffers and tasters and some people are tasting the coffers or quaffing the toasters." I smiled. "It's as simple as that."

"How long have you been drinking?"

"Hm? Now that you mention it, I had a couple with lunch, then after work, and now here we are, and...what?"

Paul was staring at me with a worried expression. "Caro, have you had bad news or something? Has Tebaldi kicked the bucket?"

I gulped. "Not that I know of. What are you trying to infer?" I made an attempt to get to my feet, which was not entirely successful.

Paul sighed. "Look, I've got to get something on tape, then we can make our way home. Stand here against the wall..." He lifted me up.

"No cactuses. Don't like cactus."

"*You* are cactus, I'd say. Think you can hold the camera?"

"Certainly."

He looked into my eyes. "Marc. This isn't like you."

He gave me a reassuring slap, threw on a media smile and whipped off into the crowd. Within seconds he was surrounded by heavily coiffured women, all shoving whisky and press releases at him. I slumped, closing my eyes. Paul would take care of me.

"There you are," piped a bright voice. My eyes opened languidly to see my old friend the waitress.

"Try this one," she urged. "It's a Kentucky blend."

"Better not."

"Oh, go on. Everyone's raving about it." She flourished the tray at me.

"Cheers," I said warily.

"Whisky sours are coming out shortly, with chicken wings."

I laughed out loud at a vision of these winged cocktails swooping over our heads.

In keeping with the farmyard theme, a pig in pin-striped trousers now accosted me, or at least a man who looked like one: rotund, pink-faced, and sweaty. He grinned on approach, then shot out a tubby hand.

"Don't believe we've met," he intoned. "Crispin Hurt. Columnist. 'Piggy' to my friends." I was right.

"Marc Petrucci. *NOW!*"

He leered. "Now what?"

"*NOW!* magazine."

"Oh! Forgive me. I'm less than au fait with the populist publications." He laughed uproariously. I joined in.

"Me too," I confessed.

"How are you enjoying the tasting?"

"I'm getting into it. You?"

He nodded casually. "Middling, middling. Of course, this crowd wouldn't know a double malt from a milk shake." He lay a hand against the wall, close to my shoulder. "I contribute a regular whisky column to *Fine Arts Quarterly*. In fact, I cover a broad lifestyle spectrum. Everything for the discriminating man of means." He leant in closer, as if imparting a military secret. "I'm on the board of the Historic Houses Trust," he whispered, emitting a toxic, alcoholic belch. "Pardon."

"That's nice. The historic homes, I mean."

He produced a handkerchief and patted his forehead. "Warm in here. I shan't be staying long." He leered once more. "You're accompanying Paul Silverton."

"Yes," I said in surprise.

"One knows *him*, of course. Between you and me, I shouldn't think his camp style will be in vogue for much longer. Look at this proposed antihomosexual legislation. Tide's about to turn and no mistake."

"Do you think the bill could get through?"

"Well...I have many influential friends on the conservative side of politics. My informed guess is it'll be too hot to handle along party lines, which means it'll come down to a conscience vote. If that transpires, I'd expect the bill to garner overwhelming support in both houses."

"You mean they'd pass it?"

"Under those circumstances, yes."

"But that's terrible," I exclaimed.

"Mm. Possibly not," he murmured. "At least it'll put paid to this stultifying political correctness one encounters everywhere. I must do another column on the subject."

"But surely you aren't in favor?"

He assumed a worldly sneer. "Constraints are not necessarily a bad thing. Of course, what some fellows get up to in private is another matter entirely."

I was suddenly aware of a warm, slightly moist pressure creeping lazily down my lower back. It was Piggy's free hand.

"Guess what I'm wearing," he whispered. I wheeled around, a little too quickly for comfort. My head reeled and I found myself clinging to the odious man for support. He glanced about quickly and pushed me away. "Careful, dear. Let's not be too *open*."

I drew myself up. "Get your hands off me," I shouted.

"Quiet now…" He made for the door but I grabbed his arm. I intended to tell this person what I thought of him.

"You pig!"

"My dear fellow," he hissed, "I believe you're drunk."

"Maybe," I answered triumphantly, "but as Churchill once said, I'll be sober in the morning."

"Don't count on it."

He wrenched free and stormed out, leaving me slightly befuddled. I was sure the snappy comeback had worked better for Churchill. Perhaps I'd got it wrong. Just then, Paul came running over.

"What are you doing, caro?" He clicked his tongue. "I had no idea you were such an aggressive drunk."

"Paul," I asked carefully, "exactly what did Churchill say?"

"Who? I've got no idea. Pull yourself together. I've set up an interview with a spokesperson from the Australasian and Pacific Rim Alcohol Association. Here she comes now." He placed the video camera in my hands. "It's all ready to go. Steady yourself against the wall, for God's sake."

My recollections of what happened after that are fragmentary and, I think, untrustworthy. I'm sure at some stage the alcohol spokesperson marched away in disgust, though I forget why. With her large eyelashes, she'd reminded me of a camel; it was quite a menagerie all round. And I seem to recall the waitress came back and held the camera while Paul interviewed me. But why would he do that? I had nothing to do with whisky—not officially, anyway.

What was clear though, even to me, was that I had quaffed one too many. Fortunately, Paul took charge, hailed a cab, and bundled me into it.

I dozed in the taxi till I was jolted awake by the driver. He reached awkwardly around his safety bubble and nudged me into the street. The moment I hit the sidewalk, the cab screeched away into the night.

With careful deliberation I made my way along the path to my door. Unfortunately, key and keyhole refused to coordinate and produce the required unlocking action. *Why,* I asked myself. *Why this? Why now?* Inside, my comfy bed awaited with open sheets. Despairing, I banged my head against the door and wailed.

Immediately, the night's silence was shattered by a barrage of barking and scratching. Someone had let a dog into my house! Who could have done this inconsiderate thing? The best option, I decided, was to keep perfectly still. This wasn't possible, however, because the door opened and I fell into the hallway.

The dog, whom I recognized as Hector, flew into a fit of yapping and face licking. Gavin shooed him away and crouched next to me.

"Marc!" he exclaimed. "What's happened? Have you been attacked?"

"I'm just fine," I mumbled into the carpet. "It's very kind of you to mind my house, but I have to be sick."

"Quick," he said. "This way."

He helped me to my feet and we stumbled to the nearest pristine bathroom. Fifteen minutes later I was lying full length on a single bed, covered by a tasteful bedspread.

"Where am I?"

"In my spare room," said Gavin.

"Oh! I'm so sorry…"

"You'd better stay here tonight."

"I only live next door…"

"Much too far to travel in your condition."

I felt I owed him an explanation. "I had a drink with lunch, you see, then I was in a pub and…the news came on. That's right. Antigay laws. I couldn't believe it!"

"Shh, go to sleep," he crooned. "That clown's enough to drive anyone to drink. Don't worry about it now. We're going to deal with it."

"Deal with it," I repeated wanly. "Why don't we just deal with it."

I daresay there is no need for me to describe how I felt next morning. Shame was the least of it. As for the Petrucci brain cells, they'd been frazzled beyond cognition. All those happy memories—my first teenage crush, family holidays, trips to Italy—gone forever, marinated into oblivion. Even the segment of the brain that recognized my neighbor's spare room took some time to get its act together. When it did, a further wave of embarrassment swept over me. Painfully I got myself dressed.

I checked my watch; to my consternation it was after 11 o'clock. I prayed Gavin had gone out, but I heard him bustling around, which totally spoiled my plan of sneaking home and avoiding him for the rest of my days.

"Up at last," he shouted gaily as he stomped into the room.

"Gavin. I'm so grateful to you and ashamed of myself," I began.

"Think nothing of it. Berocca?" He handed me a fizzing drink and began rolling up the bed cover. "I hope I'm still capable of a night on the tiles at your age," he added.

"Thanks." I took a cautious swig.

"Though you had better be careful. The gay-hate killer struck again last night."

I choked.

"It was on the news this morning. Another body was found in that park, in some clearing by the side of the road."

I was staggered. "Not the same place," I exclaimed. "I know it! It's quite bushy. You can hardly see it from the road…" Gavin was watching me intently. I cleared my throat. "Uh, I took

Hector there for a walk on election day. Remember?"

He forced a tight smile. "And have you been up there since?"

"No, luckily."

"That *is* lucky." He stood awkwardly. "Well, Marc, I have work to do..."

"I'll be off then. Um, thanks again. I'll return the favor."

"Hopefully not."

As he showed me out, he suddenly asked, "Is there any reason why music should be playing in your place when you're not there?"

My head ached. "It must be Paul," I answered. He was the only person I could think of who knew about the spare key.

As I soberly wandered back home, my sixth sense told me any lingering possibility of romance with my handsome neighbor had just been torpedoed.

I could hear Act 3 of *Tosca* blaring as I approached my front gate. Unlocking the door with no effort this time, I instantly rammed my shin into a suitcase huddling in the passage. I hobbled to the lounge room, expecting to find the usual cyclonic destruction that accompanies Paul everywhere he goes. Instead, the room appeared unusually neat. I even had the impression some of the furniture had been moved. Stepping over to the CD player to turn it down, I saw that all my opera sets had been rearranged in some weird nonalphabetical order. What on earth? It took me a moment to twig: The CDs had been stacked according to the color of their spines.

"Paul?" I called doubtfully. If Paul was the intruder, he'd evidently misplaced every one of his marbles.

"Marc! Is that you?" A pitter-patter of tiny feet came scurrying down the stairs. "I was just clearing up," sang a never-to-be-forgotten voice. "Where have you been?"

There in front of me bobbed a round, boyish face replete with red rimmed eyes and thinning hair: Andrew, my ex-partner of eleven years. I was bemused. Had I binged myself back in time or something?

"Andrew? Don't you live in Brisbane?"

"Not anymore." His lip trembled in a chillingly familiar way. "Can I stay? Just for a while?"

"Well, yes, of course. What's happened?"

Tears welled up in his eyes. He lunged at me and threw his arms around my neck. "Oh, Marc! Neil and I broke up. We had a major fight and I've left him for good. I didn't know where else to go-ho-ho...."

I patted his hair gently. "Shh, there now, all right. You can stay here. Just let go of my neck. Please, I've got a headache."

"OK." Andrew stepped aside and blew his nose. "I've just brewed some bancha tea, but there's no biscuits. Really, Marc, you're not very well stocked. I'll bake some tomorrow."

"You drink the tea. I'll pour myself a coffee, then you can tell me everything."

"I arrived last night." He followed me into the kitchen. "The spare key was still under the gas meter, thank heavens. Where *were* you?"

"Next door, mostly."

"Next door?"

"It's a long story." He started sniffling again. I'd forgotten what a crier he was. "Pull yourself together. Your nose will go bright red and you hate that."

Closing my eyes, I let the healing smell of freshly ground coffee beans assail my nostrils and began the long, arduous transformation into a living thing. At the same time a warm, malicious glow lit up somewhere deep inside me and an involuntary grin invaded my lips. So my ex had left that hideous lover of his. That pompous, self-important, tight-assed, prissy queen of a pharmacist. I'd never taken to Neil. The only surprise was that Andrew had stuck it out for so long.

I was feeling considerably magnanimous by the time we settled down with our drinks. "Well," I said, wrapping my hands around my cup. I took a sip of coffee. "Mm-m-m."

"You needn't be so happy about this," Andrew pouted.

"Of course I'm not, I'm terribly upset for you. So what was the fight over?"

Andrew sank miserably back into his arm chair. "Still got these old chairs, I see."

"All right, don't tell me a thing."

He frowned. "It was about space."

"You mean cupboard space? *Closet* space?"

"Please don't send me up, Marc. Personal space, of course."

"That's pretty vague."

"Nevertheless, that was the issue."

This wouldn't do. If my ex expected to claim sanctuary for an unspecified length of time, he could at least dish the dirt. I tried a different tack.

"I presume Neil's having an affair."

"Don't be ridiculous!" Andrew looked shocked.

"Well, what's the story then?"

"There's a club, OK? A drag club—"

I squealed. "He's been getting into a frock? Saints preserve us!"

Andrew got to his feet. "I think I'll go to a hotel," he said.

"Sit down. I apologize. I'm not myself. I had too much to drink last night."

He frowned. "I thought it was something like that."

"Please finish. You know, I might be able to advise you. That's what I do for a living these days."

His mouth fell open. "You have a job?"

"I ghost write an agony column for *NOW!* magazine. Amongst other things."

"Good for you. Neil said you'd never—" His face reddened.

"I think if you're going to stay, we'd better not get into the 'Neil says this, Neil says that' area."

He nodded. "He does have rather a lot to say."

"So. There's a drag club?"

"They got me in to do the interiors, that's all. A tranny named Scarlet Ribbons runs it. She cultivates a *Gone With the Wind* look. I designed her a big staircase, fake of course, but lots of gilt and velvet. I adore all that."

"Very Brisbane."

"You think? Anyway I'd forgotten how much fun those venues can be. But Neil wouldn't set foot in there. He hates me to enjoy myself. If he'd only relax and let his hair down he'd see there's nothing wrong. It's just a bit of a giggle. Nobody's having sex behind anyone's back."

An unmistakably guilty look flashed across his face.

"What are you going to do about your decorating business?"

"I don't know. I'll have to relocate to Sydney. I haven't thought about that yet."

I moved over and sat on the arm of his chair, stroking the familiar soft bristles of his neck.

"Get yourself settled first. One thing at a time. There's no rush. And I'd love to put you up."

"Thanks, Marc. I've got money, so I won't be sponging off you."

I chuckled. "What a relief! Hope you don't mind sleeping on the couch."

"Of course not."

"Speaking of which, I have a little snoozing to do myself. If anybody wants me, tell them I'm down with croup."

"Oh!" He sprang up. "A friend of yours rang. Paul. He needs to speak to you urgently. He seemed very surprised you weren't home."

I sighed. "I'll call him back later. Paul's version of 'urgent' is different from ours. It means he's bored."

I climbed the stairs—at last!—but no sooner had my head reached its pillowy destination than I heard the radio blaring in the kitchen. Cursing, I crept downstairs again.

Andrew was bent over, rummaging under the sink. I stood in the doorway, distractedly contemplating his chubby derriere.

"Oh!" he exclaimed when he eventually backed out and saw me. "Is it too loud? I wanted to hear the news.... What's up? Are you going to be sick?"

"No, no. Shh."

I sat slowly, struggling to grasp what I was hearing. The news bulletin concerned the second gay-hate murder. The victim had been identified. It was my "sister," Raymond.

chapter twelve

However I looked at it, I was in an unexpected, unwelcome position. Who had gotten gainful employment as a direct result of Quentin Butler's murder? Who, as Paul's minder, had rid him of a nuisance hairdresser by sending said nuisance off to meet his maker? And who was feeling guilty as hell about it? Me.

Sitting at the kitchen table, I brushed aside Andrew's irritating queries and desperately tried to recall my last meeting with Raymond. When I'd suggested he team up with some passing stranger to make Paul jealous, I hadn't meant a homicidal maniac! If only I'd stayed with him. But instead, I'd left him in the company of a very sexy Italian waiter. Had they gone off somewhere together or separated after a few drinks? Only Fabio knew the answer to that.

I thought I'd better ring Paul. Shakily, I dialled his number and got a recorded message.

"Hi!" chirped a strange, deep voice. "Brad, Zoltan, and Paul can't take your call at the moment 'cause we're at the gym running self-defense classes. So leave a message after the beep, and one of the big guys will get back to you. Ciao!" (The voice rose slightly.)

"Paul, it's Marc. Do I have the right number?"

A second later the receiver was picked up. "Caro? Is that you?"

"Yes! Who else?"

"Ah. That's the question."

"What are you talking about?"

"I'll explain when you come over."

My temple gave a tiny, threatening throb. "I take it you know about Raymond."

"Of course." Paul's voice quavered. "Caro, we need to talk."

"I'll never fit into your flat with all those karate experts. Couldn't you come over here?"

"No. Caro, *ple-e-ease!*"

It had been a while since I'd heard that particular word issue from Paul's lips. "All right."

I didn't feel quite up to driving, but fortunately Andrew was heading off to the markets for fresh produce. I got him to drop me outside Paul's building, a weather-beaten inner-city warehouse jam-packed with loft apartments. The foyer boasted a spacious central atrium with a glass roof and old-fashioned open elevator. It was here I waited after Paul had buzzed me in. Always one to make an entrance, he'd insisted on coming down to meet me. When the elevator finally creaked to a halt I hardly recognized him in a pair of heavy sunglasses and a black beanie.

"What's all this?" I inquired.

"Best I could do at short notice. Are you alone?"

"Don't rub it in."

"Let's go across the road for a sandwich. I haven't eaten today."

We slid into a greasy café designed to cater solely to workmen who convert warehouses into apartments. Having ordered toasted cheese and tomato fingers, we settled into a table in the back corner.

"When do I get to meet Brad and Zoltan?"

He lowered his voice. "They don't exist."

"Fair enough," I remarked breezily. "If you're going to make up imaginary friends, they might as well be rippling with muscles. I didn't realize your love life was at such a standstill."

He looked pained. "This is no joke. I'm a celebrity now—"

"You don't say."

"And I need to take precautions. It's only common sense. Supposing I'm next on the list?"

"What list? The ten worst-dressed?"

"Caro, there's a misfit gay-hater on the loose! Who's the voice of bent Australia? The most 'out' person on television? *Moi*! He knocks me off and he's *really* made his point. Whacking Raymond was a sign to let me know he's got me in his sights. Today, no more hairdresser; tomorrow, no more head."

I didn't know what to say. Paul really did believe the universe revolved around him. "So what are you going to do," I inquired, "apart from butching up your phone message?"

He placed his hand on mine. "We've got to find the murderer before he finds us."

"Excuse me? We? Us?"

"Well, you. But I'll be right behind you. It's not like we haven't done it before." He munched a cheese finger.

"But hold on—"

"Channel 6 News gave me the details. Raymond was found early this morning by a council worker investigating a complaint about a drainage problem. Now, that's significant. Where *is* this drain? Could a murderer hide there? It sounds extremely suspicious."

"The whole thing stinks."

He ignored my interruption. "Raymond's body was in a park by the way, the same place as the first one."

"I know."

"And listen to this: what's really weird is, the body had been sort of patched up with gauze and stuff! There's a sick little mind at work here."

I was silent. I certainly hadn't forgotten Denis's description of the bandages he found on the Quentin's corpse, though they had never been mentioned in the press reports. It was evidently a detail the police had wished to keep back. Serial killers often use some particular quirk to identify the work as their own. A signature. Is that what these bandages were? There could be no doubt the two murders were linked somehow.

"We'll throw ourselves into the investigation," continued Paul gleefully, "while the evidence is fresh. You'll be in the field, I'll be backup."

"I don't want to be in a field. What about my work?"

He mused. "Take time off. Think of it this way: You now have an extra job to do. Your undercover job."

"Great," I replied dryly. Just what I needed, another secret agenda.

"Of course, I can't stay in my apartment," Paul added. "I'd be a sitting duck. Every time that clanking lift comes up I feel like the supporting cast in a Hitchcock classic. I've packed a few bags. Take them with you now. We should go separately by different routes to confuse him."

"Go where?"

"Don't be so thick. Your place, natch!"

I smiled awkwardly. "I'm sorry. My couch is spoken for."

He frowned. "Whoever she is, throw her out. This is more important than rough trade."

"You're miles off," I laughed.

Briefly I explained how my ex had shown up out of the blue. Paul, who had heard about Andrew but never met him, was most sympathetic.

"The sponging old bitch! So that's who I spoke to on the phone, all prissy and formal. I thought he was the fem half of one of those queer cleaning couples."

"That's hardly fair."

"What's unfair, caro," he seethed, "is to walk out on a sweet, easygoing person like you after decades of wedded bliss just to shack up with some hot fuck and then come crawling back when it all turns ugly. What a lousy act."

"That's not quite how it happened."

"I hate to see my friends taken advantage of."

"'Specially when you're trying to do the same thing yourself."

He sniffed. "Totally beside the point. Andrew will turn your whole life upside down."

"I doubt it," I replied. "He's done nothing but tidy the house so far."

"And where do think this endless preening and fussing will end? You'll go stark raving mad." He nodded sagely. "I've seen it time and again. So! Out she goes."

"I can't do that. You'll have to hide somewhere else. You've got a million friends."

"But can I trust them?"

I was losing patience. "Stop being melodramatic. It's not as if you'd received a death threat."

He looked hurt. "I might have! How would *I* know? I don't answer my mail."

"Paul, I answer your mail. You haven't had any death threats. Not even reading between the lines."

Suddenly I remembered the whispering caller, although he hadn't sounded particularly threatening. I'd never told Paul about him, but now was hardly the time—not while Paul was being Princess Paranoia.

"So," he continued, "what do these victims have in common? That's the line we should pursue. You already know something about the first one, don't you?"

"A bit," I confessed modestly, and told him everything I'd learned about Quentin Butler, including the bandages and the connection with LAV.

"Off to a flying start." Paul tossed his beanie in the air. "It's just like old times, caro. I feel so much better knowing our best men are on the case."

Half an hour later, I set off for home. It was a warm afternoon in early September and a slight southerly breeze blew, bringing a whiff of the ocean into even this dry, industrial part of the city.

The phone was ringing as I walked through the door. Andrew didn't seem to be around. I snatched up the receiver. It was Angel, the giver and taker-away of opera courses.

"You *are* there," he cried. "Did you know there's been another murder?"

"Only too well," I answered, half to myself.

"Oh, you've heard." He sounded deflated. "Anyway, hon, I can't chat, I just wanted to tell you about Wednesday night. We're holding a huge concert and rally in Hyde Park—the Parliament House end. Bring as many people as you possibly can."

"Is this over the antigay legislation?"

"*Proposed* legislation," he exploded. "That's all it is and all it ever will be if I've got anything to do with it. GLEE is only one of the groups involved. Celeste—you know, the activist?—she's doing most of the legwork. She's even getting corporate sponsorship. Personally, I'm all for it. What's a few logos here and there so long as our message is clear?"

"You can count on me," I promised. "Solidarity!"

"Right on, sister!" he exclaimed. The word sent a shiver through me. "We're organizing some major talent for the concert. You can't keep these cabaret singers away from a fund-raising opportunity. And," I could almost hear him licking his lips, "our very own Stewart is going to perform a solo dance piece he's been working on. It's the story of a young guy who comes to the big city and gets into the porn scene."

"Sounds deep."

He roared. "You don't know the half of it! I must go. Be there by 7 P.M. Wear something pink and triangular."

I hung up and threw myself into one of the chairs Andrew disliked so much, wondering where he was. We still hadn't had time to catch up. I suddenly had an inspired idea: I would cook him something special for dinner! My traditional lasagna spinaci, perhaps. In the kitchen I found the fridge crammed to capacity with meats and vegetables. Evidently Andrew had come home and gone out again.

I stretched out on the couch to wait for him and fell straight into a fitful sleep. When I awoke it was dark and I was starving. The only nourishment I'd had for twenty-four hours was whisky and Berocca. Andrew still hadn't returned, so I shelved the lasagna idea and walked around to my local Italian trattoria,

Fratelli di Marco. On the way back I noticed Andrew's car parked on the opposite side of my street; however, the house remained exactly as I'd left it. This seemed rather strange. Still, I could see no point in waiting up.

I slipped *La Rondine* into the CD player, adjusted the volume to performance level and trudged up to my room. The bedroom was dark, so much so that I failed to notice Andrew's prone form spread-eagled across my bed. I practically sat on top of him, just stopping myself in time.

"Ach!" I cried.

His head lolled back at an odd angle and his mouth hung open. Immediately I wondered if he had done something desperate, but there were no notes or empty pill bottles lying about. I tried to feel his pulse, but couldn't find it. His body was still warm, at least.

"Andrew?" I whispered.

There was no response. I shook him roughly. "Andrew!"

He snorted awake. "Mm?" he yawned. "Oh, Marc. Hello."

"Is everything all right?"

"Oh, I guess so. I'm sorry about wrinkling your bedspread, but I had to lie down. I didn't sleep too well on the couch last night; it's so uncomfortable."

I breathed a sigh of relief. "Be my guest." Inadvertently I brushed the pillow. "Have you been crying?" I asked.

"Oh, you know me," he answered sheepishly. "I can't help it. Neil rang up. He knows I'm here."

"It wouldn't take Einstein to work that out."

"I've never heard him so angry." He looked at me soulfully. "He blames you."

"Me? For what, precisely?"

"Oh, it doesn't matter."

"Tell me!"

He cleared his throat. "He says you corrupted me."

"How?"

"Don't be offended. He thinks you set a bad example when we were together, because you're sort of unmotivated—'lazy,' he calls it—and when I took up with this drag crowd it was a throwback, and he should have known I'd go 'Sydney' on him! He said he can't believe he's wasted so many years of his life on me and the cat's pining, which is entirely my fault, apparently—"

I saw red. "Lazy!"

"Neil's very upset."

"Let me show you upset," I said, and with preternatural strength grabbed all three pillows from the bed and flung them out the open window.

"Marc!" he screamed. "Stop it! Quick, get them back. They'll be filthy!"

"Good."

"Please, you'll just make it worse."

Then, at last, the waterworks came on with a vengeance. Andrew sat with his knees up, rocking backwards and forwards.

"He's being so mean…" he whimpered. "He says he'll fight me in court…that he owns all our things, which is just not true, it's *not*!—and all our friends are on his side…"

"Shh," I said softly, putting my arms around him in a bear hug. "Come on now, stop rocking like that. The mattress isn't up to it."

"I can't go on. I can't."

"Shh. He's only a pharmacist. Listen," I kissed his flushed cheek. "I want to tell you something."

"Yes?" he sniffled.

"Neil's the most genuinely boring man I ever met," I whispered.

"Oh."

"But I had no idea he was stupid as well."

"Marc, what are you trying to say?"

A good question. I thought I'd covered it fairly succinctly. "I mean," I explained, "he must be stupid if he's prepared to let you go."

He lay his soggy head on my shoulder. "You let me go once."

"But I didn't want to."

"Didn't you?"

"You know I didn't."

"So why did you?"

I pondered. "It seemed like a good idea at the time."

He was quiet for a moment, then abruptly produced a neat pressed handkerchief and blew his nose.

"What led to our breakup?" he asked. "I don't even remember."

"Well," I said, "one thing I could never stand was the way you blow your nose on a folded handkerchief, instead of unfolding it first."

"It's more absorbent that way."

"Andrew, for goodness' sake, it's ridiculous!"

He smiled through his tears. "So that's it."

"Must be."

He rolled up his hanky and threw it out the window. "Happy now?" he said.

"Very."

There was nothing more to say. We'd both had difficult days, we both felt vulnerable and seriously nostalgic, we both needed each other—and so the inevitable happened. As it inevitably does.

I awoke, shivering, just after 1 A.M. Extricating myself from Andrew's sleeping embrace, I got up to throw an extra cover on the bed. Retrieving my shirt from the floor, I felt something in the pocket. Then I remembered: my assignment—Helen's extra letter for Paul's column.

No longer sleepy, I crept downstairs and reacquainted myself with the miserable office girl. The scenario was all too common: the girl was hopelessly in love with a manipulative bastard.

I started to scribble a reply in the usual flippant Paulspeak. Suddenly, it hit me: This was an extremely familiar situation! This, in fact, was the story of Paul and Raymond.

I scanned the letter more carefully. "We have great sex," I read, "but I want more than that. I want commitment." It was Raymond's problem to a T. "He doesn't want anyone to know we're seeing each other." That was true as well. I'd had the distinct impression Paul was trying to downplay the whole business, even from me, probably out of guilt at his high-handedness. He was just as indirectly responsible for that boy's death as I was.

I scrapped my first reply and crafted a new one. I maintained the fiction of the heterosexual office romance, but I let the "Paul" character have it with with both barrels. I was in no mood for niceties; he was getting what he deserved. Then I sealed the papers in an envelope with a cover note for Helen and stumbled back to bed.

Neither Andrew nor I had much to say next morning. It was as though the implications of what had happened were as yet too hard to grasp. What had led to our little historical reenactment? Mere nostalgia, or something deeper? Would there be repeat performances? I could tell from Andrew's inscrutable expression that he was asking himself the same thing.

The sex had been delightfully stimulating. There was nothing tentative about it, since we knew each other's quirks well, but because we hadn't been together for so long, it was fresh and unpredictable. The experience was like hearing a politically incorrect joke from years ago and suddenly remembering all those things you used to laugh at.

Upon waking, we scampered to the kitchen and plowed into an enormous Sunday breakfast of bacon and eggs, tomatoes and mushrooms, while maintaining a polite, noncommittal patter, never coming within a mile of the one question that was on our minds: Where do we go from here?

Out, in my case. I thought it wise to allow Andrew quality time on his own. The last thing I intended to do was paint him into an emotional corner. I was also unsure of myself. Paul had hit the nail on the head: Thorough housecleaning once a month was invigorating. Seven days a week it was pathological.

"I might go out for a while," I announced, after piling our dishes in the sink.

Andrew nodded. "OK. Run away from me if you must."

"What do you mean?"

"I mean, Marc, that you never used to face up to things and

you're no different now." He rubbed furiously at an egg stain on the table. "We made love last night, remember?"

I slumped onto one of the kitchen stools. "I assumed you didn't want to talk about it," I sighed.

"You hoped."

"Andrew, look—for God's sake, put down that sponge! Stop rubbing things for five minutes."

He did. "So what about last night?"

"What about it?" I replied. "I liked it! Didn't you?"

"Of course I did."

I smiled. "It was like remembering an old joke."

Andrew bristled. "You thought last night was a joke?"

"No, no. I just meant...it took me back."

"Oh, I see," he answered. "Well, if you imagine we're going to have some sort of casual sex arrangement in return for room and board, you can forget it. Is that what you've got in mind?"

I protested. "I've got nothing in mind. Yet."

"That's my point," he said, thoroughly exasperated. "We'll drift into it and after a while it'll be a fait accompli. That's how you operate."

Now he was beginning to annoy me. "You say I haven't changed, but you have. For the worse, if you want to know. You were obsessive before, but all these years with Neil have honed it to a fine art. Look at you, cleaning and polishing everything in sight. I won't be able to walk through the house without seeing my reflection. I don't like my reflection that much."

"So you want me out, then," he sniffled.

"Oh, no, stop that! Look, all I'm trying to say is, can we not draw up a timetable right now? I'm not ready for it."

Andrew nodded stiffly. "She dumped me too."

"Who? Neil?"

"No," he answered ruefully.

"So you *were* getting it on with the tranny! I thought so." I grinned. "Did you rendezvous behind the velvet drapes?"

His face took on a sly look. "Maybe."

"Well, well." I hopped off the stool and marched to the fridge. "Let's have a glass of champagne."

"Now? Why?"

"Why not?" I said, popping the cork. "Because you finally saw your life with Neil was a grotesque sham and threw caution to the winds. I'll drink to that."

"It wasn't a 'grotesque sham,' as you put it. Besides, I have *no* life now." He handed me two pristine glasses.

"That's not true," I replied. "You just have no road map."

"Ooh, listen to the philosopher."

We drank up.

"There's plenty of this stuff, I see," Andrew remarked. "Champagne and coffee are the only things you're stocked up on."

I shrugged. "I like it. Paul likes it."

Andrew folded his arms. "Yes, about this Paul. Is he the boy you've been seeing for a few years? The dancer?"

"He's only a friend. He's not doing chorus work now, he's on TV."

We took our drinks into the back yard, and lazing around under the old liquidambar soon brought each other up to date. I gave him an edited rundown of my employment situation at *NOW!*, making myself sound as indispensible as possible. We talked about the murders Paul and I had investigated—one of which Andrew had been slightly involved in—and I mentioned our current interest in the gay-hate killings, though I played it down. I knew he disapproved of my amateur detective work.

Changing the subject neatly, I told him I'd seen Angel and finally got the GLEE opera business off my chest. Andrew was most sympathetic; I hadn't forced Puccini down his throat for all those years for nothing.

We were happily avoiding any mention of a future together when he took hold of my hand. "Marc, I think no more sex until we've sorted ourselves out. OK?"

"Whatever you like," I replied solemnly. "What are you doing Wednesday night?"

"I'm serious."

"No, no. I'm going to a protest rally. I thought you might like to come. Angel invited me."

Andrew's face brightened. "It would be *him*. But aren't protests a thing of the past?"

"They were, until some idiot politician started talking about antigay legislation."

"My God! Of course I'll come."

Watching him scamper back inside for more champagne, I felt a peculiar tingly sensation. I'd just made a date with my ex-lover. It was as though the last twenty years had never happened.

chapter thirteen

The nerve center of *NOW!* was very subdued over the next couple of days. Of course, Raymond's death was mainly responsible. Office staff who had known him were in a state of shock, and even those who had nothing to do with the TV show found themselves pondering the awesome subject of their own mortality. The police were known to be poking around the studio, which further brought home the reality of the situation. But alongside all this something else was in the air, and whatever it was seemed to concern me. Every so often my coworkers would drop whatever they were doing to leer in my direction. Once I walked into a room and became uncomfortably aware that I'd stopped a conversation dead in its tracks. This was puzzling. No one had ever taken much notice of "Paul's assistant" before.

It was now Tuesday. Even though Paul had graciously allowed me time off for sleuthing, I couldn't neglect my responsibility to Helen, particularly to our hallowed tradition of Monday lunch. Much to my annoyance, however, she'd postponed it at the eleventh hour.

"Sonia's in too much of a flap," she'd explained. "I'm trying to get her latest overseas jaunt organized. She even cancelled today's yoga."

"Where is she going?" I'd asked.

"Oh, the usual. Milan, Paris, and New York."

"Why now? The spring fashion shows are weeks away, aren't they?"

"She's sneaking in early to snoop," Helen had answered wryly. "Sonia doesn't go anywhere because she has to. She goes because she can."

So I was killing time redirecting phone calls and soaking up the peculiar atmosphere. I was especially suspicious of Bryce, the accountant. His all-purpose smile had been replaced by a different one, more secretive and knowing, as though he were planning a big fat audit.

I had never liked Bryce. He wore smarmy Armani business shirts teamed with tasteful silk ties, and square glasses with trendy titanium frames. Paul had swiftly pegged him as gay by the deep tan he sported right through winter. Even his shirts seemed to have been tanned a darker shade of pale blue. But in this case I knew better: Helen had informed me long ago that Bryce was merely a gay wanna-be. His real name was Bruce.

I could see into his office from where I sat. The third time I caught him staring at me with that irritating half-smile, I leapt up and marched to his door.

"Is something wrong, Bryce?" I asked bluntly.

He started shuffling papers with uncharacteristic abandon. "Nothing at all," he answered suspiciously. I stomped grumpily back to my desk.

At last Helen grabbed me and we sped out to the nearest bistro: old reliable Eccocina.

"Tell me," I asked, as we made a lunge for our regular table, "why is everyone looking at me strangely?"

Helen peered about. "Nobody's looking at you."

"Not here. In the office. It's unsettling. Even that little accountant's doing it."

"*Is* he now?"

A pert girl with pad and pencil loomed up and presented us with a false, expectant smile. "Wine?" Helen inquired.

"Please."

"Silly question, really," she grinned and ordered two dry whites.

"Now *you've* got the office look! What's so amusing?"

She was blunt. "Perhaps they've all heard how you got roaring drunk at that whisky tasting. Some minder!"

"What?" I was astounded. "Maybe I had one too many, but 'roaring'? I very rarely roar!"

"I believe you almost came to blows with another member of the media."

"I don't remember that."

"Well, he does," she laughed. "I wish you had, actually. He's a real prick."

Our drinks arrived. I could hardly bring myself to touch my glass.

"Bottoms up," Helen announced. "Go on. You'll only draw attention to yourself if you don't."

"Apparently."

"But next time there's a tasting I'm taking your place. I haven't had a wild night out in ages." She examined the menu. "Shall we get the pasta special? It'll be quick."

"Sure."

"Where's your suave friend today?" she asked casually.

"Fabio? I don't know."

Suddenly, I leapt to my feet. Fabio was the main reason I'd wanted to come here! With all that mysterious whispering in the office I had completely forgotten.

"Fabio!" I croaked. "He's gone. Where is he?"

"Jesus," muttered Helen. "One drink and he's off."

I rushed towards our waitress. "Is Fabio here?" I panted. "This is extremely important."

The girl's smile rapidly disappeared. She shrugged and pointed towards the large bejeweled lady with black coiffed hair who sat at the cash register. The woman stared unflinchingly at me, implacable as a lizard on a warm rock. I marched in her direction.

"Don't hit anyone," Helen cried.

"Yes?" wheezed the bejeweled lady, flickering her lizardy eyelids at me. I took one look at her heavy make up, professionally tucked chins and plucked eyebrows and I knew: She was Roman.

"Please excuse me, *signora*," I said in my most respectful Italian, "but I must speak to Fabio, your waiter."

She flicked her wrist nonchalantly. "Gone," she drawled.

"Gone?"

"That's what I said."

"But I saw him here on Friday."

"Gone on Friday," she sniffed, with an air of utter, rock-bottom boredom.

"Where has he gone, may I ask, if you would be so kind, *signora*?"

"Milano." She shook her head. "His Australian visa runs out. Too bad. He is a good waiter." She winked. "*Simpatico* also, don't you think?"

True to form, she'd sussed me out. They're no fools, these Italian mamas. "I need to find him, *signora*," I insisted, thinking hard. "He…he owes me money."

She nodded sagely; this news was no surprise. Producing a thin, sparkly pen, she copied something onto a scrap of paper and handed it to me. The scrawl revealed Fabio's full name, Fabio Bottone, and gave an address on the Via San Martino, Milano.

I oozed appreciation. "*Signora*, I am in your debt."

She waved my thanks away. "Carpaccio of Atlantic Salmon special today. Very good. *Fr-r-resca*."

Distractedly, I ordered two specials as I pocketed the address.

"What was that all about?" Helen inquired sardonically, as I returned to the table.

"Hmm? Oh, I just wanted to get in touch with Fabio. You know, say goodbye. He's gone back to Italy." I didn't think Helen would take to the idea of Paul and I investigating Raymond's murder. I was supposed to keep Paul out of trouble, not lead him straight to it.

"The guy was only a waiter," she purred. "Goodbyes aren't strictly necessary…under normal circumstances."

I decided to use the same excuse I had given the *signora*. "Fabio owes me money," I said, "that's all."

"How much?"

"Pardon?" I might have known she wouldn't let it drop. "How much?"

I was offhand. "Oh, um, fifty dollars."

"You're getting pretty bloody excited over fifty dollars."

"It's the principle of the thing," I replied weakly.

"Show me his address," she said. "Via San Martino. That's the fashion district, isn't it?"

"Could be."

"Fashionable, anyway. No phone number. Well, whatever this is *really* about," she smirked, "I could give his address to Sonia. She'll be there next week and she does like to have a handsome man hanging off her arm. She could pass on a little note asking him to send you a postal order—or whatever it is you want."

"You think she'll do it?"

"Oh, I'd say so. After I describe him. He's bi, I presume?"

"He's an Italian waiter. That's all I know."

"Same thing."

The waitress reappeared with two minimalist plates of salmon carpaccio. She grated black pepper over them and retreated in a flash.

"What's this?" asked Helen.

"The lunchtime special. Thought we might try it."

She consulted the menu. "You'd better write that note," she quipped. "A very small fish has just eaten up your fifty bucks."

Back at the office I tried to come to grips with Fabio's disappearance. It was so astoundingly inconvenient! He was the last person I knew to have seen Raymond alive. Although I didn't seriously suspect him of the murder, it was still a possibility I had to consider.

I tried to recall the previous Friday in detail. I'd left Fabio and Raymond together at around 6:30. On impulse I checked with Qantas and Alitalia. They'd each had a flight scheduled that Friday evening to Milan via Rome, one at 8:10 and one at 9 o'clock. Unless Raymond was murdered before, say, 7:30, which was unlikely, Fabio was in the clear—that is, if he had actually boarded one of the flights. I called both airlines back, pretending to be Fabio's father, but they refused to give out any passenger information. Cursing, I regrouped and tried again. This time I evoked Justin Flynn, *NOW!* magazine, Paul and all the combined clout I could summon. It worked like a charm—I was transferred to a PR person whose only role, apparently, was to do favors for the media. She told me everything I needed to know: Mr. Bottone had flown out on the 8:10 (which, in reality, had left at 8:45 P.M. after sitting on the tarmac for thirty-five minutes).

Next I called the international exchange, hoping to find a Milan number for Fabio, but there was none registered in his name. My only hope was to write the letter for Sonia to pass on. Knowing she would read it, I limited the message to "Please telephone me urgently. Matter of life and death," plus my name and number.

Paul made one of his rare appearances late that afternoon.

"What are you doing here?" I asked, automatically vacating his special chair as he pranced into the room.

"I had to spend some time in the editing suite," he explained glibly. "Getting tomorrow's segment ready."

"Since when do you care about editing?"

He looked unusually virtuous. "I need to take more of an interest in the technical side. The stuff we've been putting together is riveting." He lowered his voice. "How's the sleuthing?"

I didn't mention Fabio, as I had no intention of Paul finding out I'd been plotting behind his back with Raymond. At least, not until Raymond's pathetic letter had been published. "I haven't really done anything yet," I lied.

To my surprise, he was sympathetic. "It's hard to know where to start. I've done some general run-of-the-mill snooping, and I discovered Raymond was an Adelaide boy. He only moved to Sydney this year. I'd never have guessed. He was so camp I thought he was born at Les Girls."

I wracked my brain from one end to the other. "Adelaide rings a bell, but why?"

"City of churches?"

Then I remembered. "City of sisters! Quentin Butler's sister lives there."

Paul sprang to his feet and began pacing as best he could in the tiny office space. "Both from Adelaide. Caro! This is our strongest lead yet."

"Our only one."

He clapped his hands. "By George, she's got it! Why don't we go down there in person and give Butler's sister the third degree? We can shoot a segment for the show at the same time. I've got nada lined up for next week anyway."

"What segment?"

"Oh, any old thing. Leave it with me. We'll whiz out tomorrow, straight after the taping."

I blanched. "I've got another commitment."

Paul threw me a shocked glance. "Work comes first, caro."

"But I'm going to a rally tomorrow night to protest against Cahill's antigay legislation."

He frowned, his enthusiasm ebbing away. "That's important too, I suppose."

"It's in Hyde Park. Why don't you come along and bring a camera crew?"

"Not my department. That's news. A different beat, as we say." He gave me a quizzical look. "Anyone else going with you?"

"Only Andrew," I answered quietly.

"Don't tell me *she's* still hanging around! All right, I'll definitely come. Meet you at your place at 7."

With that he swept grandly out of the office.

Meanwhile, it was back to the phone. I rang *Celluloid Sisters* and, luckily, Butler's partner Doff answered. I reintroduced myself, inquired about the Keanu item—the warehouse was all out of them, I was devastated to hear—and we swapped trivia for fifteen minutes. I told him I was about to visit Adelaide and thought it might be a friendly gesture on behalf of GLEE to pay my condolences to Quentin's sister. When I finally hung up in triumph, I had both the address and the phone number. I chuckled.

If I got any better at this investigative spadework, I would have to turn professional.

However, before we could wing our way south, there was Paul's spot on *NOW TV!* to deal with. As I stumbled over the now familiar doorstep the following morning, everything seemed unusually quiet. Then I realized what was missing: Raymond's high-spirited chatter. This would be our first time without him.

The floor manager came loping down the corridor, his hair as greasy and unkempt as ever.

"Ay, Marc," he mumbled. Over the weeks his early smirks had been replaced by a grunting acceptance. We had almost achieved a low-key camaraderie, as much as two creatures from different planets could.

"Quiet today without Raymond," I remarked.

To my surprise the boy took hold of me in a fierce embrace. I felt the hard muscles in his arms.

"Oh, mate, it's bad," he muttered, stepping back to release me. "Really bad. I mean, Raymond was way over the top, but he would never hurt a living soul, you know? If they ever catch the guy who did it…" He clenched a fist. "Not yet!"

"Sorry?"

He pointed to his earphone. "Camera operator was asking me if Paul's here."

"Ah. Well, I'll miss Raymond. I liked him."

"Yeah. Look after yourself, ay? And Paul too. You gays gotta be careful just now."

I was astounded, not just by the unexpected intimacy but also by the fellow's genuine concern. You never can tell about people.

Paul and Sonia arrived together, in a typical flurry, with Helen in tow, all chattering and arguing at the top of their voices.

"What are you doing here?" I managed to ask Helen.

"Still sorting out Sonia's trip. Incidentally, you're flying to Adelaide 11 o'clock Friday morning. Agh! *Scusi!*" Her cell phone was in the process of exploding.

Sonia bore down on me. "*Matt*, my darling heart. I got your little note for that boy in Milan. He's rather dishy, I gather."

"If you like the dark Antonio Banderas look."

Deep beneath the day makeup, her cheeks positively glowed. "Well, you do have an eye for them. You found Paul, didn't you! This boy lives on the Via San Martino, yes?"

"That's right."

"It's perfect! Anna Piaggi's there. You know Anna?"

"Uh, no."

"We're great old chums. You *should* see her apartment. Rooms are chocka with clothes. You seriously cannot *move*. We'll all go to that fabulous Russian tea place. Oh, it'll *make* my trip!" She dragged Paul bodily into the conversation. "Don't forget to keep an eye on my little house, darling," she whispered, "and if I hear about any wild parties, I'll want to know why I wasn't invited."

She swanned off to makeup.

"So," I asked Paul, "have you found a scoop for us in Adelaide, or is that still to be manufactured?"

"Have no fear. I can ad lib on any subject except human reproduction."

He then went into a huddle with the director and other technical people about the forthcoming segment. Normally I'd have been included—after all, I was Paul's unofficial censor—but today he blankly refused to discuss it with me. It was to be a surprise, and I would love it. Period.

Sonia opened the show with a shrewd estimate of what to expect from the top fashion houses in Italy next season, repeatedly emphasizing that she was flying to Europe for a progress report on behalf of her loyal *NOW!* readers. They deserved nothing less.

She was followed by commercials, quite indistinguishable from the program, then a preheated cooking segment. Eventually it was Paul's turn. He stared meaningfully into the camera lens, without his usual broad smile.

"Hi there," he said. "Paul Silverton with you. How's my hair looking today? OK? Maybe the hair's a little quiet, but I'm quiet too. I want you to see something."

A still photograph came up on the monitor. It was a picture of Raymond, caught throwing his head back in a big girlie laugh.

"Isn't he sweet?" Paul continued. "But he's got nothing to laugh about now. This is Raymond. He was my hairdresser here on *NOW TV!* Last Friday Raymond left the studio at about 5 P.M. and turned up the next morning in a park. Murdered."

The picture faded.

"Here at *NOW TV!* we're all a little bit quieter today."

"No!" Sonia hissed into Helen's ear. "It's a downer! He'll lose them!"

"I doubt it," Helen whispered back.

Paul's expression became more pained. "We loved that boy, every single one of us." (Somebody didn't, I thought cynically.) "If any of my friends out there saw him on Friday night, anywhere, alone or with somebody else, please! Come forward with that information. Do it for me." He pouted bravely.

My heart skipped a beat. I could be in a jam if scores of bystanders started calling in with stories of a suspicious older man buying the victim a drink. I wished I'd mentioned it to Paul after all.

"But meanwhile, the show must go on," he admitted bright-ly. "While these tragic events were unfolding, I went off to a whisky tasting. So, from *Australia's Most Wanted* to *Australia's Most Wasted!*"

Sonia nodded. "That's more like it," she muttered.

The videotape hit the monitor as Paul described the crowd and the various whiskies. To me the scene looked nauseatingly familiar. The sooner we moved on, I thought, the better.

"I spoke to Adriana Slater, chairperson of APRA, the Australasia and Pacific Rim Alcohol Association."

We cut to another part of the video, this time with sound. Adriana Slater was speaking.

"What we're doing here is letting the public know that whisky is a young, happening drink."

"It still makes me think of old colonels in big leather armchairs reading the *Times,*" Paul joked.

Adriana laughed lustily. Only her eyes revealed the truth: She could have killed him. Suddenly they both stared at the camera as the picture began swaying from side to side. Slightly flustered, Adriana returned to her theme. "That's how things used to be. But we think whisky's too good to be locked away in a cupboard—" The image now bobbed up and down. "Can I tell you, uh, about some of the cocktails you can make with whisky? They're marvellous dinner party ideas and very simple to make…"

"Oh, yes?" said Paul distractedly, stepping out of frame. Then, to my dismay, the picture gave a jolt and I appeared on the screen. I looked absolutely trashed. Adriana turned to someone off camera.

"Can we start over?" she asked. "The cameraman's drunk!"

"You look like a camel," I said to her.

"I beg your pardon?"

"A camel. Has anyone ever told y'that?" I leered straight into the lens. "Ladies and gentlemen, this is remarkable. Wash me closely."

Surreptitiously I glanced at Sonia. She was staring at the monitor. Helen was staring at me. Their mouths were hanging open.

"I shall attempt to speak to her in camel," I giggled. "Oh, wait. Whoa! Wait a second. They spit, don't they? What's that joke? Beware, the camel spits! Get it? *Be where* the camel spits. As Winsson Churchill once said."

As I lunged out of shot, we were treated to a video compilation, all speeded up à la Keystone Cops. We saw footage of me in the distance falling down a small flight of steps, slamming into the waitress and sending her drink tray spinning high into the air, and finally attempting to remove my shirt without first unbuttoning the cuffs. In between these escapades, Paul had cut in a shot of me quaffing a glass of whisky, repeating it over and over again. The tape ended on a freeze of my face, grinning with bleary-eyed satisfaction at the disruption I'd caused.

Back in the studio, Paul was shaking with suppressed laughter. Indeed, tears were rolling down his red flushed cheeks. "I'm sorry," he said in a cracked voice. "That's all from me for this week. Stay tuned for Sonia. And whoever that man is—or was—let's hope he *gets over it*! Bye!"

The floor manager, wearing the widest grin I'd ever seen on his face, cued Paul out. On came the commercials. Instantly Paul rushed over and put his arms around me. He was still giggling.

"Oh, shit! I'm really sorry. But wasn't it hysterical? Caro, speak to me!"

I had simply frozen, patiently waiting for the floor to open up. My whole life had flashed in front of me, on national television. My past, present and, emphatically, my future.

Helen and Sonia also seemed to be in shock. Helen stared vacantly into the distance. "That whisky woman'll sue the pants off us," she murmured to herself.

Sonia snapped to attention. She now had a proper crisis to deal with and she was splendid.

"Adriana won't sue," she said. "I know her. The girl used to work for me. I'll give her a little tingle. You see, I think Paul's right, it's *hysterical*. I'm sure the panel chat shows will be keen to get hold of it—they're always desperate for something to talk about. Get onto them today. The only way to defuse this is to *saturate* the airwaves with it. It's fucking *gold*. OK, everyone?" She held Paul's face in her hands. "You're a clever boy. I was worried about that down opening but you completely turned it around!"

Then she walked over to me and gently took my hand. "Matt," she said softly.

"I…I don't know how…"

"*I* know how, darling. My second husband was an alcoholic. And believe me, if anything like this happens again, you'll be shoveling shit for a living. Got it?"

"Uh, yes. Absolutely."

"Good."

chapter fourteen

The evening had turned blustery. A strong easterly breeze set the city in motion, rustling leaves, swaying overhead cables, propelling maverick sheets of newspaper and lone empty soft-drink cans on their journey to nowhere. It produced a distinct sensation of everything being stirred up, which reflected my own feelings exactly. I was still dumbstruck, hours afterward, by the shameful spectacle I'd witnessed in the studio.

Paul, Andrew, and I left my car in a poorly lit back street in Surry Hills and made our way on foot towards the park. We were late, of course. Paul hadn't arrived until well after 7—twenty-two minutes past, as Andrew informed me sotto voce several times during our journey.

Paul had unleashed a geyser of charm from the moment he and Andrew had met. Sporting his sexiest look, he'd laughed and chatted incessantly, seemingly oblivious to Andrew's indifference. Repeatedly he'd apologized for his lateness and expressed his profound regrets for making me look like a clown on television. Andrew grudgingly asked for details. I hadn't thought it necessary to tell him everything but Paul happily obliged—so by the time we arrived the two of them had formed an alliance.

Ignoring them both, I pulled my coat around me, cast my face to the wind and pressed on.

As we approached the Parliament end of the park, we encountered a large gathering of notably queer people. They milled about excitedly, filling the park's main walkway and spilling over into the well-lit square near the fountain. There, dense groups clustered under large signs displaying mysterious acronyms: CLAP, for instance, or UFUC. A token police presence hovered around the fringes of the crowd, while the wind buffeted people this way and that, occasionally wrenching a paper plate or placard up into the air.

"Where's your contact?" Paul cried in my ear.

"I don't know."

We shuffled through the crowd and I was elbowed roughly into a makeshift trestle table. Seated behind it, clutching a pile of printed pamphlets, was a man dressed in an elaborate nun's habit.

"Don't lean on the table, child," he smiled. "It's already blown over once."

"Sorry, um—"

"Sister Euthanasia of the Sublime Short Cut. Bless you, pet." He flourished a pen at me. "Sign here and you shall be one of us. Hallelujah."

"I don't have a habit," I answered vaguely.

"My child, I meant you can join UFUC." He pointed to the sign propped precariously on a tree behind him. "The United Family of Urban Communities. And we'll give you this lovely badge, which says and I quote, UFUC WITH ME AND IFUC WITH YOU. And see? There's the dove of peace. So sweet."

Paul and Andrew were moving on. If I wasn't careful I would lose them. "I'm actually looking for GLEE," I said.

"Never heard of it. Are they a nomadic order?"

"So it seems." There was no sign of GLEE anywhere. Literally. "What's CLAP?"

The nun gave a saintly smile. "As the good book says, if you have to ask, you don't want to know. *St. Paul's Letter to the Endorphins, 1:17.*"

A young woman nearby glared at him. "It's Corporate Lesbians And Partners," she snapped.

"Do you know where GLEE is?" I asked her.

"Try up near the stage."

As I'd feared, Paul and Andrew were now lost to sight. I plunged back into the mass of people, many of whom were, like me, in a frenzy to find their affiliated acronym. I could see a stage perched at the very edge of the park, the edifice of St. Mary's cathedral glowering in disapproval behind it. The stage was awash with microphones, a drum kit, and several keyboards, and was framed by black towers of enormous speakers on either side. Smaller extra speakers sat atop scaffolding at the rear. Evidently we were soon to be in for a deafening experience. *Imagine Tebaldi singing through that system,* I thought wistfully.

I had just begun to shove my way towards the stage area when blinding lights flooded the immediate vicinity and the speakers struck up a deep, nauseating hum. This was followed, but not replaced, by the twang of bass-heavy guitars and the cry of raw, screechy voices. I stood on tiptoe. A band of hefty girls in plaid shirts and well-worn boots were easing their way into perform-ance mode, their mouths swallowing the microphones and their eyes fixed downward on their guitar-playing fingers. All around me, women of all ages began to clap and sway joyfully in time to the beat, while the men carried on with their conversations as best they could.

"Don' you fret, mah honey," the band moaned in precarious harmony, "I'm doin' this for money / Then I'll dump my load and truck on home to you-u-u!"

As the band became more comfortable, they writhed tenta-tively and began to indulge in a modicum of choreography, most-ly consisting of line-dance moves and a graphic gesture on the words "dump my load." By the tenth or eleventh chorus I found myself joining in, clapping and gesturing along with everyone else. After a few such selections and encores, entirely inter-changeable, the singing truckers retired to a tremendous ovation.

Everyone was now in a mood of defiant exhilaration, primed to be harangued by Celeste Ireland. She barged across the stage to the front mike.

"Hello, criminals!" she screamed. The sound level almost shook the city to its heritage foundations. "Hello, felons! Good evening, lawbreakers!"

There was an overwhelming surge of laughter, cheers and general hubbub, which she drank in. Power was obviously her drug of choice.

"Great to see so many here. Let's keep up this level of commitment, yeah?"

"Yeah!" we replied as one.

"We are a presence tonight," she exulted. "I think the fat cats in Parliament House know we're here."

This was greeted by more laughter and boos. The crowd ignored the fact that, until recently, Celeste had been set on becoming one of these obese felines herself.

"But while we're enjoying ourselves, entertained by the cream of lesbian and gay performing talent, we mustn't forget the serious purpose of this rally. We face vilification on every side. Gay hate killings, which the police do not *want* to solve, and retrogressive legislation, which will effectively put us on the wrong side of the law. Make no mistake, these things are linked! Linked by a right wing, homophobic backlash in politics and the media. Murderers can be locked up—when and *if* they're caught—but politicians are more dangerous and a lot bloody harder to stop. Some *bastions* of the queer community—some high and mighty, self-appointed *spokespersons*—think we've come a long way. They point to Mardi Gras and similar visible celebrations. How can we go backwards, they ask? Well, let me ask you this: how did queer Berlin of the 1930s become Nazi Berlin of the '40s? We ignore history at our peril.

"I'm not saying parades and dance parties don't spell progress, but we need to put them in perspective..." With this, Celeste launched into a long-winded history of the local bylaws pertaining to homosexuality and discrimination. Every so often her voice was obscured by a gust of wind catching the microphone to produce a sonorous raspberry. This led her to curtail her political message. "Anyway," she sighed, midbarrage, "to introduce our artists tonight, please welcome one of the icons of Oxford Street, the lovely Elena Traffic!"

An extraordinary creature stumbled across the stage. To say she was tall would be like saying Quasimodo was plain. With her incredibly thin legs and large-lashed, vacant eyes she looked like a glamorous giraffe. She also seemed to have applied her makeup during an earthquake while coming out of a coma.

"Whoa!" she cried as she lunged with both hands at a mike stand for support. She gazed blankly into the crowd and stood completely still, hoping to orient herself.

"I don't think I'm a criminal," Elena crooned, entirely missing the ironic point of Celeste's greeting. "Sometimes I steal lipsticks but they're very small. Don't tell a *soul.*"

She laughed and waved casually as if to consign her witticism to the ether. There followed a second drawn-out silence. I began to suspect drugs may have been involved. Queens in the crowd tittered, but Celeste's body language told a grimmer story: If there'd been a hammer within clutching distance, Elena would now be a bloody statistic.

"Um, look. I forget why we're here but I know it's a good cause so give generously. Give with all your hearts. Give, give…give…" Very gradually, Elena's speech slowed to a halt. Celeste marched over, grabbed her by the elbow and hurled her towards the stairs from whence she'd tottered.

"Good night, everybody," Elena mumbled jerkily. "Be kind to each oth—!"

Celeste gave her one more vicious shove between the shoulder blades, then smiled with considerable effort.

"As I said, the cream of lesbian and gay talent. To start the ball rolling—are they ready? OK! Let's do it. Please welcome cabaret icon, Lena Del Mar!"

A stately matron, serene and gracious, swept onto the stage taking full control of the proceedings by sheer presence alone. She was exquisitely and expensively dressed, her hair coiffed to the consistency of concrete.

"Thank you Celeste," said the diva with welcome lucidity. Celeste receded, while a thin young man sprang from nowhere to perch, hawklike, at one of the keyboards behind the beloved songstress.

"Oh, my," Lena cooed, "there's so much love in this room. This…park. I can feel it out there! It makes me almost wish I was gay myself!"

Mystified silence reigned. Clearly, many of the audience had assumed Lena was another drag artiste.

"I'm not gay, of course." The chanteuse gave an apologetic grimace. "No, I've two beautiful grown-up children. Somewhere. But the gay community has given me so much over the years—if I can give just one tiny part back, I'll be a happy woman." This went over well, producing scattered applause. Encouraged, she added a political post script. "As for this antigay legislation…well! There ought to be a law against it."

She indicated for her accompanist to begin, then thought better of it and held up her hand. "You better sit down, kids," she announced. "I'm stayin' all night and I'm singin' 'em all!"

Immediately, everyone around me simply collapsed where they had been standing. I could now see what had been hidden before: The ground was a patchwork of picnic rugs, cushions and pillows. Unlike me, others had come well prepared. Champagne buckets and wicker baskets oozing soft cheese were strategically placed on the corners of rugs to compensate for the wind. People sat cross-legged or lay, stretched out, taking up even more space than when they were standing. I perched like a flamingo, one foot in the air to avoid stepping on a plump silk cushion. I couldn't stay like that forever so I surreptitiously squatted down on the edge of somebody's rug.

"I gotta be *me*!" howled Lena Del Mar, to an accompaniment more elaborate than a Bach toccata.

"Would you get off our rug?" A bald man was glaring at me from his prone position. He wore a three-piece suit, but had removed his tie. Next to him lounged a languid Thai boy aged about 14.

"Sorry," I said and stood up.

"Sit down!" someone else called. I quickly squatted again.

"Go to the back," the bald man grumbled. "There's no room here. This is our spot."

"I wanna *be* a *part* of it, I *am* what I *am*!" Lena sang. By now the tears were coursing down her cheeks. This gig meant a lot to her.

As I stood up again, a group of boys caught my attention. These young men were taking no notice whatsoever of the cabaret performance; in fact they had their backs to it. I saw the GLEE sign flapping in the breeze behind them and caught a glimpse of Paul's peroxided locks: they were queuing to get Paul's autograph! There he was, flourishing away and beaming becomingly. Angel stood nearby, but I couldn't see Andrew anywhere.

"Paul," I called, waving frantically, but against Lena's strident chest register my chances of being heard were nil. This didn't stop the bald man from making a courteous request.

"Piss off!" he yelled.

I had no alternative but to tiptoe through the crowd. I was just about to do so when a sharp gust of wind hit the park. It came up from behind the stage and swept down over the sea of picnickers, leaving a string of minor disasters in its wake. It knocked over mike stands, blew the accompanist's music to hell and caught Miss Del Mar's wig, heaving it sideways to reveal her wispy gray hair. Personal effects were carried aloft as the audience shouted in confusion. The cascade of water from the nearby fountain altered its course to include a group of onlookers in wheelchairs and, in an exciting theatrical moment, the stage lights and sound cut out completely.

Upright as I was, I caught the full force of the gust. It rocked me backwards. Stumbling, I heard a scream as I trod on someone's fingers. At the same time, my other foot came into contact with a

champagne bottle. It rolled under my weight and I sprawled help-
lessly to the ground on top of the bald man and his friend.

"Jesus!" the man cried in alarm.

I felt a sharp pain in my arm. I raised it to discover jagged sliv-
ers of broken glass glinting on my sleeve.

"I've cut my arm," I whispered in disbelief, struggling to pull
off my coat and roll up my shirt sleeve. Blood was already seeping through. The cut was quite deep.

Next to me squatted the Thai boy, his eyes wide. "Oh," he
exclaimed. "The crystal."

"What?" screamed the bald man. "I knew this would happen."
He glared at his friend. "I told you not to bring the crystal glasses."

"But I like them," the boy answered simply.

"I'm very sorry," I stammered. "The wind...um, I'll pay for
the glass."

"You can't, it's a priceless antique," the bald man moaned.
"You'd better wash that cut before you get lead poisoning. There's
a loo on the far side of the park."

"I should go with him," the boy suggested.

The bald man seized him by the wrist. "Stay right where you
are," he snapped. "I'm not letting you near a men's toilet again."

The toilet in question was one of Sydney's most historic beats,
having been consecrated half a century before when a prominent
international concert pianist was discovered there tickling more
than the ivories. It was a staid, stone building, probably designed
by someone famous, with additions from later generations in var-
iously colored bricks. Pressing a handkerchief to my forearm, I
trampled my way to the crowd's edge and hastened into the
depths of the park.

Reaching a grotto of Moreton Bay figs, I was struck by how
dark it was away from the rally. This part of the park remained
unlit. Only the pathway farther along was illuminated, and that
very dimly. I stopped to rearrange my soggy hankie and glanced
up just as a dark figure stepped furtively behind one of the wide
tree trunks. At least, that's what I thought I saw.

Slightly rattled, I hurried on towards the toilet. I was almost there when a dishevelled young man in track suit pants and a singlet came racing out of the bushes opposite. He almost ran into me but veered to one side at the last moment, slamming his left hand into my arm.

"Ow!" I cried.

"Oh!" he exclaimed breathlessly, skidding to a halt. He lifted his hand to his face and stared. "What's this?"

"Blood," I answered.

A look of panic came over him. "Oh, fuck!" he said. "Did he get you? Did he get you?"

"Who?" I asked, but he was already running off.

"I'm out of here!" he shouted wildly.

Whatever he was talking about, something had badly upset him. My heart pounded as I heard more footsteps behind me.

"Marc!"

I turned. This time I was relieved to see Andrew bustling towards me. It was a moment before he could summon up enough breath to speak.

"Oh...dear..." he panted. "I think I'll have to join a gym or something. Are you all right? I saw you fall over...oh, my lord!"

I revealed my shredded forearm.

"Quickly, quickly," he babbled. "You must get that looked at. What are you doing over here?"

"I was going to the toilet to wash."

He shook his head. "Sometimes I think you're just plain mad. There's a first aid place next to the nuns. For heaven's sake, you were right on top of it! Didn't you see it?"

"No," I admitted.

"Come on. You're completely useless. Paul's dead right about that."

As Andrew had said, a first aid tent had been erected on a grassy patch not far from where I'd been injured. We rushed towards it, but it was unmanned.

"Damn!" said Andrew. "Isn't this typical."

"Maybe we could find a swab or something."

"You need somebody who knows what they're doing," he snapped. "I'll go and find them. Sit still and don't faint."

I was glad enough to rest, although the cut on my arm had almost stopped bleeding. I peered blearily at the stage. In spite of her threat to stay all night, Lena Del Mar seemed to have been removed. In her place was a dizzying light show, complete with smoke machines. A figure walked to center stage and hit a pose. I tried to concentrate but found it impossible. I closed my eyes. A soft tap on my shoulder roused me from my torpor. Wearily, I looked up. It wasn't Andrew, but Gavin, my next door neighbor.

"Marc!" he exclaimed. "What's happened here?"

"Oh, Gavin, hi. Cut myself on a champagne glass."

He examined my arm and plunged into the first aid kit. "We'll patch that up in a jiffy," he said efficiently. "Sorry I wasn't in residence. Had to take a leak. So how did you do this? Glass slip out of your hand?"

"It wasn't my drink," I protested. "It was someone else's."

"Right, sure. OK. This stuff may sting—"

"Aargh!"

"That's it." He chatted away as he worked. "Your friend Paul's on a roll these days. I thought he was kidding when we watched his show reel, but he's huge. Several of the companies I deal with would like to get hold of him for corporate events. After dinner speeches, emceeing, that kind of thing. Does he have an agent?"

"I suppose so. He was an actor," I answered without much interest. "*NOW TV!* keeps him pretty busy."

"I don't like dealing with agents," Gavin went on. "They're more trouble than they're worth. Perhaps we could organize a little luncheon *chez moi*. It's easier doing business face to face."

"I'd love to."

"You're invited too, of course."

He finished smoothing thin gauze over the worst part of the cut and began binding my arm in a tight bandage. "There we go. And to set it off, a tiny gold safety pin. Presto! A charming accessory."

I felt much better. "Thanks. I admire your healing skills."

Unusually for Gavin, he looked sheepish. "It's always worth-while to have first aid up your sleeve. The trouble is, one gets roped in to do it."

Carefully I pulled on my coat. I didn't feel like waiting for Andrew but skirted the crowd till I reached the section nearest the GLEE club. Every head was riveted to the stage. I spotted a familiar broad back which could only have belonged to Angel. As I approached him the lights dimmed and, after a moment's awed silence, the whole place erupted into prolonged applause.

"Angel," I called out.

The head swivelled, the fish bowl lenses honing in on me. "Ah! There you are," he beamed. "Your famous boyfriend said you were around here somewhere. He introduced himself. Lovely! He's volunteered to be a guest speaker at GLEE."

"Paul's not my boyfriend."

Angel ignored this correction. "What did you think of that?" he wheezed.

"What?"

"Stewart!"

"Has he been on?"

"That was him just now." Angel appeared unnaturally flushed. "Who'd have thought high art could be so...*filthy*? And yet, the piece had a kind of erotic integrity. Young Stewart's really learning how to communicate with his audience. All that television stuff he's been doing at Channel 6 is obviously paying off—not to men-tion the three days a week he spends with his personal trainer."

Angel's comment started the little beige cells working in my head. Of course! Stewart had been linked to Quentin Butler, but his work on *Precinct Hospital* could link him to Raymond as well. They could easily have met in the studio. What's more, just before he was killed, I had advised Raymond to latch onto the most mouthwater-ing hunk of man he could find. Stewart fulfilled the criteria com-pletely. Could Stewart have had the same trouble with Raymond as he'd allegedly had with Quentin? Stewart always appeared so vague and dumb, but you don't need brains to attack somebody.

"Wakey, wakey," said Angel, snapping his fingers in front of my face. "The fun's over and the work begins. I've got you a placard. Hope it suits." From under a table he produced a sign. It read, in a hasty scrawl, I'M LEGALLY FUCKED.

"It's a bit blunt," I complained.

"All the better! Shock 'em into submission."

"I don't think I can hold this thing. I've injured my arm. Look."

"Ooh," he clucked. "Neat work from nursey. Well, never mind. You just relax, hon."

Meanwhile, Paul had seen me and excitedly beckoned me over. "Caro, where have you been?" he cried, flinging his arms around me and causing considerable pain. "Front row, smack in the middle, I presume."

"I'll tell you later," I answered flatly. "Is Andrew back yet?"

"Still looking for you. When we lost you he insisted we split up and comb the place from top to bottom." He flicked my nose good naturedly. "Andrew's very fond of a certain person."

"Don't be coy, it's revolting."

He murmured in my ear. "Don't you worry, *caro mio*, he won't get you in his clutches again. I'll see to that."

"What if I want him to?"

He looked dumbfounded. "You don't *really*, do you? He's hideous!"

"Paul, you are so two-faced!"

He shrugged. "He's just not for you. Trust me, I should know. I write an agony column."

I rolled my eyes.

"Now, caro, direct your gaze over to our left." He pointed across the crowd. There sat a distinctly leathery group of men with a sign that simply said LAV. "It's Quentin Butler's outfit. I've been chatting them up. They all know me. It's amazing how many old leather queens watch daytime TV! Don't ask me why. And guess what? They invited me to their next meeting."

"Bravo," I said. "You haven't been wasting your time."

"No, caro. Not a bit. In fact, I think I've charmed my way into a new relationship."

"With an old leather queen?"

"Don't be silly."

"Who, then?" I inquired.

Paul smiled like a transfigured Renaissance madonna. "They call him Stewart," he whispered.

chapter fifteen

It was obvious as we boarded our flight to Adelaide that Paul hadn't slept a wink. Rarely had I seen him so drained of energy; you'd have thought it was the day after Mardi Gras recovery. When I mentioned this, he only smiled. No further confirmation was necessary; he'd spent the last thirty-two hours restaging Stewart's cabaret act in intimate and strenuous detail. The moment our plane left the ground, passing within millimeters of my roof, Paul curled up and began alternately snoring and purring.

Still, it was a relief to hear him breathing. I'd been on tenterhooks until that morning and hadn't done a great deal of sleeping myself. Just as I'd reappointed Stewart to my very short suspect list, Paul latched onto him. But nothing untoward seemed to have happened—only the reenactment of the entire Catalina video repertoire.

When I'd arrived early that morning to pick him up, Paul had insisted on phoning Quentin Butler's sister then and there.

"I should have done it yesterday," he apologized, "but I was flat out."

He dialed, listened briefly, then abruptly hung up.

"Didn't anyone answer?" I asked.

"They said "Hello, Mardi Gras." I must have hit some international fag hotline by mistake."

He tried once more.

"Uh, hello," he said with a shrug in my direction. "I'd like to speak to Laurie Butler please…Paul Silverton." He held the receiver at a discreet distance. "They still claim to be Mardi Gras," he whispered. "Uh, yes, Laurie? Paul Silverton. I host a segment on *NOW TV!* I'm sure you know the show.… You don't? We're a fashion-infotainment program on Channel 6." His eyes lit up. "Look, could you tell me something about this mardi gras of yours? We're officially fascinated…"

He continued in his most amiable style for about five minutes, jotting down the odd note. When the call was finished, he glowed in triumph. "Well! It's certainly Butler's sister, and she's given us a perfect reason to talk to her."

"What's this mardi gras?"

"She lives in a town in the Adelaide hills called Munchstadt. They have an annual celebration there, apparently—a local shindig tied in with the church—and it's called the Lutheran Mardi Gras. Isn't that cute? We're going to interview her about it."

"A church fete? Sounds exciting."

"Don't worry, I can cut in some footage of the Sydney parade, spice it up a little. You know how good I am at editing."

I gave him an icy look. "I wouldn't bring that up if I were you, unless you'd like to see a murder from the victim's point of view."

He remained sleepily sheepish all the way to the airport.

Now, winging my way south with Paul drifting in R-rated dreamland, I could only hope Laurie Butler would provide us with some fresh information. With Fabio uncontactable and Stewart my sole unconvincing suspect, our investigation had gotten nowhere fast. On top of that, I had to face the possibility that the two murder victims had nothing in common but the person who stabbed them. There was no way Paul or I could solve random serial killings—we didn't have the infrastructure. That was a job for the police, with their forensics and profilers.

Idly, I wondered what a profile of our antigay killer would look like. He would have to be strong to have overpowered Raymond. For all his queeniness, Raymond had muscle where it counted.

Of course, the hairdresser's high camp style might easily have inflamed antigay feeling in anyone that way inclined. Even I had tended to shy away from Raymond in full cry. Quentin Butler had been similarly open; Doff had complained that his partner "announced his sexuality from every street corner…"

I remembered a point Celeste made in her speech at the rally. She'd claimed the murders were linked to Cahill's legislation, that it was all symptomatic of a homophobic backlash—although I can't say I'd noticed any such thing. To my mind, society's attitudes are pretty well set. Australians are basically apathetic. Stanford Cahill only spoke for an extremist minority. Most people probably did care more about the state of the roads.

Cahill clearly had some difficulty with homosexuality, otherwise why would he make such a fuss? Most politicians hate to stir up trouble, and while picking on minorities is a sure way to keep conservative voters onside, that alone failed to explain Cahill's hatred. It seemed more personal.

"Newspaper, sir?"

My train of thought was interrupted by a neatly dressed flight attendant with shaving cuts on his chin and dark circles under his eyes.

"Oh, yes, all right," I answered, but the attendant didn't move. He was staring at my sleeping companion.

"Is that Paul Silverton from *NOW TV*? He's so excellent!" The attendant gazed at Paul in awe, hardly daring to believe.

"I'll have the paper, thanks," I said.

"Mm? Oh. Here." He dropped it in my lap. "Why don't you buzz me when Paul wakes up? First Class is full but I can bring you two a bottle of bubbly." He oozed off down the aisle. Although I'd seen this sort of thing before, I still found it incredible. Why would anyone think that because a face appears on television the person behind it is somehow special or even worth knowing?

I opened the paper and a picture on page 3 leapt out at me. It showed Celeste pushing the stoned drag artiste Elena Traffic away from the microphone, though from the angle of the photo she might have been plunging a cleaver between Elena's shoulder blades (as she no doubt had wanted to). I was surprised our protest cabaret had been covered at all, but the headline explained the paper's ongoing interest: "Gay Serial Killer On Rampage."

I devoured the article. It had come to the police's attention that the antigay killer may have been present at the rally. An unsuccessful attack had been made on one Sean Tunnicliffe, 26, of East Sydney. Sean had not managed to get a close look at his attacker's face but he'd seen the knife well enough and, having been a champion sprinter at school, he'd sprinted like a champion. "It was there right in front of my eyes," Sean said, referring to the knife. If the knife had been in front of his eyes, I could only conclude that Sean's eyes were somewhat lower than head level at the time.

Sean told police that, running away, he had bumped into another man who also seemed to have been attacked. There were no further details.

Of course, I knew the second "victim" intimately: It was me! The boy who ran into me and asked "Did he get you?" must have been this Sean Tunnicliffe. The incident suggested even more strongly that the victims of the gay-hate attacks were being chosen at random.

I broke into a sweat as I recalled the dim figure I'd spied, skulking among the trees. How chilling to think that someone in that happy crowd had been harboring thoughts of cold blooded murder, his true purpose concealed behind a thin facade of political commitment.

With a shiver I leafed through the rest of the paper. An update on the issue of Cahill's antigay legislation was buried at the back of the real news, under the banner Premier Rules Out Conscience Vote. It read:

> NSW Premier John Garland ruled out a conscience vote on the antigay issue at a press conference yesterday. He emphasized that no legislation was before Parliament, and talk of a conscience vote was premature and unhelpful. The

Premier said he was currently in dialogue with Mr. Cahill and understood his concerns. He assured the public these talks would be fruitful.

Paul slept until we touched down at Adelaide airport. I liked the fact that this was still that old-fashioned type of airport where passengers could descend the stairs to bustle across the tarmac.

Blank faces were pressed up to the glass at the entrance, waiting for us—or for Paul, to be precise. A mixed group of young gays and lovers of daytime television pressed him for autographs. Heaven knows how these people knew he was coming.

"Are you goin' out tonight, Paul?" one of the boys whined. "Come to the Tow Bar!"

"You'll get in for nothing!" promised another. This kid had so many metal studs in his face I thought he must have been catapulted through the window of a hardware shop.

"Aah!" squealed one of the girls, pointing at me. "It's the funny drunk guy!"

I nodded and smiled regally. The girl rushed over to thrust her autograph book under my nose. "Can you sign this?" she asked sweetly.

"Certainly. Why?"

"You were on TV with Paul." She scoffed at my naivety.

I signed, utterly mystified. "Sorry to be blunt, but I suppose you know he's openly gay?"

She nodded enthusiastically. "Yeah. That's so cool." Oscar Wilde, I reflected, would be revolving in his grave, if only out of confusion.

A chatty work experience girl from the local TV studio drove us to our accommodation, which Paul referred to as digs. (He was still a chorus boy at heart.) Helen had been on the blower, galvanizing the Adelaide TV people into providing us with anything we might need for our segment, including a list of potential topics.

"Deathly quiet, isn't it?" Paul remarked as we sped along through the flat, spacious suburbs. "Stephen King's favorite city. Everything looks still on the surface but evil's bubbling away underneath."

I had expected *NOW!* to put us up in a ritzy hotel, but the reality was quite different: a sprawling 19th century family manor encased by ancient gnarled trees and old vines. The house, erected by some long-impeached governor, currently functioned as an upmarket bed-and-breakfast. The walls of our suite were host to a complete photographic history of the old governor's extended family. Five overdressed generations scowled down at us, and a simian lot they were too, considering their high social standing.

We were supposed to report to the studio as soon as we'd unpacked, but Paul sent our work-experience girl away with the message that he'd phone in later. He was now sprawled across my bed, munching on a wizened slice of melon from my complimentary fruit basket.

"OK," he announced, "two plans. Three, if you count a lavish dinner somewhere chic overlooking the Torrens River."

"Aren't we supposed to be working?"

"Work, work, work! First, we take these and flash 'em around the Tow Bar tonight." He produced a cutout newspaper photo of Quentin Butler and a blurry shot of Raymond, his eyeballs reddened by the camera's flash. "The Tow Bar's been around for aeons," Paul continued. "If our boys were ever part of the scene, they'd be known there."

The Tow Bar was on the other side of town, namely the wrong side. The dive itself was hidden in the basement of a very plain old building in a block which was otherwise completely deserted. Inside the club was noisy and dark. With its shiny dance floor and carpeted booths it resembled a servicemen's club from the 1960s—one where they'd neglected to replace most of the light globes. Unlike gay dance clubs in Sydney, which opened and reopened several times a year, there was no evidence here of any refurbishment. The fittings and the mirror ball were antique, and a stickiness against the underside of my shoe indicated several decades' worth of spilled drinks.

We arrived around 11 P.M. Paul immediately plunged into the crowd to a frenzied welcome, while I was left to lounge against the bar, nursing a double vodka and tonic.

Gazing around the room I observed another aspect of the Tow Bar that separated it from the trendy Oxford Street scene: the clientele. The club's customers were a remarkably diverse group. Not only was it mixed, but the men came in all sizes and ages— from heroin chic waifs (a term Helen liked to use) to avuncular scoutmasters with trimmed mustaches and long socks. There were bottle-blonds and musclebound barmen, just like at home, but instead of following the accepted pattern of ignoring every-body, they seemed to be openly chatting. I saw couples boogying on the dance floor or holding hands in a corner who astounding-ly were not mirror images of each other.

I sipped my drink. Perhaps it was the vodka working, but I start-ed to feel my sad lack of attachment. One by one I ran through my litany of lost opportunities, the most recent additions being Tim (the boy from GLEE) and my next door neighbor. Somehow I'd scared Tim off, but I should have worked harder on Gavin.

Meanwhile, a man on my left who'd arrived at the bar to buy a drink was staring at me. It was a little disconcerting.

"Sorry," I said, turning. "Got enough room there?"

"Yep. Thanks."

His hair was graying but he had a young face. The body seemed nice, strong in the chest area but spreading a little below that. Lightweight, snug-fitting tops are merciless, of course.

I remembered Raymond's photograph. "'Scuse me," I said. "Do you know this boy?"

He took hold of the picture and peered at it, then nodded imperceptibly. "Friend of yours?"

"Not really. Someone asked me to look out for him."

"I used to see him around here. Not for a while now. Don't know his name."

"How long ago was he here?" I asked as I put Raymond away, his work done.

"Oh...Christmas." The man smiled. "What are you drinking?"

"Vodka and tonic. Allow me."

"No, I'll get it."

In between the ordering and arrival of our drinks, he pulled my head close to his, placed his lips onto mine and kissed me for all of twelve seconds.

"Whew," I remarked. "I..."

Now he put his finger to my lips. "No names," he said.

"Sorry, what?"

"I'm not telling you my name and I don't want to know yours."

I smiled. "All right then. But why?"

He got a certain glint in his eye. "Better sex."

At that moment a song began to blare from the several cheap speakers positioned around the room. It was Donna Summer's "Last Dance." A literal blast from the past.

"Oh!" I gushed. "I haven't heard this for years."

"C'mon."

He grabbed my hand and we made our way to the dance floor. Normally, even if I feel like dancing, I think twice about making a buffoon of myself, but here it was different: Here, nobody knew the buffoon's name. I flung my arms around gracefully, while my nameless escort kept his hands firmly planted on my hips. At one point my eye alighted on Paul, bopping away at the other end of the room. He winked. I winked back.

"Who's that?" asked my dancing partner.

"Just a guy I know," I shouted.

"You're hot."

"Pardon? Didn't hear you!"

"*Hot!*"

"Yes. There's no air conditioning."

"Sorry?"

"*It doesn't matter.*"

"Let's go."

"OK," I indicated.

I shook as the cold air hit me, but soon warmed up in my

anonymous friend's car after we enjoyed more passionate kisses in the front seat.

He hardly spoke a word as we rumbled off into the night and pretty soon, warning bells began to ring. Away from the easy atmosphere of the night club, it became uncomfortably clear that I had let myself get carried away. I didn't know where I was going, or with whom, or how I could get back if anything went wrong. Stupidly, I hadn't told Paul I was leaving, nor introduced him to my new acquaintance: the classic precautions a person is supposed to take under these circumstances. I decided I'd feel safer if I knew something about my abductor.

"I don't know what to call you," I ventured, stroking his thigh.

"No names." His eyes never left the road. "We're men. We're hot. That's all."

We drove on.

I tried again. "I work in the media…" I began.

"Look, if you really want to talk about something, talk about what we're gonna do to each other. Or let's just fuck." He hit the brakes.

"Where are we?"

"We're home," he said grimly.

The car swung into the driveway of a typical Adelaide cottage: stone walls, a wide veranda on all sides, and a leafy yard. I relaxed a bit. At least it wasn't some remote, deserted spot, and the yard didn't seem to have been dug up recently.

"I got a great big bed waiting for you," he crooned, slipping his key into the front door lock. Inside, it was pitch black. He pushed me ahead into the dark entrance hall, carefully easing the door shut behind him.

Suddenly I was blinded by light.

"Leslie, is that you?" came a voice.

I peered into the glare to see an old woman in a shabby dressing gown emerging from one of the doorways down the hall. Between her fingers she clasped a glowing cigarette. "Who's this?" she added.

My new friend stepped in front of me. "Mother, what are you doing up?"

"Couldn't sleep."

"Are you sick? Is anything wrong?"

She coughed. "I heard something."

"What? When?"

"I dunno. Aren't you gonna introduce me to your 'friend'?"

"Hello there," I mumbled.

"No I'm not," he replied sternly. "Get back to bed."

"I can't sleep, Leslie. Make me some cocoa."

"Make it yourself, you're not paralyzed," he snapped. "Sorry. Wait in here, would you?"

This last request he addressed to me as he opened the closest door and flicked on the light. I stepped into a room filled with bookshelves. At one end, under French windows, stood an old-fashioned love seat with piles of papers stacked on it. A computer hummed on a table against the wall, alongside pencils, graph paper and other drawing paraphernalia. I stood, staring vacantly at the computer's screen saver: a night sky with stars, crescent moons, and a witch on a broomstick darting across the scene at regular intervals.

After a few minutes, Leslie poked his head round the door. "That was my mother," he said, with an embarrassed grin.

"Ah."

"I didn't think she'd still be up. She heard noises outside. Cats or something." An awkward pause followed. "I guess you found out my name."

I extended my hand. "Marc," I said. "We meet at last."

He stepped into the room and gave me a chaste peck on the cheek. "Mother's sort of killed it, I guess," he sighed. "If you want to go back now, I can take you."

I almost laughed. It was refreshing to find somebody even more inept at this sort of thing than I was. "I'm sweaty after the disco," I whispered seductively. "Maybe a shower…?"

"Sure. I'll show you the bathroom."

I slipped my arm around his waist. "You might need one too, stranger."

chapter sixteen

Munchstadt was a perfectly preserved haven in the Adelaide hills. It had been settled by German immigrants, like much of South Australia, but the architecture hardly reflected their influence. The main street was flanked by solidly Australian country-style shops with wide verandas and tethering rails, so evenly spaced you would swear they'd been built as recently as the 1970s. And you'd be right. Munchstadt, we discovered, had undergone a complete makeover at the height of the authenticity boom. Only the squat, limestone church at the town's entrance had survived intact, save for the addition of a neon cross. The town residents probably did their shopping elsewhere, unless they existed entirely on a diet of preserves, pottery, and recycled junk —the sole items available in the main street.

We drove there in a rented car, courtesy of the studio. A camera crew (thoughtfully arranged for us by Helen) were due to appear in Munchstadt after lunch, which left us the morning to give Ms. Butler the third degree.

Our trip was totally devoid of conversation. Whatever Paul had been bouncing on the night before, it wasn't his four-poster. I'd cabbed it back from Leslie's well after 3 A.M., and had discovered Paul's door open and his bed untouched. I think he may have got in around dawn. To leave early the following morning had required a superhuman effort which used up all our conversational energy.

By 11:30, however, when we arrived in the spruce hamlet, we had perked up considerably. The prospect of coffee beckoned, so our first port of call was the Munchstadt Tea Shoppe, a chintzy, flyblown establishment. As well as providing refreshments, the store was host to an exhibition of ineptly cast pottery.

Over a mug of hot milk posing shamelessly as cappuccino, we discussed our ground plan.

"I don't think you should mention the Mardi Gras," I said. "I mean the real one. She may be touchy about the comparison."

"True," Paul replied, "but I think we're too late." He pushed a newspaper across the table. It was the *Hill Country Courier*, open at the editorial page.

> It's Mardi Gras time again, and as per usual Munchstadt has to put up with a lot of jokes about the name. Let's get one thing "straight"! We had it first. The Munchstadt Lutheran Mardi Gras has been going since the war. It originated in a spirit of forgiveness and reconciliation with our German brothers after we thrashed them in that unfortunate conflict. There's nothing "gay" about our Mardi Gras, except in the real sense of the word, denoting joy, love, and family values. Isn't it time this Sydney mob found a new name for their parade? I'll start the ball rolling. What about "The Big Fruit Salad"?

"How witty," I muttered. "Do you think we'll end up nailed to a signpost pointing the way out of town?"

"God knows! By the way, how did you go at the Tow Bar last night?"

I demurred. "What do you mean?"

"With Raymond's photo, natch! Or didn't you have time to whip it out?" He leered salaciously.

"As a matter of fact, someone had seen Raymond last Christmas. But I didn't learn anything useful."

"How about later?" he chuckled.

"Oh, later..." I mused enigmatically, "I learned that a boy's best friend is his mother."

Laurie Butler ran a shop called Buried Treasure. It was closed. I peered through the tinted window to see rows of cabinets crammed with *objets de trash*: incomplete sets of crockery, bent cutlery, faded LPs, photographs of deceased nobodies, and other bric-a-brac. I suppose some people like that sort of thing, but speaking as a potential tourist the stash held no attraction for me whatsoever. I was appalled to see an entire wall of shelving given over to the same hideous pottery we'd seen in the Tea Shoppe. Perhaps half-glazed bowls with gaping cracks and vases with mis-shapen, impractical lips were a traditional local artifact? If so, the Lutherans had a lot to answer for.

I pressed the buzzer adjacent to the doorway. We heard a faint stirring within, then the door was flung open by a sturdy, middle aged woman.

"Are you Paul Silverton?" she asked, extending her hand to me.

"That's me," Paul smiled, stepping forward and practically bursting with star quality. "This is my producer, Marc Petrucci."

"Laurie," she barked. "Sorry about that. Don't watch much TV I'm afraid—only the occasional BBC costume drama."

We followed her into the shop, then stepped through a red and purple bead curtain into a large room. This area contained an enormous heavy wooden table and ten or so chairs. In one corner stood a small sink, and next to it a desk. Unlike the Olde Worlde gloom of the shop, this back room was bright, courtesy of a spacious skylight.

"Take a seat, fellas," said Laurie. "This is my office. Would you like some tea?"

"Thank you," I said, prodding Paul.

"Fabulous idea," he gushed.

As she bustled around making tea, I tried to size her up. Her broad back suggested the genuine countrywoman, and there was a rough practicality about her closely cropped hair, thick woolen shirt, and military-style khaki jeans. She wore a necklace of chunky amber, and more amber accessories adorned her wrists and earlobes.

"Thought there'd be more of you," she observed over her shoulder.

"The crew will be here after lunch," said Paul. "That'll give us a chance for a cosy little chat before we start." He beamed radiantly.

"Mm," she answered, slopping down two cups of milky tea in chipped, ill-matched cups. "I'm kinda busy today." She pulled a pouch of tobacco out of her shirt pocket and began to roll a cigarette. When it was lit, she strode to the back door and called out "I've made tea!"

"Will there be a parade?" Paul asked.

She sniffed. "Oh, yeah. A fete too. Crafts, local produce, cake-making competition. I do tarot readings. Very trad." Her face broke into a smoky smile. "I know what you're up to."

Butter melted in Paul's mouth. "What?"

"You're thinking of using footage of the Sydney Mardi Gras and cutting the two parades together."

"Uh…"

"Don't know why no one's thought of it before."

"You wouldn't object?" I asked.

"Might put us on the national stage for once. Course, there's some round here wouldn't see the funny side."

"I know," said Paul. "I've read the paper."

"Lutherans." She spat the word out.

"But isn't it a Lutheran event?" I asked.

"That was ages ago. Everybody mucks in now. It's fun in an old-fashioned way."

"Darl?"

I looked around as a second woman entered the room. She was of a similar age to Laurie but an utterly different shape. Buxom, it used to be called. She had tied up her bleach-blond hair with a scarf and, in place of the plaid shirt, she wore a tight fitting sweater. She wiped her hands on the sides of her jeans, adding to the splotches of tan-colored muck already accumulating there.

"Ciggie time," she announced. Sliding her arm around Laurie, she gave her a fond peck on the cheek, then transferred Laurie's cigarette to her own mouth.

"My partner, Merilyn," Laurie said proudly, then chuckled. "You thought I'd be some old high-church spinster, did you?"

"But this is great," Paul chirped, after the requisite introductions. "You two can be the focus of the story! It's what we call human interest."

Merilyn piped up in a husky, nasal voice. "I don't know that we wanna be outed on national TV."

"No," Laurie agreed.

"We marched in the Sydney parade once," Merilyn added, "but that's different."

Laurie glared at her as she took back her cigarette.

"Oh, I'll be sensitive," Paul pleaded. I was stunned that he even knew the word.

"I don't think so," Laurie stated.

For a split second her eyes strayed to the desk. I followed her gaze. It had alighted on a framed photograph of a happy, blue eyed family: dad and mum smiling at the camera while a fearful little boy clung to his mother's side. The picture was not recent but I easily identified the woman as Laurie. If she was an escapee from an unhappy marriage, that was all the more reason to keep her current status out of the limelight. It was quite understandable and, equally, none of our business. We were only interested in her brother.

But the man in the snapshot seemed disconcertingly familiar, and my gaze kept returning to him as I tried to place the face. Surely I'd seen him quite recently.... When I finally realized who it was, I was astounded.

"How about this?" Laurie was saying, as I forced myself to pay attention. "After I chat a bit about our little mardi gras, you could ask Merilyn about her pottery! She's famous in the area."

"Aw, cut it out!" Merilyn simpered. I realized the muck on her jeans was clay.

"That's a great idea," said Paul, with feigned enthusiasm.

"Good. Well I guess we'll see you down at the oval," Laurie concluded.

Feeling our opportunity to do some detective work slipping away, I took the plunge. "I wanted to mention how sorry I was about your brother," I said gravely.

Laurie stubbed out her cigarette butt and gave me a laconic stare. "Aw, Christ," she sighed. "So *that's* why you're really here."

"We've said all we're gonna say on that subject," Merilyn snapped.

"No, no…" Paul smiled reassuringly. "News isn't my area. Besides, it's a pretty old story now."

"Don't bullshit *me!*" Laurie shot back. "There's been another murder. We don't live at the bloody South Pole! Well, it's not to be mentioned, clear?"

"Understood," Paul answered.

"Sorry if I upset you," I said, "but I worked at GLEE myself."

"Oh, yeah? Were you a friend of Quentin's?" Laurie asked.

"I didn't know him personally." I mentally crossed my fingers. "But everybody at GLEE is wondering why the police haven't made an arrest."

"You're telling me!" she exploded. "What the hell are they doing up there? Haven't they talked to all those bloody old sleaze-bags he was hanging around with? Take 'em all in, I reckon!"

"You mean LAV?"

"Yeah," she said disgustedly. "LAV!"

"Do you think he might have been killed by someone he knew from there?"

"Wouldn't surprise me."

"Anyone in particular?"

"How would *I* know? Look, I'm busy." She took our empty cups and rinsed them in the sink, then turned back to us. She was furious. "I don't know what was wrong with Quentin. His whole personality had changed. Out all hours, a different boy every night. When he was visiting over Christmas I hardly saw him at all. We had a big screaming match. Grow up, I told him.

You're not 20 anymore! If I'm pissed off about somethin', I tell people!"

"That's for sure," said Merilyn proudly.

"He even started neglecting his shop. I invested good money in that business! I told him over and over again: keep your eye on the place or that partner of yours'll rip us off. What did Quentin do? Washed his hands of it! When he was here at Christmas—"

She stopped dead.

"Are you OK, babe?" asked Merilyn.

"I didn't think it'd be the last time I'd ever see him," Laurie concluded in a small voice.

She sat, stony faced. Merilyn took her hand. "We should cancel the interview," she said.

An awkward silence fell.

"Well, that's up to you," Paul said brightly. "Can I see some of your pottery?"

Merilyn beamed. "Oh, sure!"

"Is this your work?" Paul sprang up and strolled to the desk. "It's exquisite."

"Oh, that's just an old teapot. There's lots better stuff." She pulled Laurie to her feet and we all bustled into the shop.

The craft work was even more hideous up close. Examining the texture in horrified fascination, I could make out the occasional blond hair or broken fingernail imbedded in it.

"It's so earthy," Paul extemporized, roaming intently from shelf to shelf. "So completely…of the earth."

"They're clay," Merilyn confirmed. "Originally."

"Which one do you like, caro?" Paul turned to me with an expectant air.

"Hard to say."

"We'll take the big one," Paul announced suddenly, pointing to a remarkably grotesque piece. It resembled a toilet bowl excavated too late from the ruins of Pompeii. "This'll be perfect for that shrub of yours, caro."

"What shrub?"

"Six hundred and fifty dollars," said Laurie, instantly achieving closure. "Six hundred, cash."

"I've only got Visa," I mumbled.

"What a bargain," Paul exclaimed as I swiped away a fortune. "So we'll see you girls later?"

They glanced at each other. Laurie nodded.

"Wonderful! And don't forget to remind me, I want to get a shot of your beautiful artwork."

I grizzled as we shoved and prodded the pot into the back of our car. It weighed a ton. "Why do you always make me do these stupid things?" I whined.

"We had to sweeten those two somehow," Paul complained. "We can't fly back without a story."

"We can't fly back with this thing either!"

"Don't worry, caro. The taste police will smash it at the border."

As we ambled along the main street, I was thinking hard. "What did you make of Laurie Butler's outburst?" I asked Paul.

He shook his head. "We know Quentin was here at Christmas, and so was Raymond. There must be a link, but I haven't got a clue what it is. We'd better get ourselves to LAV quick smart. We're not finding out very much down here."

It was clear he hadn't noticed the old wedding photo in Laurie's office, and, for the time being at least, I decided not to mention it. I was supposed to be Paul's minder, after all. It was my brief to keep both him and *NOW TV!* out of trouble, and frankly, after the whisky story, I didn't trust him an inch. We walked on in silence.

The mardi gras festivities were taking place at the Munchstadt oval on the far side of town. For the occasion the oval was decorated with trucks and caravans, selling disposable food and offering precarious joyrides for the unwary. We spent an hour or so eating hot dogs and drinking ice laced with raspberry cordial while the oval filled with families from all over the surrounding districts. Everybody looked exactly like everybody else, even the children. Some entrepreneur had made a killing in flannel shirts and broad brimmed hats. Our crew arrived and set up just before the official celebrations got underway.

Like all mardi gras, this one opened with a grand parade. Instead of dykes on bikes, however, it began with men on mobile farm machinery, all of which was brightly polished and draped with MUNCHSTADT and LUTHERAN MARDI GRAS banners. These monsters were followed by a combined scouts and schools band, performing rousingly ragged renditions of the theme from *Rocky* and "New York, New York."

A group of men in silk shorts and white singlets came next. They weren't young, but were certainly in the peak of fitness.

"Now it's looking more like a mardi gras," Paul remarked.

"Who are they?" I asked.

"Judging from the sexy arms, I'd say wood choppers. Mm!" He called out to the camera operator. "Shoot those guys! Shoot the wood choppers."

A family within earshot nervously moved away.

The sexy wood choppers were succeeded by horse riders and an elderly man with a herd of dogs and ducks. The ducks had been dressed in awkward but colorful costumes, while the dogs carried miniature saddles and dolls on their backs. Understandably bewildered, the ducks were prone to wander, but the dogs kept them in check.

"Excuse me," I said to a girl nearby. "What's this supposed to be?"

She stared at me as though I were an idiot, then drawled, "That's Lester and 'is farmyard circus."

"Ah. And what do they do?"

"They go in the parade. Been doin' it for years."

Finally we came to the crowning moment of the procession. From a horse-drawn open carriage, festooned with ribbons and balloons, a beautifully dressed girl grimaced and waved to the crowd. She was all decked out in tiara and tulle and looked radiant, if ever so slightly inclined towards obesity. A sign on the carriage's side proclaimed: TINA, QUEEN OF THE MARDI GRAS.

"Lucky her name isn't Priscilla," Paul roared.

The procession then dissolved into a general melee of children, animals, and mercenaries of the carnival circuit. In their midst we spotted Laurie and Merilyn, chatting to a man carrying a load of sound apparatus.

"I want to do that interview before some local windbag gives a speech," whispered Paul.

Our crew followed as we selected the perfect spot to film Paul's piece: directly in front of a hand-painted banner which read CONGRATULATIONS TINA, MARDIE GRAS QUEEN. As I had no technical task to perform, it fell to me to keep the gawking locals out of the way.

"Move back, please!" I thundered.

"I wanna be in the pitcher," a thuggish spectator shouted.

"Please be quiet so Mr. Silverton can get started."

"He's a poof," the thug shrewdly observed, in the same awed tone he might have used on coming face to face with an extinct Tasmanian tiger.

"We're rolling. Quiet, please."

Paul eased his way into the interview with a host of queries about the town, the celebration and even the voting procedure for Queen of the Mardi Gras, which was unbelievably complicated. (I suspected the present incumbent had slept her way to the top.)

After covering these generalities, Paul's questions took a more personal turn. "How long have you been living in Munchstadt, Laurie?"

"Four or five years. She's a great little town."

"It's an inspiring place for a creative person," Merilyn added proudly. "You can rebuild your life here. Forget the past and start again."

Paul beamed. "You obviously have a happy and fulfilling life." He paused. "Together."

The girls nodded uncertainly.

"They're good people," said Merilyn. "They respect you as an artist. When are you gonna take those shots of my work?"

"You mean people respect your open lesbian relationship?" Paul continued, then addressed the camera. "Looks like

Munchstadt's a real mardi gras town after all!" He turned to Laurie, sympathetically. "But the gay hate murder of your brother Quentin reminds us nowhere is safe."

"That'll do," Laurie interrupted him, but Paul was not to be stopped.

"So, Ms. Butler, do you have a personal message for the Sydney police? I'm sure you'd like to see your brother's killer in court."

She made no comment but simply glared at the camera.

"I think we've had enough," said Merilyn.

"OK then, that's it." At Paul's signal, the crew began packing up. Laurie was livid. "You lying bastard!"

Merilyn grabbed her friend. "We're going," she announced, but Laurie stepped up to Paul and poked him in the chest with her forefinger.

"I'm not givin' you permission to use that interview," she barked. "If you do, I'll sue the pants off you and your TV network."

My heart performed a double somersault. This was the precise wording I'd always had nightmares about. I froze.

"But what would you get out of that?" Paul asked deftly. "Wouldn't it be better to stick it up the police? Get them moving again?"

Laurie frowned.

"Some people in Sydney have a theory," he continued. "They think the police don't care one way or another if a gay man dies in suspicious circumstances. There's a lot of homophobia around. It goes all the way to the top."

I watched as Laurie's expression turned to one of cool fury. "Gimme that microphone."

The camera man had already set up again, displaying a foresight born of long experience. Paul eased Laurie into frame and nodded.

"My brother was murdered months ago," Laurie said, "and now there's another one. I want to see justice done. We don't pay the police to be *incompetent!*" She threw the microphone back into the paws of the startled sound man. "Happy now?" she snapped.

By this time the crowd was considerably larger, but I'd had no trouble keeping them quiet. They had watched everything in open-mouthed silence. As Laurie and Merilyn made a hurried exit, Paul grinned. "That's all, folks!" he said breezily to the onlookers, and strolled over to me.

I had to remind myself to breathe. "Paul," I said, "that was so close to disaster."

"Wasn't it?" he agreed. For once, he didn't appear too cocky. On the spur of the moment, I gave a him a hug. "What's that for?"

"You were extraordinary," I said.

"Caro, thank you!"

"I just wanted to tell you before *you* told *me*."

As we were speaking, a tall, balding man sidled up to us. I had seen him in the parade, leading the scouts band, though out of uniform he looked unprepossessing and a bit rumpled.

"Do excuse me," he mumbled in a quiet, breathy voice. "Paul, I always watch your segment on *NOW TV!* I'm a great fan." He smiled, revealing tobacco-stained teeth. "How do you like Munchstadt?"

"Adorable. The mardi gras is so bright and gay!"

Our friend chuckled wheezily. "Hardly that, dear."

"You're the band conductor," I said.

"For my sins."

"I'm not sure how much of your band will be in the final piece," Paul said solemnly. "With our time constraints…"

The man scratched his head. "Oh, don't worry. I don't want publicity, not at all. And neither does Laurie Butler, I see."

His eyes twinkled. Instantly Paul scented a fellow gossip. "She's very touchy about her relationship. Is she worried about a Lutheran backlash?"

"The locals aren't the problem. Her past is." The bandmaster lowered his voice even further. "It's difficult for someone in her position while her ex-husband is making such a great public fool of himself in parliament."

"And who might that be?" Paul asked.

A triumphant look stole over the man's face. "Why, Stanford Cahill, of course! Didn't you know? Laurie and her girlfriend moved here to get away from him. Anyway…" He held out his hand, which Paul shook warmly. "I must run back to the kiddies. Very nice to meet you."

"You too."

Paul turned to me. "Wow!" he said. "Did you hear that? Laurie Butler is the lesbian ex-wife of the ranting homo-hater!"

"My God," I said quietly.

"Oh, *caro mio*! I wish we'd known this juicy little piece of info when I was doing the interview! That would have really spiced it up."

"Too bad," I agreed, concealing any sign of relief. Of course, I'd known about this revelation for hours.

chapter seventeen

I had a lot to think about on the return flight to Sydney. The link between Quentin Butler, his sister, and Stanford Cahill was tantalizing, but I didn't yet know what to make of it. Did it implicate Cahill in the murders? He hated homosexuals, unquestionably, but he'd found another way to deal with that little bugbear. On reflection, it was probably lesbians—rather than gay men—who really got under his skin. And then, it was one thing to go nosing around the odd bric-a-brac shop in Munchstadt, but quite another to march into Parliament House and start asking a Member of Parliament whether he ever felt the urge to dump dead bodies in a public park.

Paul thought we should wait and pour all our meagre resources into LAV. He was convinced we would find a few answers there. I confess, the prospect made me uneasy. I certainly didn't relish getting involved in any S/M scenes. (When it comes to sex, I'm your basic cassata: vanilla with a little spice and a few preserved fruits thrown in.)

Strangely enough, the subject of sex was already on my mind. It was all Leslie's fault. While less than volcanic, Leslie had definitely created a ripple. I yearned for more—it had been too long between eruptions—which is not to say Leslie struck me as soul-mate material. Definitely not! Fifty is slightly past the stage of gritting your teeth in case the old lady wakes up.

No, as I headed back home, my thoughts turned instead to Andrew. I found myself looking forward to seeing him again. I knew we had more areas of conflict than I could count on four hands, and our relationship had floundered more than once, but who had he turned to in his time of woe? There was something deep and permanent there. What more could I hope for?

I recalled his plaintive request: no more sex until we'd sorted ourselves out. Well, I decided it was time to get sorting and perhaps sex was the best way to do it. He'd complained tirelessly about sleeping on the couch. It was time he snuggled back into the marital bed and let nature take its course.

It was odd that my old couch was in my thoughts because, when I arrived home from the airport, said piece of household furniture had vanished—in its place was a harsh, sleek, alien sofa. We took an instant dislike to each other.

"Where's my couch?" I cried, chucking my bag at the interloper.

Andrew flounced out of the kitchen. He wore an apron, as usual, and a devil-may-care facade which almost certainly concealed deep guilt and shame. "I'm doing a field mushroom risotto for our lunch," he squealed gaily. "Welcome home."

"Where's my couch?" I repeated.

Andrew dropped the risotto face. "All right," he said. "I bought a sofa bed. Don't you adore it? That hideous old thing was breaking my back."

I was flabbergasted. "This is my house! I *liked* my couch."

He contradicted me. "No you didn't. You just stopped noticing it."

"It was full of old memories."

"Full of old stains, you mean. I suppose it could have been recovered, but why bother? This one is very swish, and it's a bed too."

"So now you're redecorating! How long are you planning to stay? If you can afford furniture you might contemplate the mad old idea of rent."

"I told you, Marc, I'll pay rent as soon as I get a job. I thought we agreed that was fair. I'm doing my bit. I bought field mushrooms for the risotto. They're not cheap. I could've got ordinary, boring mushrooms...." He was beginning to get his familiar flushed look. "I *am* a decorator, you know. Stupid me! I thought you would appreciate my input." He bolted from the room.

I kicked myself; this was hardly the homecoming I had envisaged. "Andrew," I called wearily. "You might have asked first."

"I'm scraping our risotto into the trash," sobbed a voice from the kitchen.

I wandered after him. Predictably, the rice was still bubbling away on the stove. Andrew could never have brought himself to carry out such a threat. I slipped my arms around him.

"Why don't you sleep in my bed from now on?" I whispered, gingerly testing the waters.

"So you can have the new sofa bed?"

"Don't be obtuse. Sleep with me."

He sniffed. "I don't think it would work. You fly off the handle at the slightest thing."

I was insulted. "Oh, like when my home is turned upside-down without my knowledge?"

"See?" He pushed me away. "I'm going for a walk. There's your lunch. Give it another ten minutes and rinse the saucepan before you eat."

I gave up, and served myself. Down the hall, I heard the front door close pointedly. The risotto was delicious; there was a subtle flavor to it which I couldn't quite place. (Not strychnine, hopefully.) Andrew was good in the kitchen, it was undeniable. As I wallowed in *La Rondine*, I determined to smooth things over— but he didn't return until very late, long after I'd gone to bed, and then next morning he lay huddled on the horrible new sofa, dead to the world, when I left for work. Our reconciliation and subsequent romantic interlude would have to be postponed.

As it was, a further confrontation was in store for me at *NOW!*

No sooner had I seated myself at my desk than Bryce the bean-counter came scuttling over with a malicious twinkle in his eye.

"What can I do for you, Bryce?"

"I hope you had an enjoyable weekend in Adelaide," he drawled.

"Oh, yes. I'm afraid we ran up a few bills."

"I daresay." He inhaled slowly, savoring the moment. "Flynn wants to see you in his office at 10."

"Flynn! What about?"

He smirked. "He would hardly tell *me*."

I panicked quietly while Bryce cavorted back to his nest. I'd never even met Justin Flynn. What could he want? The very fact that he knew of me by name was somehow threatening.

Never having visited the top brass before, I got lost and arrived slightly late for our appointment. His secretary asked me to wait.

"Mr. Flynn is in a meeting," she explained. She was so glib I actually believed her. Then she eyed me warily. "And how are you feeling today?" she sniffed.

"Fine. Just fine."

Of course, that was it! My drunken debacle. It had merely taken a few days for it to be brought to Mr. Flynn's attention. Well, I'd had it. For Marc Petrucci, *NOW!* was about to turn into *THEN!* Could I invoke unfair dismissal laws, I wondered? There were such laws, though I doubted they covered making a national alcoholic spectacle of oneself. Flynn was probably viewing the segment on his office VCR one last time, to build up a full momentum of outrage.

The secretary answered a buzz. "You can go in."

I felt a pressing desire to rush to the toilet, but fought the impulse with every sinew I could muster. Really, this was ridiculous: a man of my age quaking like a schoolboy! I couldn't allow my nerves to get the better of me. I had to pull myself together. Take control of the situation. Gain the upper hand…

"Mr. Petrucci?"

"Yes," I answered confidently.

"Mr. Flynn will see you now," she said patiently.

"Oh. Right."

I strolled nonchalantly into a luxury office. The harbor view was so perfect you'd swear it had been commissioned specifically for this window.

Seated behind an uncluttered desk was the mogul himself, his oft photographed features looking even more astute in real life. He was dressed neatly, a gray suit matching his thick gray hair. A maverick he may have been, but he still wore the corporate business uniform.

He stood, hand outstretched, to reveal an expensively lean physique. "Please sit down. May I call you Marc?" he said, with a smile which inspired instant and lifelong trust.

"Thank you, uh, Justin."

"Mr. Flynn will do. Best to keep this on a business footing."

We sat. He leaned back in his chair. "How is Paul going? Is he fulfilling the brief, in your estimation?"

I wasn't prepared for this! He seemed to want an opinion. I hedged. "Well, um, what do *you* think?"

He nodded imperceptibly. "Good answer. I think he may be developing his own agenda. I noticed it last week when he mentioned the death of the hairdresser."

"Yes." I sounded suspiciously like a yes-man.

"I'm not saying it's a good thing or a bad thing necessarily, but to be blunt, queer politics are of no interest to our demographic. None whatsoever. Zilch."

I nodded back. Flynn's natural authority had now transformed me into the humble village mute.

"Murder's always of interest, however," he continued, "so I let it go. In future we won't head down that track. OK?"

"No."

"It's *not* OK?"

"I mean no, we won't. Yes, it is OK. That's what I meant."

There had to be more. This was stuff Helen could easily have passed on. Of course, if Flynn had seen Paul's piece on Raymond then he'd seen my performance too. How long, I wondered, before he got to the part where he grabbed me by the collar and threw me down the elevator shaft?

"There's something else, Marc." I watched his lips contract.

Here it comes, I thought.

He opened a drawer in his desk and removed a sheet of paper which he thrust across the desk. It was a page from the magazine proofs.

"You ghost write Paul's column," he said. "Perhaps you'd be so good as to read the highlighted section."

I took the page and immediately recognized Raymond's letter. "Dear Paul—"

"Not aloud. Just refresh your memory." He smiled encouragingly.

Quickly I scanned the copy. It read:

> Dear Paul,
>   I have a serious problem, and I think that while you're funny and everything you're also v. wise about relationships. I would really like to "get over it," so here goes.
>   I am 20. I love this successful guy. He's very hot when we're together but he can just as easily turn it off and pretend like he doesn't even know me.
>   The thing is, I work for him. At work he doesn't want anyone to know we're seeing each other and this is making my life impossible.
>   We have great sex but I want more than that. I want commitment. I want everything! Is he just using me? Will he change? Or will I have to leave him and my job? I don't want to do this as it's a good job. Please tell me what to do.
>   Caroline

Paul's answer—or, rather, mine—followed.

> Dear Caroline,
>   You're pathetic! Can't you see all the power's with you in this situation? That lousy creep is playing you like a cello. He's taking everything and giving nothing. This has got to stop, girl!
>   Now's the time to drop a few hints round the office.

Apply some pressure. You ask: Will he change? Not unless you make him. Change always hurts, but this egomaniac needs downsizing. He owes you. It worked for Monica Lewinsky! (I hope you kept the frock.)

Whatever happens, don't play his game. We all know what happened to Tosca in Puccini's wonderful grand opera of the same name: She ended up jumping off the balcony. But if anybody's going over the balcony in this scenario, it's him. He just doesn't know yet.

My work seemed like a triumph of Paul impersonation, and I'd written it with a purpose. Raymond hadn't deserved the high-handed treatment he'd received from Paul. I had been extremely angry about it at the time, although in the cold light of Justin Flynn's harbor views, my reply may have suggested a slight over-reaction. I looked up.

"Well?" Flynn asked. His smile had disappeared.

"Well," I answered. "There it is."

"You tell this reader to push her employer off a balcony. That's an exaggeration, is it? For comic effect?"

"Yes. Of course!" I laughed lightly.

"What a relief. And here you suggest she drop a few hints around the office about their…affair." He cleared his throat. "This letter being the first such hint, I presume."

Whatever was this heavy ironic tone all about? "Ah, well," I faltered, "I suppose it could be shorter."

"Exactly what I thought. Rest assured, the edited version is considerably shorter. It has been shortened out of existence."

I nodded and grinned idiotically.

"There's no place in *NOW!* for satire or in-jokes," Flynn continued. "Watch your step, Petrucci. That's all for the moment."

I realized I had been dismissed.

Outside Flynn's office I tried desperately to make sense of what had happened. His objections to the reply were out of all proportion. It was just a typical example of Paul's casual advice as far as our readers were concerned, even though it was really about

Raymond. Or was it? Had I jumped to the wrong conclusion? It seemed odd the way Helen had produced the original letter out of the blue. In fact, it was not even the original. Hadn't Helen transcribed it?

As the elevator hauled me back down to my designated level, the puzzle began to fall into place—particularly my gut feeling, right at the start, that Helen enjoyed a special relationship with Flynn. My face flushed, a flood of retrospective humiliation. It was so obvious: Helen was having an affair and she'd used me as a pawn. She had forced the fake letter on me because it was her own story, and I'd more or less told Flynn in print that he was an asshole. On top of that, I'd advised her to shove him over the railing!

By the time I reached Sonia's office I'd worked up a nice head of self-righteous steam.

"Helen! A word?" I adopted Flynn's style of sarcastic politeness.

"Ah, Marc. Adelaide went well, Paul tells me. I just got off the phone from Milan. Sonia's having a marvellous time squiring your friend around."

This took the wind out of my sails. "She found him?"

"Oh, yes. She's good. And guess what? He claims he doesn't know you. Has no memory of you at all, and knows nothing about any debt."

"What? But you've seen us together!"

"My memory's rather sharper than his. He said he couldn't remember every odd bod who came into the restaurant."

"He's lying." I could only imagine Fabio had somehow heard about Raymond's death and thought he was under suspicion. Maybe Sonia told him.

"Let it go, Marc. Whatever it was, it's over. There's plenty of waiters around, God knows. I'll help you look for a new one."

Closing the door, I returned to the purpose of my visit. It was time for straight talk (so to speak). "Helen, I've been upstairs chatting with Justin Flynn."

She raised her eyebrows as she picked up the phone. "Take my calls," she barked to the switch operator, then settled back in her chair, regarding me with a resigned expression. "Well. I suppose I owe you an explanation."

"You used me."

"I did."

I held up a hand. It was time to reveal the fabled Petrucci powers of deduction. "Don't bother, I've already worked it all out. You and the Great Justin Flynn are having an affair, although it could be more than that if he would only come around to your way of thinking."

She raised an ironic, amused eyebrow.

"I don't mean to suggest you're after his money," I continued, a trifle warily. "I'm sure it's a mutual attraction thing. But like most men of the heterosexual persuasion, he needs a little persuading. I only wish you'd told me what you were up to."

"Yes, I should have," she admitted. I waited, trying not to look overtly smug. "You guessed it," she said finally, "more or less. You're only wrong about all the details."

"Ah."

"For beginners, I wouldn't seriously consider having an affair with my dad, even though he's rich and good looking. Now if he had a slightly younger friend…"

My jaw dropped. "Justin Flynn's your father?"

"I don't spread it around, for obvious reasons. He and mumsy went their separate ways when I was small. Her separate way was to London. When I came back a couple of years ago, daddy very sweetly secured me this job. Nepotism in its purest form, really."

"But, the letter—?"

"Reverse psychology! As you of all people should understand, no man can be blackmailed into love. Our letter was designed to scare daddy off. Once our correspondent—what did we call her?"

"Caroline."

"Ah yes. Once 'Caroline' started dropping hints and making veiled threats, I figured she'd be out of his life and out of a job in one fell swoop. Or that was the idea." She grinned slyly. "My favorite line was *I want everything.* If that hadn't put the wind up him, nothing would."

It was becoming clear. Helen was even more cunning than I'd imagined. "Who are we talking about exactly?" I asked. "Flynn and who else?"

"Did you happen to catch sight of his secretary while you were up there hobnobbing? A gold-digger from way back. Daddy needs to be protected from women like that. One day he'll thank you."

"That secretary: Her name's not Caroline, is it?"

"Well done. Though to be quite accurate, I believe Caroline is her anglicized name."

I buried my head in my hands.

"Don't worry," Helen cooed. "Daddy won't fire you. He quite likes people who are a bit cheeky. I'll put in a good word, I promise." She paused. "Did you say I had anything to do with the letter?"

"No."

"Phew! Listen, I really am sorry. Lunch is on me. As usual."

I peeked out from behind my fingers. "OK," I replied.

She put her desktop computer to sleep and tidied away a few papers. "I hope you'll keep my secret, Marc," she said quietly. "Nobody else around here knows. Not even Sonia. I daresay they'll all find out one day, and then my job will be a million times harder."

"Mum's the word. I mean, Dad."

She laughed. "You know, I believe in name dropping as much as the next person, but sometimes it's better not to tell people who your father is."

chapter eighteen

At the very moment I was being hauled over the coals by Justin Flynn, all hell was breaking loose in certain pink pockets of the city. I was too preoccupied with work to hear the news, but when I arrived home I found Andrew and Gavin perched on the edge of my ghastly new couch, staring at the television like a suburban couple. I hadn't realized they'd met.

"Andrew—where did you run off to last night?" I demanded. "Hello Gavin."

"Shh," said Gavin rudely. "Here it is. Listen."

The 7 o'clock news bulletin was on. Ignored into submission, I sat. The sober face of the news reader appeared, following the usual stirring views of Australia, the globe and the universe (in order of importance).

"In tonight's bulletin, a controversial update on the New South Wales homosexual bill. Responding to statements made by the independent Stanford Cahill, Premier John Garland held a press conference this afternoon."

Garland's face flashed onto the screen in a revealing close-up. He smiled encouragingly, but his beady eyes betrayed discomfort. "I have spoken at length with Mr. Cahill, and he has abandoned plans to draft a private member's bill which would recriminalize homosexuality in this state. I pointed out to Mr. Cahill the antidiscrimination legislation already in place—which his proposed bill would possibly contravene—and I think everyone would agree we have moved beyond such a stage of hysteria."

"What's the trade-off?" cried a voice that could only belong to Celeste Ireland.

The premier glowered. "At the same time, my government is aware of a level of concern in the broader community over this issue. I have always said we cannot deprive citizens of their civil liberties. But at the end of the day we stand for an economically rational society. A level playing field. Why should the majority fund the minority? Our new tax legislation reflects this reality. My government will impose a special levy on those antifamily groups and organizations which fall outside the accepted norm. Let me emphasize: This is not a discriminatory move, it's a simple economic one."

"A *gay* tax, Mr. Premier?" asked a subdued, disbelieving voice.

"It's a fair and valid tax," the Premier said, choosing his words with caution. "We already tax luxury cars, for example. This is a tax on a luxury lifestyle. I might add that we have moved on the advice of some highly respected economists as well as senior churchmen."

I watched in stunned disbelief as members of the public—carefully vetted, no doubt—expressed their support in a series of vox pops.

A tired, untidy woman told the camera, "It's fair enough. I've got nothing against them personally, but they ain't got nobody to spend their money on but themselves. I'm a mother of four, with another one on the way, and we're struggling."

Gavin was crimson with rage. "The politics of envy, is that it?" he screamed. "I don't see any law forcing her to have five kids. If anything, she should be sterilized! I'll happily do it myself."

"Calm down," whispered Andrew.

I thought Gavin was about to attack the TV set. Fortunately at that point Celeste came on like a fire-breathing dragon.

"The premier says this tax isn't prejudicial. Not much, it isn't! This blatant discrimination will have a roll-on effect. There'll be more gay bashings, more people sacked because of their sexuality, more murders—where will it end? This is a basic human rights issue. I have already contacted the appropriate international agencies. If Garland wants to see a peacekeeping force in Oxford Street, he's going the right way about it!"

"Don't kick my TV," I begged, as Gavin leapt to his feet.

"It's appalling," he panted. "Garland's even worse than Cahill, the sleazy little rat! I'll murder the both of them with my bare hands." He stared at Andrew and me.

I gulped. "Gavin. We're on your side."

He exhaled, slowly and carefully. "Nobody treats me like a second-class citizen. Look, I'm sorry, I'll have to go. I must call Celeste." He marched out, slamming the door behind him.

"Is he often like this?" Andrew asked nervously.

"I don't know; he's new. So where were you last night? You were gone for hours."

He sighed. "Can't we talk about something else?"

I shrugged it off. "All right. But I trust you'll be staying in this evening?"

"Oh, yes." He smiled meekly.

"Good."

"Angel rang earlier," he called after me, as I popped upstairs to change.

"Probably organizing a protest," I replied.

On my return, I noticed Andrew had a glass of wine waiting.

"Oh, Marc," he muttered quietly, no doubt referring to my ensemble of gray track suit pants teamed with a rust-brown woolen jumper full of holes.

"I know I look putrid, but it's been a hard day. Can't we take it easy?"

So we put our feet up and soon fell to reminiscing, which I regarded as a very positive sign. I'd almost forgotten, but Andrew actually spent a night in prison after the first mardi gras march.

He was an entirely different person then—a baby!—and only landed in the clink because he was in a '70s kind of relationship with an outspoken activist.

Now Andrew reminded me about the first time he'd ever seen gay porn—at Angel's rundown terrace in Darlinghurst. Magazines, of course, from the prevideo Stone Age.

Angel's terrace had eventually been demolished to make way for an expressway. A lot of Sydney was like that, we agreed. Places which were once so important disappeared all the time. If they weren't pulled down they were enclosed in smoky glass and rendered unrecognizable. Soon the new millennium would be in full swing and we'd have nothing to show for the old one. What's more, nobody would care.

The conversation was becoming maudlin, but I didn't mind. I was thoroughly relishing our renewed intimacy. Then the doorbell rang.

Andrew hopped up. "Who can that be?" he asked, in the tone of a Harlequin Romance heroine pretending not to be expecting a visitor. He looked disappointed when he returned with Paul in tow.

"Are you ready, caro?" Paul asked, then stared at me. "Jumpin' Jesus! What are you *wearing*? We're not going to a charity soup kitchen."

"Are we going somewhere?" I replied coolly, although Paul's costume rendered an answer superfluous: a clinging black top and snug, black leather pants. His hair was slicked down and he'd strapped a tight, studded dog collar around his neck. His left arm sported a barbed-wire tattoo which I'd never seen before.

"Interesting tattoo," Andrew said, reading my mind.

"I just did it in the cab with a marker. See this squiggly bit? That's where we ran a red light."

"Where'd you get the dog collar?" I asked.

Paul glared at me. "From a dog! Stop asking inane questions. We'll be late. Get dressed. Wear all your leather accessories."

"Where are we supposed to be going?" I repeated.

"The LAV meeting. I told you!"

"You didn't."

"I did. At that concert in the park."

"You never said it was tonight."

"Oh, didn't I? It is. Now, chop-chop. What leather do you own?"

I frowned. "A belt."

"Is that all?"

"Um," Andrew coughed. "I have a little jerkin."

Paul laughed. "Perfect! A little jerkin goes a long way."

I glared at him. "Why are we dressing up? They'll see through us in a second."

"I thought we should do the right thing, clothes-wise, as a mark of respect."

I lost my temper. "No! Go on your own. I've had enough punishment today already. I'm always answering your boring phone, tagging along on your errands, jumping whenever you click your fingers. I'm not your slave, you know. I'm over it, to coin a phrase. Nothing will get me out of these trackies tonight."

Paul and Andrew shared a spontaneous glance. "Kitchee-kitchee-e-e..." Paul whispered.

Within seconds the three of us were rolling around the floor screaming—and my tracksuit pants and I were soon parted. I'm a martyr to ticklishness. As the others lay back laughing like special children, I resigned myself.

"What's a LAV meeting?" Andrew enquired breathlessly.

"Leathermen Against Vanilla," Paul grinned. "I guess they prefer chocolate."

"You might consider easing up on jokes like that," I warned him.

Andrew merely nodded. I had the sneaking feeling he was glad to be rid of us. He located his little jerkin and I struggled manfully into it. The buttons wouldn't meet around my middle (although I am by no stretch of the imagination fat.)

"It's not supposed to do up," Andrew explained.

Paul spun me around and pronounced the outfit "cute."

"I'm cold," I remarked.

"Don't worry," said Paul. "Nothing warms you up like a night of S/M."

The meeting was taking place at the private home of one of the LAV bigwigs. The address surprised me; it was smack in the money belt of the eastern suburbs. We crept along Oxford Street in the post-post-peak hour traffic. Unfortunately, Paul filled in the time with a torrent of personal questions.

"So what happened in Justin Flynn's office?" he asked hungrily. "Tell me everything. Leave out nothing."

"You've heard about that?"

He scoffed. "Are you kidding? Everyone in the worldwide *NOW!* empire knows you got into trouble."

I had to give him something—"It was over a letter in your column," I confessed.

"Oh, dear, what have I done now?" he giggled.

"Nothing, as you well know. I just got this letter and wrote a reply which Flynn thought was too, uh, inflammatory. OK?"

"Why did you do that?" he asked. "You should take more care with my reputation."

The traffic had slowed to a halt. I clenched my hands on the steering wheel to control myself. "It was a pathetic letter," I said slowly, "from somebody who was being treated like dirt, and it made me angry. I thought it was from Raymond, though, as it happens, I now think I was wrong—"

"From *Raymond*? Why didn't you tell me?"

"I didn't like the way you were treating him," I snapped. "Calling him a star fucker and so on. You really get on my nerves sometimes."

"Caro," he replied hotly, "you don't know the first thing about it!"

We sat in silence, stewing.

"Why don't you tell me, then?" I suggested.

He sighed. "Basically, Raymond was making my life hell," Paul said, in a subdued voice. "I know I led him on, but that's me, isn't it. I wouldn't have if I'd known he was going to get obsessive. He never stopped touching me, and turning up in all sorts of odd places. The phone would ring and wake me up at every hour of the morning, and there'd be no message. Or it would be somebody whispering! It had me totally freaked out, remember? Now I know it was him: It stopped right after he was killed."

"The whispering man," I said. "He rang for you at the office too. You should have said something."

He smiled bravely. "I didn't want to worry you, caro. And maybe I'm a mad fool, but I thought I could get him to stop." He took my hand from the steering wheel and held it tightly. "How guilty do I feel? I wished him dead—and I hated what he did with my hair."

I flushed. "We've both kept things from each other. I'm guilty too." Making a clean breast of it, I told Paul everything: how I'd met Raymond, taken him for a drink, left him with Fabio and, above all, given him that fatal advice. Neither of us spoke when I'd finished. Simultaneously, we found objects of interest to stare at outside our respective car windows.

"So," Paul said eventually, "do you suspect this Fabio person?"

"No. He couldn't have done it. He didn't have time."

"I see."

We paused once more. He was still clutching my hand. "Paul," I said, "I want to apologize."

"Caro..." He broke off. "Raymond said he loved me. He even wrote me long, rambling love letters, which I threw straight in the garbage. Love's not a word I bandy about. I don't think I even know what it means. It's not something I'm looking for, except as a sort of casual souvenir." He squeezed my hand tighter. "Have you ever been in love? I mean the full romantic bit?"

"I thought I loved Andrew once," I admitted.

"Not now."

"I suppose not. But it's a hard thing to define. Nostalgia buggers it up."

He leaned over and gently kissed me. "Friendship's more important to me," he said. "That's something I do understand. You're my best friend, Marc."

"And you're mine. Why *is* that?"

"Peculiar, isn't it! But who cares? You're not going to lose me. We're not going to lose each other. Just no more secrets, all right?"

"All right."

He slapped my thigh. "Good," he declared. "Enough of the lovey-dovey stuff. Take me to an orgy."

chapter nineteen

Our destination that evening was a mansion, looking down on the world from its smug vantage point atop Bellevue Hill. The houses in this smart road had been built by millionaires at a time when that word still meant something. The homes were all of a style, set in sprawling, elegant grounds with weathered stone gates at every entrance. I parked at the manicured edge of a pebbled driveway, next to a pair of gleaming motorbikes.

"I feel ridiculous in this little jacket," I whispered.

"Don't fuss, caro," Paul replied, "Let me do the talking."

We tripped up the sandstone steps to discover the front door standing open. A pair of distinguished leather-clad gents stood chatting at the other end of the vestibule. If one disregarded their leather shorts and harnesses, they could have been two high powered executives discussing marketing strategies at an exclusive club (as indeed they were).

The elder of the two, a white haired, statesmanlike chap, beckoned us in while his companion scuttled off down the hall.

"This is the guy who invited me," Paul confided. "James! Hello-o-o!"

The man's smile dropped slightly as we came closer. Something he'd seen seemed to have ruffled him. (My jerkin, no doubt. I, for one, found it hugely disturbing.) Nevertheless, he rallied, thrusting out his hand to me.

"Come in," he huffed. "James Thurling. Delighted to have you as our guest tonight."

"Oh, thank you," I answered. "Marc Petrucci."

He nodded. "Marc. Do I have your permission to address your friend here?"

I blinked. My permission? His tone hadn't held even a smidgen of sarcasm. I turned to Paul, whose expression, a combination of confused and insulted, was utterly priceless.

"Allow me to introduce Paul Silverton," I announced with pompous amusement.

"We've met," said James. "Good to see you again, Paul."

"Likewise," Paul returned.

"Follow me into the study if you would," James continued. "It's very informal. Drinks are set out on the sideboard, Paul. I'm sure you'll find something to Marc's liking. Minimal alcohol tonight, though." He smiled knowingly at me.

"Naturally," I agreed, vaguely wondering whether news of my binge drinking had reached even these remote shores.

We were led into an impressive wood-paneled room. One entire wall consisted of bookshelves stuffed with old volumes, their mismatched spines suggesting they'd been acquired for reading rather than appearance. The remaining space comfortably encased two long leather-upholstered divans, a few leather armchairs, several low tables, and a side table. In one corner sat a screen: a Japanese print depicting sumo wrestlers in a particularly unsavory hold. Ambient music wafted from hidden speakers and the lighting was on the intimate side.

Eight or ten men, wrapped in a variety of hides, lounged in the chairs. A few were clearly couples: older, wiry men with saucer-eyed younger men sitting next to them, bolt upright. The older men stared at us imperiously, while the young men looked at the carpet or at the older men. There was a whiff of the ancient Roman senate about the whole thing.

"Well," said Paul with awkward bonhommie. "How about a drink?"

"Just water, thanks," I answered.

"Tomato juice," barked our host, quite rudely, I thought. As Paul sashayed to the drinks table, James whispered to me: "You must understand, Marc, when I met Paul and invited him here, I didn't realize he was with you. Do forgive me."

"Oh, we're not—" I began.

"Everybody," announced James, "LAV welcomes Marc and his boy, Paul."

"Welcome, Marc," chorused the assembled leather throng.

A young man of about 20 walked into the room carrying a tray of hors d'oeuvres. He wore nothing but tiny leather shorts. His marble skin reminded me of a photograph I'd seen in the newspaper of the partially exposed body of a mountain climber which had been preserved for sixty years in the ice. The boy had eyes for nobody but our host.

"This is Poppet," James said. "If you need anything, tell him."

Poppet turned to me, although he still failed to make eye contact. "If you wish to smoke, sir, we would request you do it next door."

He indicated a partition doorway, half open, leading to an adjacent room.

"No, no," I said, as I casually glanced through the doorway. "I don't...Jesus! What's that?"

In the next room sat a long, low table with a man lying face down on top of it. The only visible parts of his anatomy were a pair of full, round buttocks, protruding from the cutaway rear of his leather pants. The buttocks were fairly unattractive, dotted with red welts and weird patches of gray. To my astonishment, a second man emerged from the smoking room and, as he passed, casually stubbed out his cigarette on the closest buttock. The slab of seared flesh quivered slightly and the prone figure moaned. I registered the faint odor of something like oysters Kilpatrick.

"Him?" said James dismissively. "He's only an ashtray." I'd heard about such fetishes but actually seeing one in action was a jolt.

"Don't worry," James added, "he's been good lately. He deserves it."

"I'll have that drink now," I replied.

I scurried over to the drinks table.

"Here you go," said Paul, handing me a mineral water. I put it down and poured myself something stronger. "Come on now, caro, don't do the whisky routine again. We should assimilate."

"I don't want to meet any smokers," I muttered.

He took my hand and led me over to a couch where Poppet was getting rid of the last of his snacks. Two leather men were sitting there.

"Mind if we join you?" asked Paul brightly, grabbing a pâté biscuit from Poppet's tray. Neither of the men answered, so Paul simply shoved me down next to the younger one and sat beside me. "I'm Paul Silverton," he said with his mouth full. "If you're wondering where you've seen the face, I host a segment on *NOW TV!* And it's fabulous."

I raised my eyes to heaven. Paul can be shameless.

"I've seen you," whispered the boy.

"Be silent," snapped his companion.

"Sorry, sir."

"And don't apologize unless I tell you to, or there'll be real trouble. Fetch me a snack."

Poppet had moved on but the boy hopped to his feet and wandered after him.

"The kid's in training," the man said to me. "He's a good lad. Deep inside."

"And pretty stunning on the outside," Paul added.

The man completely ignored him. "Training's everything. Training and discipline."

"How true," said Paul. "Hitler thought so too." (Paul is never happy when he senses his charm is not working.)

I leapt in. "It's generous of LAV to allow us strangers in, to see how it all operates," I purred. "I heard about it from Quentin Butler before he...well, I'm sure you know the story."

"Wasn't it dreadful," the man responded with gusto. "A thing like that could give sadism a bad name."

"Do you think sex might have been involved somehow?"

The man shook his head. "I doubt it. Quentin was a top."

The well-trained friend returned with a small plate of biscuits and runny cheese.

"I've changed my mind," said the man. "Offer them to Marc, then take one yourself."

"Thank you, sir," the boy answered.

Paul curtly swiped a handful. "Mm. Tasty!" He gave the boy a seductive smile. When this was by no means reciprocated, Paul turned grumpy. "Who's got the cards?" he exclaimed testily. "Let's play 'Old Maid.'"

Luckily for everyone, our host chose that moment to address us.

"A couple of things to report," he began. "First, some bad news. The rack is still being repaired…"

This information elicited groans all round.

"But there are some special surprises for those fortunate enough to be using Playroom B. I won't tell you what they are, except to say I'm dreading the next quarter's electricity bill."

He chuckled at this apparent bon mot while the assembly made various noises of anticipation.

"Now some old business. Leather Pride Fair Day will remain on the first Sunday in May. I know we had problems this year, but our international affiliates tell me it simply can't be changed."

"But it's Mother's Day," moaned the man next to me.

"Only in Australia. I'm afraid you'll have to get mom out of the way in the morning. Or else go to the Fair, take mom out to dinner, then come back for the party. That should be easy enough, surely."

"I don't want to be getting in and out of my leathers. I wanna wear them all day long, head to foot, with pride," The man beamed, as his young friend gazed at him in awe.

"Tell your mother you're going deep-sea diving," Paul quipped.

There was a stunned, frozen silence. Everybody, with the possible exception of the ashtray, stared at Paul, who shrugged good-humoredly.

"Marc, please don't be offended"—James was seriously concerned—"but it's time you took your boy aside for a little chat."

With a sweep of his hand he indicated the smoking room.

"In there?" I peeped.

"If you'd be so obliging," he said, with a stern nod.

"What the fuck is the matter with those queens?" raged Paul as I closed the door behind us. "Talk about a humor bypass."

"Shh!" I cautioned. "The ashtray will hear you."

"The what? Oh, yuck!" Paul marched over to the figure on the table. "Cover yourself up," he spat, "or at least go to a gym. You're repulsive."

"Mm-m-m," the ashtray agreed.

"Paul, calm down," I hissed.

"I'm buggered if I will," he replied, pacing up and down. "These wankers invite me here then treat me as if I'm Typhoid Mona! Why? Don't they like my show or something?"

"I don't think that's it," I said drily, wondering how I was going to tell him.

"Well," he continued, "whatever it is, leather is starting to give me a rash. This joint is nothing but a piss-elegant abattoir."

As if on cue, the buttocks moved, accompanied by a little groan. Abattoirs evidently figured in the ashtray's sexual fantasies.

Paul's face lit up with mischief. "Caro, hand me that cigarette." He winked. "The one you're holding now: that red hot, burning, sizzling fag." The ashtray inhaled noisily. "Thank you. I believe I'm going to grind it into this person's big fat bottom!"

The buttocks tensed with delight. Paul snatched the drink I was still clutching, shoved his fingers in and pulled out an ice block. In a flash he strode to the table, placed the ice block squarely between the quivering cheeks and gave it a hefty whack with his fist. "There!" he cried.

"Ar-r-rgh!" The buttocks heaved as the man snapped his head up like a meer cat. I instantly recognized him: It was the pompous columnist I'd tackled at the whisky tasting.

"Oh! Hello again," I said. "What a surprise."

"Uh?" The man stared straight at me, but no sign of recognition registered. His eyes merely glazed over as he gradually lowered his face to the table once more.

"Let's go," said Paul, "before he farts and knocks one of us out."

"I haven't finished my drink. Besides, we're supposed to be doing some detecting."

He snorted. "All I can detect is a shitload of attitude."

I chuckled. "Can't you see what's happening? They keep referring to you as my 'boy.' They assume we're a couple."

Paul clapped his hand to his forehead in horror. "No! They *don't* think I'm your...*bottom*? Nothing personal," he added to the ashtray.

"Yes! And you're my slave. That's why they're talking only to me." I laughed. "How ironic. If anyone's the slave in this outfit, I am."

Paul was appalled. "It must be because of this stupid dog collar," he whined. "Help me get it off." He started tugging at the leather strap around his neck. "Ow! Fucking thing!"

"Keep still!" I couldn't get my fingers behind the strap. It was awfully tight. "Did you put this on yourself?"

"It must have shrunk. It's so dry in here."

I let go. "Couldn't you play along till we know a little more?"

"You just want to boss me around."

"Nonsense!"

Paul looked doubtful. "OK...but I'm not licking the soles of your Nikes or anything."

"All you need do is pour us both a stiff drink and keep your mouth shut."

"Hurry up then. I'm choking. This thing's torture." The ashtray quivered and moaned. "Oh, get over it," snapped Paul, giving its right buttock a vicious pinch as we left the room.

"Ah," cooed James as we reentered the fray. "I hope you didn't think me rude before."

"No," I answered. "Everything's under control now."

Paul nodded like a demented puppy.

"Get me another drink, slave boy," I commanded. Paul gave me his "if looks could kill" smile and slunk to the drinks table with exaggerated humility. Glancing around the room I noticed the couple we'd chatted to had vanished.

James moved surreptitiously to my side. "Marc. I was wondering—since you are clearly *simpatico*—whether you and Paul would be interested in joining LAV. We've no political affiliations; we're merely a group of like-minded men."

"Ah, well," I answered cautiously. "We should certainly think about it."

"I have two fully equipped playrooms here, for my own use and that of my LAV associates. Playroom A is presently occupied but I have reserved Playroom B for you this evening, should you be so inclined." He oozed generosity.

"Oh, no. It's a great honor but we wouldn't dream of putting your rotation system out of whack. I mean, out of sync."

He took my arm. "You're most thoughtful. At least inspect it." Before I could reply he was leading me away. Paul glanced up as I passed. "Paul," I said, "I order you to drink a glass of wine and strike up a conversation with somebody."

James took me through a sumptuous hallway to a staircase which led down to the basement. Once there he unlocked a metal door and escorted me into a dark, sweetly dank-smelling room. Dim illumination bled from hidden lamps built into the ceiling and floor.

"Lighting from below was my own initiative," James murmured hoarsely. "It creates more imaginative shadow play."

The result was like a set from a silent film. Manacles were attached to the walls, a series of whips were displayed by size in a rack like pool cues, a full sling hung down from the ceiling, and most surfaces seemed to be coated in thick black rubber. Adjacent to the door was a low table with a neat stack of white towels on it and jars of lubricant. I stared at a sinister blue light, high up on the far wall, until I realized it was merely a mosquito zapper. He'd thought of everything!

I must admit I had seen something similar to this setup before, in equally unexpected circumstances, but it certainly hadn't included a strange little machine with dials and terminals, resembling a small sound-mixing desk.

"What does that do?" I whispered.

"My newest toy," James beamed. "It's a dynamo, producing an electric charge of up to 8 amps." He shivered. "A quick zap at the right moment, and bingo! Nirvana. And it's not connected to the mains, so if there happens to be a blackout, one's ritual is not compromised unnecessarily."

"Ah, yes, well," I gulped. "Blackouts are a damn nuisance. Is that why you have all these candles here?"

"Not the only reason." He glanced at them lovingly.

"You'd have to know what you were doing with the electrical goods."

"Of course, but that's true of anything. We're very strong on setting parameters in LAV. Sex play must be safe, sane, and consensual. We won't have it any other way."

"But when things do go a bit far…" I left the inference dangling, so to speak.

He grimaced. "Naturally, we've plenty of first aid equipment and know-how. Goes without saying, Marc."

I picked up a cane from the table and flexed it briskly. "You know, James, Quentin Butler mentioned LAV to me once or twice. Later, I naturally couldn't help wondering if his sexual predilections had anything to do with his murder."

Gently, James took the cane from me and placed it back exactly where I'd found it. "The police are of the opinion Quentin's death was a senseless, random act," he said simply.

"But you and I know a little more than that," I said, pressing on cautiously. "Things we would hardly expect the police to understand."

He seemed to relax. "I've discussed it at length, of course. I honestly believe that Quentin had found, through leather sex, a means of self-expression which had eluded him all his life."

"I know," I said, bending the truth a little. "He was leaving his partner because of it. He confided in me, you see."

James nodded. "The partner wasn't one of us. So you must know all about his bottom?"

I blinked. "What about it?"

James frowned. "Quentin said he was training a bottom."

The penny dropped. "Oh! Because he was a top."

"Of course. Tell me, Marc, have you heard of 'top's disease'?"

"Uh, remind me."

"Sometimes when tops get heavily into what they do they can lose a sense of reality. They expect to be treated as a top by everyone—in the leather scene and out of it. Topping goes to their head, you might say. They become abrupt and demanding."

"Did that happen to Quentin?"

He sighed. "I was beginning to wonder."

This probably accounted for the behavior that had so riled Angel and Quentin's sister Laurie.

"And you've no idea of the identity of his bottom?" I asked.

"Unfortunately not. Quentin didn't wish to introduce him to LAV until the boy was fully trained."

I took a pot shot. "Does the name Raymond ring any bells?"

"You mean in conjunction with Quentin?"

"Yes. Or anyone else."

James shook his head. "I can't say it does. Do you think that might be it?"

"Probably not," I hedged. "Just a name I heard once. What about Stewart?"

"No, no." He sighed. "I suppose we'll never know. Poor Quentin. So close to fulfillment, but all this was never to be his." He gazed around the playroom with a benevolent eye, then gave a kindly smile. "Are you absolutely sure?"

"I don't think Paul's up to it yet."

"I could let you have Poppet. He's exquisitely sensitive."

"You're too kind, but no."

It struck me as odd, to say the least, how well-mannered these people were before inflicting pain on each other. I found both tendencies equally off-putting.

"Well, there are others who will," he remarked smugly. Grabbing the pile of towels, he led me out of Playroom B and back upstairs. I didn't dare imagine what Playroom A must be like. Probably stocked with everything but the kitchen guillotine.

All the LAV members gazed up in anticipation when James and I rejoined them. He nodded in the direction of a hungry looking couple. "Wayne and Caleb," he said. "Playroom B is yours. Play safe."

The two men leapt to their feet with joy and hastened out of the room. Meanwhile, Poppet had taken possession of the towels and was casually distributing them to the remaining company. The lights began to dim.

"I've received some new porn from Amsterdam," James said to me. "Inspiring stuff. If you'd care to join us, we're going to jack off."

"No, thanks, I…I already came at the office." I smiled weakly. "Paul! Get over here! Bring my coat. We're leaving."

Paul trotted over. "You don't have a coat."

"Don't answer back!" I slapped him gently on the cheek.

"Ow! Watch it! You just struck a celebrity."

I sensed Paul's role as a slave was wearing pretty thin. I turned to James. "LAV has definitely aroused my interest. Now, you get started. We'll see ourselves out."

I don't think I took another breath until my car reached the main road. Then I filled Paul in, telling him about Butler's bottom-in-training and the scourge of top's disease.

"So the murder could have been a bout of nonconsensual S/M that backfired," Paul mused. "Maybe his bottom turned on him."

"It's possible," I agreed. "There's no link to Raymond, though. Our host had never heard of him."

We drove on in silence for a while.

"What are you thinking about, *caro mio?*"

"Just wondering if I've had a boring sex life."

"You fancy a bit of pain?"

"Well, I've never tried it."

"My darling, in ten years' time you'll be riddled with arthritis, gall stones, and every little twinge under the sun. You'll have all the pain you want!"

He hooted at this droll observation. Personally, I failed to see the humor in it.

chapter twenty

I must admit, I had been shaken rather than stirred by the sight of James's basement hideaway. Nipple-zapping electrodes are surely one short step removed from bad taste. When people torment each other for kicks, how do they know if they've run into someone who's heart is *really* in it? By expiring, presumably. Paul thought the leather sex scene amusing. He might not have been so tickled if he'd found himself cast as Plaything C in Playroom B.

When I dropped him outside his flat, he glared at the building with something less than a heart full of joy.

"I'm getting out of this poky dump first thing tomorrow," he announced decisively.

"Why? I thought you loved it."

"I've outgrown it, caro. I feel the need to throw huge parties."

"Where are you moving to? Oxford Street?"

"Bigger than that. Sonia's waterside mansion. She gave me the keys in case I wanted to stay a few days. You know I like to be helpful. I can water the aspidistra, flick the dust off the Picasso, etcetera."

"Don't get too used to it," I cautioned. "She may want the place back."

Andrew wasn't around when I got home to Villa Petrucci. Again! Something was definitely afoot. Where was he spending all his time? I felt as if I was running a private hotel for gadabouts. I knew there was no point in waiting up, and after all those tops and bottoms the evening had thrown at me, I was ready to collapse.

While I prepared for bed, I listened to the single message flashing for my attention on the answering machine.

"Darling, it's Angel. We must talk. I understand you and your famous friend have been poking around asking people about Quentin's death. Just like a trashy novel, eh? The lovely Stewart told me everything. He always seems to find out what people are up to. But I won't wag my finger and say 'watch yourself'" because I've been doing exactly the same thing!

"We should pool our resources, Marc. It's probably too late tonight, but how about tomorrow evening? Zip around to GLEE. I'm always here even when there are no workshops. I'm forming quite a little theory about poor Quentin's demise. I've found out something the police have been keeping back.

"Oh, which reminds me, have you heard about the latest atrocity? A gay tax! Fucking unbelievable! The conservatives see every issue in terms of their bank accounts. We're going to have to nip old 'Judy' Garland in the bud. See you tomorrow."

The message was intriguing, and not the least significant part was that Stewart had been blabbing about our investigations. I hate to mix metaphors, but Paul would let any number of cats out of the bag in order to jump into the sack. I've never known anyone whose decisions are so libido-led. How many others had he blurted this information out to over postcoital caffeine?

Still, I was interested to hear what, if anything, Angel had discovered. The secret information possibly concerned the strange, posthumous bandaging linking the two deaths. If it suggested something to him, I wanted to be the first to know.

That night I lay in bed in a half wakeful state, my mind kicking around all kinds of images: dogs and couches, politicians and potters, whips and ashtrays—all the things that had occupied it during the preceding months. I cursed my mind for behaving like this, but there are times when it will not be dictated to. Now was

one. It must have sensed that deep in this whirlpool of discon-
nected information was the beginning of a gleam of a way out.
Sensibly, I dozed off and left my mind to its own devices.

My thoughts were drifting along these lines at work the next
day when Helen appeared beside my desk and slapped an open
newspaper down in front of me. The page was full of pictures of
bleary-eyed people captured in unnatural lighting.

"What's this?" I asked.

"Last week's Adelaide *Gay Times*," she answered. "Bryce found it."

I glanced towards the accountant's partition just in time to see
his beady-eyed face dip out of sight.

"Here's Paul on the dance floor at a dive called the Tow Bar.
And who could *this* be?"

I stared at a group shot. There, clearly visible at one side,
was yours truly, arms high in the air, cavorting opposite a man
who later answered to the name of Leslie. The photographer
had caught me tilting my head back, sticking my tongue out
and going cross-eyed.

"What an awful pose," she laughed.

"Just my usual 'candid camera' look."

"Bryce is working through the receipts for your trip with a fine-
tooth comb," Helen added. "I thought I should warn you."

My eye strayed over the other portraits. "May I keep this?" I asked.

"You can't destroy it, it has to be filed."

"I'm not busy," I said. "I'll take it down there myself. Second floor?"

"Yes. Give it to Trish. And intact, please. No razor blades!"

NOW! received copies of just about every other magazine and
newspaper in the country, mainly for gossip research. I found the
filing room and soon located Trish, a bright, chatty girl with a
painful-looking cold sore.

"I don't know why that guy from accounts wanted it, do you?"
she asked slyly, as I handed the paper back.

"I'm surprised we get it at all."

"The gay rags are good on music and clubbing."

I had an idea. "Paul is interested in certain back issues of this paper," I said.

"I only keep them for twelve months."

"Around Christmas?"

"Wait a sec."

She disappeared briefly and returned with a stack of newspapers. "Here's November to February. OK? Wait, you have to sign."

In the lift I dropped the papers and while crouching to pick them up, I sailed past my stop—one of the hazards of corporate life. When I finally made it back to my floor, there was Paul, lounging on our chair and chatting on our phone.

"Around 4, OK? Beer would be lovely." Paul motioned me to sit opposite. "Look forward to seeing you, babe. Bye-ee." Dropping the receiver, he broke into a wicked grin. "Caro, I'm throwing a party! I thought of the idea last night and it firmed up this morning when I checked out Sonia's place. She's got outdoor dining with seating for twenty million! And the bed's not tiny either. So, Saturday afternoon: your full-on pretentious rich queens' luncheon. Be there or be elsewhere."

"I can't come," I shrugged. "I'm not rich."

"Don't worry, neither is anyone else." He flicked his head towards the phone. "That was Stewart. Remember him?"

"Vaguely."

"I want no one there but gorgeous spunks. You'll have to bring a pretty young date. No fems or fatties. Actually, you can come around early and help me throw a salad in the oven." He leaned forward and adopted a conspiratorial whisper. "I'm really here on business. Can we be overheard?"

I looked around. Bryce was on one of his lengthy toilet breaks.

"What is it?"

"Something occurred to me last night when I got home from the Blue Room."

"You went to a bar after I dropped you off?"

"Only for five minutes. That's not important. Remember I

told you that Raymond wrote me love letters? I thought I'd thrown them away but voilà! I've still got one."

He pulled an envelope out of his back pocket and extracted from it a wad of crumpled lavender paper. The pages were covered in a small, neat script—quite the opposite of the expansive style Raymond had favored in conversation.

"Read this bit!"

I peered at the section Paul had indicated:

> I am having such bad luck with boyfriends up until now. My last boyfriend was so fucked up about being gay! I mean, that's cool, it doesn't *have* to be an issue, I didn't want to *make* it an issue, but he was weird about it. Not like you. You're so proud, so together. Anyway don't worry about him! He was just a quickie. I've forgotten him forever.
>
> He lives in Sydney. I saw him out the other night, first time since Xmas. He looks different—but he hasn't changed inside I bet. He just stared, and I'm waving to him like a silly girl, and he's giving me this Greta Garbo treatment, like, who am I? I'm shit or something? So from this I gather he's still as fucked in the head as ever and I would have to be majorly desperate to go back. In fact, I wouldn't. I'm over closet queens and him specially. There's nobody for me but you.

"What do you think?" Paul was beside himself. "I wish I'd found this before we went to Adelaide."

"I'm sure we're on to something," I said. "This ex-boyfriend of Raymond's might be our missing link."

"We should have checked harder in the Tow Bar," Paul moaned, "but some of us were a bit distracted by other things."

I raised my eyebrows. "Did you show Quentin's picture to anyone?"

"How could I? I was dancing."

"Well," I said, shoving the newspapers at him, "start looking for it in here. These are the Adelaide *Gay Times* from November to February. The paper prints a selection of club and dance party snaps each week. It's a long shot, of course."

We browsed through the few dozen pages of passé party pics, Paul cavorting with glee every five seconds and squealing, "Look at this tragedy!" Having seen my own recent photo, pure glass-house material, I was disinclined to throw stones. Bryce returned from his sojourn and cast a patronizing glance in our direction, but we paid him no attention.

Our first trawl produced nothing, but Paul kept returning to a vast double-page spread of the big New Year's Eve dance party. It was a single photograph taken from above, next to a glitter ball, showing a dance floor packed with gyrating boys and girls in various stages of ecstasy, real and artificial.

"Caro, hand me your trusty magnifying glass."

"I don't have one."

"Some detective," he scoffed. Jumping to his feet, he bounded across the room.

"Bruce," he breezed. "Got a magnifying glass I could borrow?"

The accountant seethed. "It's *Bryce*," he mumbled.

I coolly inspected my fingernails.

"Whatever. Magnifying glass? Enlarger? Anything like that?"

It so happened Bryce did have one. He handed it over reluctantly.

With the aid of this implement, it took Paul a matter of seconds to locate Raymond "I've found him," he whispered excitedly. "And guess who he's dancing with?"

"Show me! Who?"

"Nine hundred other people."

I peered at the picture. Although grainy, the image of Raymond was clear enough. A ray of light from the glitter ball fell directly across his face. "He *is* dancing with someone," I said. "See? The other man's in shadow, facing away from the camera."

"Mm. Nice physique. At least we know it's a male."

"That's all we know," I said despairingly. "We can't see his face."

Paul brightened. "I don't suppose the photographer climbed up there and took only one shot. We'll get him to send us the proof sheets!"

"Why would he do that?"

"Because we're NOW! and we hire photographers, that's why."

"I'll ask Helen to do it. She owes me a good turn."

Things were moving quickly. Carried along by the momentum, I made a deliberate decision. It was time to broach a certain subject with Andrew: the subject of the future. His, mine, and ours. Perhaps we could discuss things over an intimate Italian meal at Fratelli di Marco, as we had done in the long-distant past. I phoned him immediately. He was home, for a change, but he hadn't planned on eating out.

"I'm preparing our dinner right now. Chicken cacciatore," he whined. "It used to be your favorite."

"All right, it was only a suggestion. By the way," I added, lightening the mood, "do you want to go to a party on Saturday? Paul's house-sitting and he's having a few people around."

"Can I bring a friend?"

I hesitated. "Uh, well. Why not?"

"Fantastic! See you later."

I was not entirely happy with this outcome. Since when did Andrew have a "friend"? Also, through some ancient racial memory, I tended to associate chicken cacciatore with guilt. For once my intuition was spot on.

"Can we talk?" Andrew asked as we sopped up the thick tomato sauce with crusty bread.

"Yes, we should," I answered. "I've been meaning to have a chat about the future."

He held up his hand. "Let's not beat around the bush, Marc. I'm moving out next weekend."

"What? Why?"

"Please, let me say what I've got to say. First of all, I think you're the most wonderful person in the world. You took me in here, out of the blue, and let me disrupt your routine, such as it is. You looked after me when I was so upset about Neil and everything."

"You're not going back to him?"

"No, no. I'm moving on. I've sponged off you for too long."

This all sounded fairly permanent. "But Andrew! Remember what happened between us just after you arrived—that night?" I reached over and took his hand, squeezing it gently.

"Marc, your sleeve is in the sauce."

"Shit!"

"About that night…" He flushed. "I wasn't totally in control of myself. It was a silly thing to do. It's thoughtful of you to understand."

"I…well. I'll miss you."

He beamed, his eyes predictably watery. "You won't have to. I'll be right next door."

"Next door? With the Chinese couple?"

"No, the other side. I'm moving in with Gavin. To tell the truth, I've been seeing a bit of him lately."

I pursed my lips. "Which bit is that?"

"Now, stop it. I thought you liked him. I think he's lovely. He's so tidy! The house is spotless. Have you seen inside?"

"I've slept there."

He blinked. "Oh, yes, when you were drunk. We talked about it. We talk all the time! We've got lots in common: decorating, politics…"

"Dogs?"

"Hector's fine when you get to know him. Honestly." He began to clear away the dinner plates.

"Don't do that just now."

He sat down again. "You know, it's through you that Gavin and I met," he confided. "If you hadn't left me waiting at that first aid tent in Hyde Park, I'd never have started chatting to him."

I gave in. It was fate. "Well. You want to bring Gavin to Paul's party?"

"We'd love to come. I'll be moving my things out Saturday morning—not that there's much stuff—but then we can all celebrate and be together. It couldn't have worked out better."

"No," I concurred. "It's so neat, it's frightening."

His expression suddenly changed from elation to one of

slight discomfort. "Oh, I hate to mention it, but the couch I bought.... Do you mind? I don't think you care for it anyway."

"Take it. Wear it in good health." I eased myself up from the table and moved behind him, placing my hands on his shoulders.

"We'll always be friends, Marc," he said softly. "I can never be closer to anyone than I am to you. I'll always be here if you need me."

"Will you drop in every night to cook dinner?"

"No."

"Any chance of a threesome?"

"I'll let you know. You are *so* tacky!" He turned his head and kissed my hand.

"No harm in asking. One more question: Would you do the washing up tonight? I have to go out."

He nodded. "Yes, sure. I understand. You need a lot of space right now."

"I'm not going to Mars."

He made a little choking sound.

"Don't cry, Andrew."

"Why should I?" he sniffled. "I got the couch."

As I drove off to keep my appointment with Angel, I reflected that, as always, a major decision concerning my life had been made in my absence. Fate had accomplished it's usual fait accompli. I couldn't decide whether to feel annoyed or relieved, so I settled for both.

For the sake of consistency, fate had provided no parking spaces near the GLEE building. I finally found a spot miles away in a matrix of narrow one-way streets. Trekking back to the main road, I felt quite excited at the prospect of seeing Angel. Paul and I had made some headway on Raymond; if Angel could sort out the confusion surrounding Quentin and his partners, sisters, bottoms, and what have you, everything might snap into place.

By the time I reached GLEE I was in full Sherlock mode, so it was doubly irritating to find the place shut up and completely dark. There was even a hastily scribbled sign stuck to the back of the glass door: CLOSED. BACK LATER. I peered as best I could through the filmy glass but saw no sign of life. I felt suspicious and irritated. Should I wait? Did the sign mean Angel had just slipped out for sushi, or did "later" mean later in terms of the great universal scheme of things? Why set up a meeting if he didn't intend to be there? Why do these things happen to me? (A general query.)

Pondering my next move, I pushed the door. Instantly it sprang open and slammed into the wall with a resounding bang. I tiptoed inside, gently closing the door behind me. If I was going to wait for Angel, I might as well do so in the comfort of his office. He couldn't be far, I reasoned, if he hadn't bothered to lock up.

The downstairs space was packed with folding chairs and placards. They leaned against the back wall at jaunty angles, casting surreal shadows in the neon light which shone dimly through from the street.

I had only taken a few steps into the room when I stopped in my tracks, frozen with terror. Peering at me were dozens of eyes, all filled with evil intent. And blood! There was blood wherever I looked. I shut my eyes tightly and took several deep breaths. When I finally felt calmer, I risked a cautious peep. Aha! The blood was still there, but it was paint. The walls were covered in paintings and murals, each one depicting some graphic act of slaughter. This grisly display must have been the result of Gerda's art project.

Averting my gaze and shaking slightly, I groped my way toward the staircase. There seemed to be light upstairs, but when I reached the landing I found it was only more neon, flooding through the window and bathing the second floor in a deathly pale glimmer.

I was feeling about for the light switch when I stopped still. Someone else was in the building. I was sure I'd heard the shuffle of a shoe, soft but unmistakable. I held my breath and waited, but I heard nothing more.

"Angel?" I called softly. "Angel, is that you?"

There was no answer. A large truck rumbled past in the street, creating a hell of a racket. It was a noisy neighborhood at the best of times, I reassured myself. Cautiously, I tiptoed across the room towards Angel's office. The office door was locked. There was clearly no point in my hanging around.

I was halfway back when the door downstairs opened and closed again, quite loudly, and I heard the sound of footsteps.

"Angel?" I cried hopefully.

The new arrival came bounding up the stairs and suddenly the room was filled with blinding light. I lifted my hand and squinted through my fingers to see a familiar figure.

"Oh, hello," I stammered. "Tim, isn't it? We're always running into each other here."

The boy nodded, his beautiful blue eyes wide with surprise.

"I was looking for Angel," I explained nonchalantly, "but, ah, he's not in."

"Where is he?"

"I don't know." I smiled as confidently as I could. He smiled back, revealing the dimples I had found so mesmerizing the first time we'd met. They still were.

"He told me to come round," the boy said, obviously puzzled.

"Me too. Odd, isn't it?" I crossed my fingers, hoping he wouldn't ask me why I was waiting in the dark. Luckily, the question didn't seem to occur to him.

"I thought somebody'd broken in," he said. "The door was unlocked."

"Yes. Angel's office is locked though."

"You gonna wait?" He tossed back his dark hair.

"Perhaps for a little while," I murmured. "So, how are you these days? Got work?"

"Some part-time stuff." Fiddling with his one of his nose studs, Tim glanced around the room. "I signed up for the new opera course."

"What, here?"

"Yeah."

"That's nice," I sniffed. "I'm not running it, you realize."

"Aren't you? Too bad. I liked your session."

I felt all warm inside. "Look, it seems silly to sit here when we could wait in a pub or, you know, a café or something."

A sweet, panicky expression spread over his face. "I can't, I've got things to do."

I should have known better than to try again. Besides, even if we made it past the front door this time, we would still have to put up with Andrew puttering around the house.

"How about tomorrow?" he muttered.

My ears pricked up. "Sorry?"

Tim smiled uncertainly. "Tomorrow? For a drink, I mean. I kind of left you standing before. A bit rude."

"Oh, forget about that. Yes, um…" I had to think quickly. Andrew would be out of the way by Saturday. "I know—would you like to come with me to a party? On Saturday? There'll be food and I believe the place is very swanky. I could pick you up if you'd like. Everyone there will be gay. You'll knock 'em dead!"

His face froze. *Damn,* I thought. I'd ruined everything by getting too excited. Why do some people find enthusiasm so confrontational?

Then he relaxed. "Sounds good to me," he said.

"Wonderful! How will we make the arrangements?"

"I've got a cell phone."

I soon located a pen and we exchanged phone numbers; a remarkable development.

"OK. I'm off," he announced, lingering awkwardly by the stairs, clearly expecting me to leave as well. There seemed no compelling reason to stay.

Once outside, I gave his arm a friendly squeeze and, much to my surprise, he kissed me lightly on the neck. "See you Saturday," he said.

"Saturday it is! Need a lift anywhere?"

"Nah."

We walked off in opposite directions, and I can't deny I had a spring in my step.

Over the next few days I remained unrelentingly cheerful, so

much so that Andrew began to suspect I was more than accept-
ably pleased to see him go. Maybe I was. It would actually be a
relief not to have to worry about him in future. I also looked forward to playing Italian opera after 11:30 at night again. Tebaldi
had been in the cupboard for too long.

Buoying up my mood even further, the broadcast of Paul's
Munchstadt piece was postponed to make way for a live interview
with the visiting star of an American sitcom. Paul was put out, but
I couldn't have been happier if I'd paid the woman's airfare
myself. It gave Helen and I another week to run the Adelaide
piece under the noses of the various *NOW!* legal advisors in case
Laurie Butler changed her mind again about suing.

Finally, to crown my pleasant week, a package arrived on
Friday morning at the office: the proof sheet from the Adelaide
photographer, accompanied by a personal note from Helen. The
note read:

> Marc. I hope this is what you wanted, and I feel sure you'll
> tell me the *whole story* over lunch on Monday.

The tiny prints inside were even harder to see than the newspaper shot. Using Bryce's magnifying glass, which Paul had never
returned, I isolated three of the brightest pictures and sent them
down to be enlarged. Two hours later the enlargements landed
back on my desk.

One shot was the picture they'd used in the Adelaide paper.
The others had evidently been taken in quick succession. The
third of this series seemed to be what we were looking for. I examined the photograph closely. The dancers were still in much the
same configuration, but Raymond's partner had turned towards
the lens and was considerate enough to face the light. His face displayed that hard, intense look frequently seen on the dance floor.

Slowly, I put down the magnifier. I hadn't expected to know the
face, let alone to have seen it so recently. And never in my wildest
dreams had I imagined it would belong to my next-door neighbor.

chapter twenty-one

The distinctive sound of bongos and sleazy saxophone harmonies regaled my ears. I was cutting leaves of spinach, using a large, sharp knife, and found myself chopping in time to the beat. Every so often, I would pause to gaze out the window at an expanse of deep blue ocean dotted with white sails and spots of sludgy foam. It was breathtaking in a souvenir snow-dome kind of way.

Paul danced by, wearing his Calvins and frilly apron combo.

"Tequila!" he sang at the top of his lungs. I almost chopped my hand off at the wrist.

"You're not drinking already?"

"Caro, 'Tequila' is the name of this song. And you call yourself Queen of Retro." He circled around me, clicking his fingers. "This is the only music for a party."

"I prefer *Tosca.*"

"*Tosca-a-a!*" he screamed. "Yes, that works. You finished yet?"

"No. Why can't you do you own cooking?"

"You said you'd help! And I have so much else to do."

"Like what?"

"Making up the video compile, for one. Whoever heard of a party without videos playing incessantly in the corner? Besides, I don't know where anything is in this kitchen."

"Neither do I," I protested. "While you're here you can mix the onions and ricotta."

He plunged his fingers into a bowl of creamy goo. "So tonight, our mission, should we choose to accept it, is to trap Gavin into a full and frank confession."

I pursed my lips dubiously. "Paul, I don't think we should jump to conclusions. I've always found Gavin charming—"

"Typical serial killer!"

"And the pictures from Adelaide are only circumstantial evidence. He's absolutely nothing like the man Raymond described in his letter. If we had something more definite..."

"His dog ran straight to where the bodies were," Paul nodded meaningfully. "The pet always knows."

I sighed. "Plenty of people walk their dogs in the AIDS glade. Anyway, if I truly thought Gavin was a murderer, I'd never leave him alone with Andrew."

"No, it was an excellent plan. If he kills Andrew, then we'll be a hundred percent positive!"

I waved the knife in his face. "Take that back!"

"OK, OK. Don't turn into Joan Crawford. *Boom! Tequila!*"

The knife jumped out of my hand. "Now I've cut myself!"

Paul giggled. "Here, show us your gash, as they say." He inspected my finger closely, then went to suck it.

"Stop that! I don't want it to go septic! Where's the first aid?"

"In the bathroom, I suppose. Use the en suite in my bedroom. Top floor."

Sonia's house had a most unusual layout. It was built into the side of the hill on a semicircular design. It had four stories, if you counted the garage and cellar underneath, and each of the top three boasted a balcony facing the sea. The first floor opened onto a large paved patio which featured an outdoor jacuzzi, while the main bedroom up top had a far-reaching view of the ocean and a superb view of the lower balconies. A curving staircase against the back wall linked the three floors inside and featured a chair lift. This gizmo had been installed for a previous resident, an elderly billionaire, but apparently Sonia got a kick out of using it, especially when she was drunk.

I rode the chair lift to the top floor. In the main bedroom, the walls and furniture were orange and white respectively. The decor stood out in stark contrast to the sedate pastels elsewhere in the house. This, I suspected, was the room upon which Sonia Porter-Hibble had put her personal stamp. I rushed through to avoid bleeding on the furry white carpet.

Madame's medicine cabinet was stocked with exotic prescription drugs, but I soon unearthed a roll of gauze and a bandage. I'm famously accident prone, but even for me this was bad luck; it was the same hand I'd injured at the protest rally. My poor paw had only just healed.

I clumsily wrapped my finger. Gavin had done a much more proficient job, I reflected. He was neat with a bandage—another damning piece of circumstantial evidence.

I had already been going over the events of that day in my mind. Near the toilets, I had bumped into the boy who'd been attacked. I had then gone directly to the first aid tent. Gavin, who was supposed to be there, had shown up five minutes later saying he'd been to the toilet. He might simply have gone behind a tree, of course.

I couldn't decide whether to suspect Gavin or not. I had hovered about at Villa Petrucci that morning helping Andrew with his things, and Gavin had been the personification of bonhomie and good fellowship. I was reminded what a splendid first impression he had made when he'd moved in, and first impressions die hard. However, if I didn't make up my mind about Gavin by the end of the day, Andrew could be placing himself in a very dangerous situation. A lot was hanging on this party.

My future love life, for one thing. I had left it until late in the week to call Tim. He'd seemed uncertain on the phone, but nevertheless our date was on. He didn't want me to pick him up, which was handy, seeing as I'd been pressed into unpaid domestic service for the day.

Chair-lifting my way back to Paul, I decided to play down my suspicions. My plan was to lead Gavin aside sometime, ask a few probing questions, and take it from there—all very subtle and clandestine. I didn't want Paul getting in the way.

"Let's just relax and enjoy the party," I said, as we concluded our preparations.

Much to my surprise, Paul agreed. "You're so right, caro. I'd hate to let messy stabbings spoil our fun—and all that time-consuming bandaging! We can decide what to do about Gavin later. I mean, he's only a vague possibility, isn't he? Here, finish this champagne so we can open a cold one."

People began arriving at 2 o'clock: a cluster of Paul's friends. Some of them were familiar to me by sight, although they looked virtually identical in their tank tops and baggy shorts. The delectable Stewart made his entrance in a tight orange shirt and cream hemp trousers, possibly chosen to team with the bedroom decor. His body and hair were as perfect as ever, though he looked tired in the face. No doubt a certain person had been up all night sitting on it.

More boys arrived, and I was kept busy providing them with drinks and nibblies. One or two flirted outrageously with me under the impression I must be the owner of Sonia's luxurious pile. I couldn't find it in my heart to correct their mistake.

Paul switched on the jacuzzi—he'd spent an hour that morning working out how to do it—and a few boys hopped in. When Stewart stripped down to a flimsy g-string to join them, every conversation sputtered to a halt and hit the ground.

Andrew and Gavin arrived with *couple* written all over them. Andrew immediately shoved a large bowl into my hands. "It's an apple and blueberry crumble," he said. "Gavin made it."

"Just for emergencies," Gavin added. "It's easy to underestimate the numbers. I've done that plenty of times."

Can this man be a homicidal maniac, I thought? He whips up his own crumble! All the same, I decided not to serve it unless I had to.

Predictably, there was more than enough to drink and everyone seemed happy to do just that. The weather stayed warm and accommodating, the jacuzzi bubbled away, the sea sparkled in the required manner, and Paul swanned around as though he not only owned the place but had personally designed and built it, brick by brick. My lasagna spinaci was lightly picked at but highly praised. All in all, the party was a conspicuous success apart from one tiny, niggling detail: My date hadn't showed up.

At 5 o'clock I decided to try Tim's mobile. I crept away from the crowd and slipped upstairs to the bedroom to make the call. Opening the door, I heard a strangled yelp and saw Andrew straighten up hurriedly. He was standing by the dresser. He turned to smile, red faced, in my direction.

"Oh, Marc, it's only you," he breathed, dropping the smile.

"Are you snooping?" I asked pointedly.

"Oh, well, who wouldn't? My God, isn't this orange nauseating?" He lowered himself onto the bed.

"I like it." I sat beside him. "Where's Gavin?" I asked, giving the wardrobe a cursory glance. "Why isn't he with you?"

"He's talking to Paul."

"Oh, no!" I struggled to my feet. I'd been waiting until the party wound down to have my heart-to-heart with Gavin. If Paul got there first and started throwing accusations around, Gavin would clam up completely.

"We shouldn't interrupt," Andrew went on. "Gav's organizing a big corporate function in Adelaide and he wants to sound Paul out about being the emcee. It's his first interstate event. He flew down last New Year's Eve specifically to check out the venue. He's so thorough."

"Oh, really? Isn't Gavin from Adelaide originally?"

"No. He'd never been there before in his life. That's why this is so exciting. Do you think he'll ask me to decorate?"

"Mad not to."

I lay back down on the bed and breathed a sigh of relief. At least one piece of circumstantial evidence had been accounted for. Maybe Andrew would be safe after all.

"What are you thinking about?" he inquired.

"Nothing. It doesn't matter. Say, have you seen Stewart?"

"Which one's he?"

"Paul's current plaything. Let me show you. It's well worth a look." We stepped out onto the balcony. "There! The red-headed god of the jacuzzi."

Andrew bit his lip. "Yummy." He turned to me. "Poor Marc. We'll have to find you a date."

"I've got a date already."

He clucked. "Don't be crude."

"No, really. He just hasn't arrived yet. Although—wait a minute…"

As I spoke, a car swerved off the road and screeched into a clearing opposite, a hundred meters past the house. The car was an expensive-looking red.

"What a beautiful BMW," Andrew remarked. "Neil has one like it."

"I hope it isn't him," I said flatly.

"Neil's is gray."

As we watched, Tim leapt from the driver's door, locked the car with a blip of his key ring, and began walking determinedly towards the house.

"That boy is my date!" I exclaimed. Babbling an apology to Andrew, I rushed downstairs to answer the door.

Tim looked quietly sexy, wearing simple lightweight clothes which showed off his tight arms and chest. Even his nose studs had had a spit and polish for the occasion. A tentative smile lit up his face. I realized I'd never seen him in full sunlight before. A tingly sensation fidgeted with the back of my neck, a feeling I recognized at once: Lust. And it was the Real Thing.

"Hello," he muttered. He looked so incredibly young.

"How old are you?" I asked.

"Hey?"

"Sorry. Just thinking aloud." I smiled fondly. "Come in."

"I'm 20," he answered, mystified.

"I thought you weren't going to make it."

"Got held up," he answered, slouching past me. "Where…?"

"The party's upstairs. You look great. Just…beautiful!" Neither of us moved. "May I give you a hug?" Without waiting for an answer (in case it was the wrong one), I took him in my arms. "Thanks for coming," I whispered, ever the perfect host.

"I'm not real good with these sort of parties," he replied.

"Don't be shy," I said, leading him by the hand. "I'll stay with you. In fact, there's no way in the world I would leave your side for a second."

We joined the throng. Andrew, of course, was a mass of winks and surreptitious raised eyebrows. Paul reacted as though I had produced five aces in a hand of poker.

"She's rough but she's ready," he declared, as soon as he had the chance. "I know I asked you to bring a boy—I didn't mean you should raid a kindergarten."

"Refill the punch," I replied, "and weep."

Tim knew Stewart from GLEE, but Stewart only vaguely remembered him—which was Stewart's general attitude to everyone but himself.

When I introduced Gavin as my next door neighbor, Tim showed no glimmer of recognition. He'd probably blocked all memory of that unfortunate night when Gavin had caught us at my front door. A good thing too. Much to my annoyance, however, Gavin's face broke into the same predatory look he'd had the first time he saw Paul.

"I'm sure we've met somewhere, Tim," he said urbanely.

"You must be mistaken," I remarked, trying my best to nip this unwelcome flirtation in the bud. The man may or may not have been a killer, but he was certainly a sleazebag. I'd gone right off him.

"No," Gavin went on doggedly. "I'll think of it. Do you live with anyone I might know?"

"Nah," Tim answered laconically. "I move around a fair bit. Been staying with my old man for a while, but it'd be good to find somewhere a bit closer to the city."

I resolved to keep this useful information in mind.

"Was it a dance party, maybe? Mardi Gras?"

"Tim!" I exclaimed, physically dragging him away. "Have you ever ridden a chair lift?"

The guests spent the remainder of the day lazing in the late afternoon sun. Paul turned up the party video, which appeared to be a combination of song clips, dance numbers from B-grade musicals, and hardcore porn. It was very popular. Then, as evening came upon us, the bulk of the crowd dispersed to sober themselves up for the long night ahead. The remaining few moved inside. Stewart pranced over to us to say goodbye.

"Are you leaving?" asked Paul, dragging Stewart to one side. "I thought you might like to hang around and…you know."

Stewart looked dumbfounded. "It's Saturday!" he answered.

There were five of us left, so Paul and I removed ourselves to the kitchen to make coffee. Blind Frederika could see Paul wasn't in the best of moods.

"Isn't life unpredictable?" he whined. "Here's me spending the night alone while you've got a luscious young thing to take home. Whoever would have thought it could happen in a billion years?"

I smiled smugly. "Blame the chaos theory."

"I'll never speak to that hussy again."

"You'll recover."

"Oh, yes," he pouted, "I go on singing. Everything is fine, as far as my public's concerned. But underneath, my self-esteem is in tatters." Suddenly, he clapped his hands. "Now!" he hooted, rushing back to the others. "This is the opportunity I've been waiting for! Serve the coffee, will you?"

Paul's sudden relish made me uneasy. I quickly poured the coffee, located a tray, and hastened towards the living room. I was greeted by a circle of pale, strained, smiling faces and an incessant stream of cheery babble. The babble was prerecorded: Paul was playing the compilation tape of his TV appearances.

"Paul, we don't want to see this again. You already made Gavin sit through it once," I protested.

"No," he squealed, "that was the old tape. This one's right up to date. I made it especially for tonight. It's got everything: laughs, tears, and cutting-edge adult drama. Sit! Enjoy!"

A dull way to end a chic party, I reflected; it seemed like the

gay equivalent of watching sporting b
passed around the coffee and grudgin_

I had to give Paul his due: He had edit_
ly. We had the odd famous face, a couple of o_
representing the "tears," Paul's short eulogy of Rayn.
tle speech was accompanied by a still photograph of the
dresser and I began to sense the method behind Paul's maa.
He'd deliberately included this image to see whether a flicker o.
recognition crossed our suspect Gavin's face. Unfortunately, at
the precise moment Raymond's picture appeared, Tim slopped
his coffee onto the floor and, being a bunch of anal queens,
everyone looked at that.

"Sorry," he stammered.

I rushed to the kitchen to find a sponge. By the time I'd wiped
up the mess the tape had moved on. In fact, it had moved on to
the side-splitting whisky tasting segment.

"I think we'll fast forward through this," I suggested, but was
howled down by Paul. The excruciating piece seemed to last for
decades, which I spent trying to avoid Andrew's thin-lipped disapproval and Paul's malicious amusement. I dared not look at Tim
at all. I could only hope he found the little episode endearing.

Luckily, images of the Munchstadt Mardi Gras interrupted my
humiliating vaudevillian routine.

"Oh, this is priceless," Paul whooped. "They've got a mardi
gras in this backwoods town, there's even a mardi gras queen!
Only one, although I had my doubts about the bandmaster. And
look, here she comes! A-a-ah!"

Sarcastic laughter filled the air. Paul and his editor had con-
trived to make the Munchstadt parade appear even tackier than
it really was: a sad imitation of a glamorous event. I found myself
protesting. "It's only a local show," I complained. "It's not trying to
be anything else. This makes it look ridiculous."

"There she is, Tiny Tina!" Paul screamed. "Looks more like the
Queen of Tonga." He roared with laughter, and even Gavin per-
mitted himself a politically incorrect smile as the plump Mardi

queen swanned around, gracelessly greeting her subjects.

Text up on the screen flashed the faces of our disgruntled interviewee Laurie Butler and her girlfriend Merilyn. "This is where it gets interesting," Paul said, instantly focussing all his attention on Gavin. "That woman is connected to the gay-hate killings. She's Quentin Butler's sister."

"So, Ms. Butler, do you have a personal message for the Sydney police? I'm sure you'd like to see your brother's killer in court."

Laurie glared into the camera, almost as though she were accusing the viewer of complicity in the murder. Paul flicked his remote and the video paused, midframe. Now Laurie's image was shaking, as if in rage and frustration.

Gavin was sitting forward in his seat, his demeanor serious. In fact, the mood in the room had changed abruptly. Tim hadn't uttered a sound throughout, but the color seemed to have drained from his face. We were all hypnotized by the furious, fluttering image on the TV screen.

"What do you think of this, Gavin?" Paul asked pointedly. "Is it making you feel just a teeny bit uncomfortable?"

Gavin stared at him in bewilderment.

"For heaven's sake!" Andrew suddenly piped up. "Turn it off."

Paul pressed the remote. The screen went dark.

"I know what you're up to," Andrew fumed. "I've heard all about your stupid murder investigations. Why don't you two grow up? I mean it!" He glared at me fiercely. "You'll end up with your throat cut, that's what'll happen."

"Not before you do," Paul spat back. "You're the one risking your neck."

"What do you mean? Are you threatening me?"

"Now, let's not have an argument," Gavin interjected, in an authoritative tone. "I agree with Andrew. We were discussing it on the way over. We feel you may be getting into dangerous waters. This is a matter for the authorities."

"They've done fuck-all," Paul replied hotly.

"The police don't make every step of their investigations

public. I'm sure they've already spoken to that woman."

"Oh, really?" Paul blurted out. "So why haven't they arrested anybody? Face it, it's going to take someone with a comprehensive knowledge of the scene to solve these murders and that someone is *us*! I'll have you know I've done some pretty fancy sleuthing in the past—with Marc's help—and we're following this case closely. Maybe you'd be interested to hear what else we discovered in our bungling amateur way. Butler's sister used to be married to Stanford Cahill. What do you think of *that* connection?" He stood. "Or maybe you already knew! Maybe you know *all* about it?"

Tim was on his feet too. "I have to go now," he announced and made a dash for the doorway.

"What? Don't go," I began, but he had.

"What's wrong with *her*?" Paul asked.

"I don't know," I snapped, "but it must be your fault."

Paul sniffed. "No sense of timing."

"Go after him," Andrew urged.

"Uh, yes. Good idea. Excuse me."

I ran to the kitchen, down the internal stairs and through the garage in an effort to catch Tim up, but the roller door had some sort of incomprehensible digital lock. Eventually I found a side exit which led to the street. As I stepped outside, all the security lights snapped on automatically, flooding the scene in a harsh glare. Tim was near his car. Startled by the light, he stood motionless: panic stricken and dazed, like a lost little boy.

"Tim!" I cried, breathlessly, and began to walk towards him. "What's wrong?"

I didn't get another word out. He uttered a peculiar cry and bolted into the bushes by the road. I ran to the spot. There seemed to be a rough track heading down through thick scrub to the beach. Peering in, I could see no sign of Tim. I called his name again, and was about to set off down the track when the security lights from the house clicked off. Now it was difficult to see anything at all.

I was unsure what to do next. It would be silly of me to go chasing anyone through the bush in the dead of night, but I was worried. What in heaven's name could have panicked the boy this time? I decided to hop in my car and search for another way to the bottom.

The road wound downhill then curved back on itself, leading to a reserve adjoining the beach. This area was lit by two or three dim lamps. They cast long shadows and made the surrounding bushland appear unusually black. I could hear waves crashing close by. I parked the car and strode towards the beach, calling Tim's name every now and again.

A scuffle and cracking of twigs caused me to almost jump out of my skin. Someone was there, in the dank scrub beside the picnic tables. "Come out," I said loudly. "I don't know what's going on, but can't we please talk about it?"

Everything remained still. Obviously I'd been addressing a possum or some such thing. Feeling a trifle silly, I walked on.

"Don' worry. It's just some dirty old perv."

I spun around hastily. There in the spot I'd just vacated stood a dishevelled pair of teenagers, a boy and girl of about 16.

"What are you two doing here?" I stammered.

"Whaddaya think?" answered the boy with shaky bravado. "Piss off or I'll flatten ya."

"I'm sorry," I said. "I didn't mean to, uh, interrupt anything."

"Let's go, Rich," the girl whined. "There's nothin' but old pervs round here."

I ignored her. "Have you seen a young man?" I asked brightly.

"You're fuckin' pathetic, mate," the boy uttered under his breath.

They marched back towards the road. By this time my patience was wearing pretty thin. "Tim!" I cried at the top of my voice. There was no answer. "Look after yourself, then," I muttered crankily and returned to my car, relieved to be quitting this hive of nocturnal vice.

Back outside Sonia's mansion, I slowed to a gradual halt. The red BMW had gone. A wave of misery rolled over me, and I knew I wouldn't be seeing Tim again in a hurry. I glanced up at the house. The only light still on was in the upstairs bedroom. I suppose I could have gone back inside, but the last thing I felt like was company.

During the endless drive home, I tried to fathom what had caused Tim to cut and run. Twice! The boy evidently had something to sort out, and I began to see what it must be: his sexuality. Either he didn't want to be gay or he was simply uncomfortable with out gay people. Of course, if that were the case, why did he sign up for queer-themed workshops? Why did he break down during the soppy bits of grand opera?

The young always have these dilemmas of where they fit in and how they're perceived by tout le monde. The truth is, once you're over 35 you realize all your youthful angst was a waste of time and effort. You probably don't fit in anywhere, and however they perceive you, tout le monde are probably wrong. If Tim needed to work that all out, I was perfectly happy to help him.

As soon as I arrived home I rushed to the CD player. I could hardly wait to get a hefty dose of Tebaldi. I selected a mixed recital by the great diva, put it on endless repeat, and at once the soothing tones and essential truth of "Vissi d'arte" spread over me like a favorite blanket. It had been an exhausting day, what with all the drama, adolescent coitus interruptus, and what have you. From now on I, like Tosca, would live only for Art.

Settling into one of my comfortable armchairs—which had somehow escaped Andrew's culling process—I closed my eyes while Tebaldi warbled away at a low, intimate level. Dozing off during her singing would be sacrilege; I simply allowed myself to be carried away to a higher realm.

When I woke up the CD was still playing, but I could feel a chill in the air. It must have been after midnight. I needed to go to bed, but felt too dozy to make the effort. I had been dreaming about Tim, or rather revisiting a sort of dream picture with Tim at its center. This wraithlike Tim wore the same lost expression which had struck me so forcibly earlier on…not unlike that other picture. I shook my head in confusion. What other picture? What was my sleepy brain trying to tell me?

Then I got it: There was a photograph of a mother and father and a little boy with dark hair and light blue eyes…and the boy had a fearful look on his face. I'd seen it at a shop called Buried Treasure. With that particular father, the boy had every reason to be fearful, especially if he was different or unacceptable in some way.

The face in the photograph hadn't had studs on either side of the nose, of course, but the face in the shadows did. I gradually became aware of it, watching me intently and silently from across the room.

"How did you get in?" I asked quietly, still not entirely awake.

"Laundry window."

"Ah. I must have it fixed." I took a deep breath. "I hope you're not going to kill me."

"Don't want to."

I noticed he was holding my sharpest kitchen knife. Now I *was* awake.

"I don't suppose you really wanted to kill the others either." He made no answer, so I crossed my fingers and went on. "Quentin, your uncle, wasn't a very nice man, was he. I think he tried to do weird things to you. It must have been a shock, when all you were looking for was a bit of support. An ally against your father."

"Uncle Quentin was sick."

"Yes, well. Not all gay men are into that stuff, you know. And not everyone in the S/M scene has top's disease. You were very unlucky."

He took a step towards me.

"Quentin brought you to GLEE, and you kept coming back after you'd killed him, otherwise it might have looked suspicious. That was smart. Uh, would you like to sit down? I'm not going anywhere."

The boy hesitated, then carefully lowered himself into the other armchair. He didn't relinquish the knife, though.

I continued with all the feigned calm I could manage. "Let's talk about Raymond."

"No!"

"Believe me, Tim, I understand. He gave you a hard time too—when you were both in Adelaide. Last Christmas, wasn't it?"

His eyes opened wide.

"Oh, yes, I've discovered quite a lot about you, except until tonight I didn't realize it was you. You must have been surprised when Raymond wanted the two of you to get back together."

"I saw him in a bar. He was all over me again."

"That's my fault, I'm afraid. I told him to get hold of a good-looking boy to make a certain person jealous…. Anyway, it doesn't matter. The point is, he was the last person you needed in your life. Right? I can hardly imagine you and Raymond as a couple."

"He was pretty full-on."

"I'm sure he outed you at every given opportunity."

"They all want me to be something I'm not," he muttered.

"Surely your mother understands?" I asked gently.

"She doesn't care about me," he answered darkly. "I just remind her of *him*."

"Does Cahill know about your…gay side?" He shook his head. "But maybe he suspects."

"Not a chance."

"If he found out, he wouldn't be too happy."

"He's not gonna find out."

I nodded; the implication was all too clear. "Is that his BMW you were driving today?"

"One of 'em."

"The same car you drove when you…when you dumped the bodies?"

He frowned. "It's clean."

"So, where did you kill those people?"

"Dad owns a warehouse."

"Near the park?"

"No. It's in the city."

In the background Tebaldi warbled on, undeterred. My heart leapt as I heard the familiar strains of *La Rondine*. I'd been hoping we would get around to it sooner rather than later. I pointed the remote control.

"Mind if I turn this up?"

"Turn it up loud."

I swallowed quietly. "Ah, you remember, then. It's Magda's aria from *La Rondine*, Act 1, that you enjoyed so much. It's so lyrical, isn't it?" (And so short, I thought to myself.) I hummed along for a few bars. "Listen to this phrase. Glorious!"

Tim's eyes, I noticed, were starting to get watery.

"You shouldn't kill people," I said.

"I had to! I didn't want to! But Raymond knew about me and Uncle Quentin. When he was in Adelaide it kind of didn't matter, but then he comes up here and won't leave me alone. What else could I do? I—like, I couldn't believe it had happened. Afterwards."

"Shh, it's OK; just relax. Listen with me. I really wish we'd listened to opera together."

"We are now."

The track finished abruptly, followed by silence. I had a sudden dreadful thought. "Where's Angel?" I asked. "You didn't—?"

"He wasn't there. Remember?"

"Thank God. But you were expecting him that night."

"I heard him on the phone telling some guy about the murders. I didn't know it was you."

"You were waiting in the building when I arrived. I heard you! You must have had a key."

"Uncle Quentin had one. I took it."

The opera recital began once more from the beginning, with "Vissi d'arte." I had to raise my voice to be heard over it. "I'm sorry to tell you this, but Angel knows everything. So even if you were to kill me—"

"He's next!"

Tim lurched to his feet and before I could make any sensible decision about the future (such as running like buggery), I felt the knife's blade at my throat.

"Wait! Can I have a last request?" I panted. "May we listen

to this aria all the way through? Please? I won't speak."

We remained frozen in our melodramatic pose as Renata wrung out her touching plea.

"*Nell'ora del dolore,*" she implored pointedly, "*perche, perche Signore, perche me ne rimuneri cosi?*" (In my hour of grief, why, why, my lord, do you repay me like this?)

It was a celebrated climax: On the second *Signore* the word would expand on a heart-rending high note while the orchestra had a brief orgasm in the background. I bit my lip. If this didn't do the trick, I would shortly be in a position to tell Puccini how much I enjoyed his work.

"*Signo-o-or-r-re,*" sang Tebaldi.

"Uhh!" The flood gates opened. Tim retreated unsteadily and collapsed back onto his chair in a slump. "I'm sorry," he wailed, and flung away the knife, which landed in my lap. "What'll I do?" he sobbed.

"It's all right," I mumbled soothingly, removing the sharp implement from my thigh. Fortunately it was a flesh wound. I slowly stood up, turned down the opera and sat carefully on the arm of Tim's chair. Gently, I stroked the back of his neck as he groaned and sniffled. "It's over now," I whispered. "It's all over."

At that moment, the doorbell chimed.

"I won't answer it," I said.

The damn thing rang again, followed by loud knocking. A voice called out "Police!"

Tim tensed. "Wait here," I reassured him. "Everything's all right, I promise."

I hurried to the door and opened it slightly. On my doorstep were two police officers, accompanied by Andrew.

"We've had a report of some trouble here," announced the younger of the police.

"Gavin saw someone breaking in," chirped Andrew, bobbing up behind him.

I opened the door wider, quite forgetting the bloody knife I was clutching. "There's no cause for alarm—"

"Oh, my *God!*" Andrew shrieked. "What's *that*? What's *happened*?"

"That'll be all, sir," the second policeman snapped at him testily.

I stepped aside and put down the knife. "You'd better come in, officers. I'm Marc Petrucci, and this my home. The situation is under control."

"Is that your car outside, sir? The red BMW?"

"I wish it was. No, it's owned by Stanford Cahill. His son is here and I think you should speak to him right away." I ushered them into the living room, then stopped dead. Tim was nowhere to be seen. "Oh! He must have escaped through the window again."

"Quick!" the policeman shouted. The three of us ran to the back door, which I fumbled to unlock, then out into the yard. One of the police flashed a torch. The beam of light revealed a startled Tim midscramble on the fence.

"Don't shoot," I said hastily. "He's unarmed."

"Halt!" cried the police.

"Fuck *you!*" Tim screamed. (Not the most effective way to discourage officers of the law.)

He struggled to the top of the fence, clumsily grabbing an overhanging branch of the liquidambar to steady himself. Suddenly he slipped, ripping the branch down with him. He landed with a crack on a raised fence post, back first. Letting out a scream of pain he flopped over into Gavin's garden amid a tornado of barks and snarls. At the same time, Gavin appeared in a blaze of light on his back porch. He was holding a gun.

"Don't let that man get away," the officer shouted. "We're coming in."

"Don't worry," Gavin called back. "Hector's got him."

chapter twenty-two

"Boo-o-o!" we yelled, crowding along the wrought iron fence of Parliament House. "Shame! Resign!"

Stanford Cahill, the man who had caused this surge of abuse, scuttled down the steps of the parliamentary chamber, escorted by a pair of placid security men, and quickly disappeared into his limousine. He didn't so much as glance in the direction of the protesters. His mind was elsewhere.

The car sped away, and the vocal clamor instantly dissipated. Our valiant band of thirty committed men and women wandered back to the alcove where we'd set up all the creature comforts necessary to maintain our vigil. Angel and I resumed our canvas-backed chairs. I held my breath until the throbbing in my thigh subsided, then returned to my soggy brioche at the point where I had unceremoniously abandoned it. Sunlight burnished the rooftops and bounced off the plateglass windows. It was a balmy November afternoon.

"Well," Angel sighed, "if we can't hound him from office, at least we can more or less guarantee he never gets reelected."

"I hope so," I added, "though the man can't be held responsible for his son's actions."

"Not legally, no," he agreed, "but no politician likes to be at the center of a controversy, whether it's his own doing or not."

I shook my head sadly. "Poor Tim. I still can't believe it."

The aftermath of Tim's arrest and full confession had been swift and dramatic. He hadn't even been behind bars long enough to be sentenced when the poor confused boy had tried to hang himself. Luckily, prison officers had found him in time.

He'd immediately become a cause célèbre. Articles had appeared in all the papers, and even the most rabid right-wing journalists had condemned the system for its insensitivity and lack of foresight. As for Celeste, she and her fellow activists were keeping up an extraordinary diatribe against Cahill.

Before the man himself had appeared, I'd been reading the latest installment in the ubiquitous *Queer Scene*. I picked it up again.

"Homophobia: All in the Family" screeched the headline.

> We're all concerned about the reaction of our parents when we come out. Sometimes we seriously underestimate their love and understanding—but not Timothy Cahill. Why was he so sure of rejection? Because his father intended to turn him into a criminal! Stanford Cahill virtually drove his own son to murder and attempted suicide.
>
> Why is this monster still in parliament? Why hasn't he resigned? Is there anyone left who still wishes to be associated with this callous individual?
>
> The Coalition for Queer Action demands Cahill's immediate resignation, and further demands that the premier bow to community pressure and back down on his homophobic Gay Tax. Protests continue this week outside Parliament House. Make a stand for compassion and let's teach these bastards a lesson.

" 'Bastards' is a bit strong," I remarked to Angel.

"Yes. *Queer Scene* may run into legal difficulties with that. After all, Cahill and Garland weren't born out of wedlock, so far as I know. 'Assholes' would have been better. Nobody's an asshole in the literal sense, but everybody's familiar with one." He chuckled, his fleshy frame wobbling in all directions.

"I'm so glad you're all right," I said. "If you'd shown up at GLEE that night, something terrible might have happened. Tim was waiting for you, you know."

I shuddered. Even now my nerves didn't care to be reminded of my last meeting with Tim. I prayed my taste for opera would not be permanently affected.

"He was the last person I'd have suspected," Angel confessed. "All I knew was, the police were following a lead involving a red BMW—and when I heard that, I remembered seeing one parked outside for the Tuesday sessions. I was working on a process of elimination, but I didn't think of Tim. He didn't seem like the type."

"He didn't know what type he was."

Angel put a friendly arm around my shoulders. "He was your type, though, wasn't he."

"I did fall for him just a bit," I admitted.

"Good! Excellent. Don't forget to include all that personal stuff in your talk. It's going to be absolutely sensational, our little seminar on gay-related murder. A real coup! It's completely sold out, you know. I could have sold it ten times over with no trouble at all."

I smiled dubiously. I wasn't entirely comfortable that Angel had bullied me into this new venture. "I don't know everything," I reminded him. "I've got no idea what the bandaging was all about."

"Oh, that's easy," he answered glibly. "It was a cry for help. The boy wanted to be stopped."

"Hm. I suppose so. Incidentally, why didn't you show up for our rendezvous? I never asked."

"Ah." He assumed a revoltingly coy look. "I can answer that in one big, juicy word. Stewart!"

"Stewart?"

He pouted. "Yes, Stewart."

"Well, That explains everything. But for God's sake don't tell Paul. He's miserable enough already."

"Speak of the devil."

Skipping around the traffic, which our little demonstration had brought to a disgruntled standstill, came two figures carrying a clutch of take-out coffees. It was Paul and Helen, both smirking openly.

"Here we are, with macchiatos all round for the yuppie protesters," Helen chuckled. "Had any effect yet?"

"Garland's sticking to his gay tax like glue," Angel replied crankily. "He keeps saying it makes economic sense—which it doesn't—and anyway, is that the only thing that matters anymore? *Stealing* makes economic sense too."

"I know a sneaky way we can get around the gay tax," Paul chirped. "How?"

"Marry a lesbian and have ten kids."

"That makes even less economic sense," Helen remarked.

"You've cheered up," I said to Paul.

"Oh, yes," he shrugged. "Look on the bright side. It's not like I've been replaced on *NOW TV!* The whole show's been axed."

"So what exactly is the bright side?" I asked.

"My agent was on the phone this morning." Paul's beam became pure Cheshire. "She's already getting some nibbles. There's a perfect role coming up in *Precinct Hospital*. A sexy administrator with a mysterious and tragic past."

"That's you to a T," I quipped.

"Why was your show axed?" asked Angel. "Wasn't it a big cult hit?"

"As a media personality, I kicked ass," Paul admitted in all modesty. "But it wasn't my show. The TV tie in with *NOW!* was the chief editor's idea. It was over the minute she resigned to accept a cushy job in New York."

"Completely out of the blue," I added.

"Not entirely," said Helen. "Sonia had been negotiating with Murdoch for months. We weren't supposed to know about it."

"Good God! *NOW!* magazine has more secrets than ASIO."

Helen grinned. "That's what makes it so much fun. I'd go bonkers otherwise." She tapped me gently on the arm. "Marc, could we have a little chat in private?"

"Sure." I hoisted myself out of my seat. "Let's wander over to the park," I suggested. "I'm supposed to keep this leg active."

It was a gorgeous day. We strolled past the stately old parliament buildings and into Hyde Park, stopping next to the fountain—an Italianate fresco, chock full of statues representing some unidentifiable ancient crisis.

"Sorry about your job," she said. "I did tell you right at the start it could be over at the drop of a hat."

"I don't mind."

"Something else may come up. I mentioned to Daddy what an asset you were to us, how keeping Paul in check would have been impossible without your help."

"Thank you."

She smiled facetiously. "I hated to tell such an outrageous lie, but I think he bought it."

We laughed. I gazed thoughtfully across the park.

"Last time I was here, at a protest rally, there was an attempted murder," I said. "The strange thing is, Tim claimed to know nothing about it."

"Do you think he was telling the truth?"

"Yes, I do. The other victims were people he knew. He wasn't a random serial killer."

"So you're telling me this park is full of maniacs?"

"So it would seem."

We found a seat in the shade of a stately old Moreton Bay fig. Helen took my hand. For one extraordinary second, I wondered whether she was about to propose.

"I have to tell you some bad news," she said. "At least, I think it's bad. I know you pretty well by now, Marc. You hide your emotions—I'm the same—but still waters run deep."

"What is it?"

"Don't be upset. It's about Sonia. The reason she's stayed on in Italy all this time is, well, she's married again. To your waiter friend."

"She married Fabio?"

"'Fraid so."

"How odd."

"If it's any consolation, all her marriages fail."

I didn't know what to say. The truth was, I couldn't have cared less.

"What's your favorite Italian restaurant?" Helen asked spontaneously.

"Hm? Oh, I often eat at Fratelli di Marco. It's named after me."

"Truly?"

"No."

"We'll have dinner there tonight. My treat, OK? Now I'm going to leave you alone here for a while with your sorrows, and if you're smart you'll take my advice."

"And what's your advice?"

"Get over it, of course!" She winked.

Watching Helen walk away, I had plenty of time to call her back and explain, but I didn't. Damn it, I mused, why should Paul be the only one with a mysterious and tragic past? Instead, I stretched my legs out in the sun, shaded my eyes, and thought about the state of the world. Here I was, right back where I'd started: alone, not a day younger, and facing the prospect of poverty again. Life is never what you'd call easy. On the other hand I was still alive and living it. That had to be a plus.